Cathrne

MW00412299

Fade to Blacque

Thank Yu For
your Support

God Bless

Joe Dall

Fade to Blacque

J. P. Dallas

ISBN-13: 9780692860649
ISBN-10: 0692860649
Library of Congress Control Number: **2017903952**
Back2Back Publishing LLC, Lanham, MD

GOD'S GRACE

All praises and honor to the one true Living God. I thank you for all the Blessings in my life, big, small and everything in-between. You started me on a journey that had me questioning the hows and the whys. I cannot imagine where this journey will take me, but with you in control I have no worries. Maybe this was your way of making me trust you reminding me that you were here all the time, waiting for me to get out of my own way. I thank you for the many chances I have been given, it has not always been easy, but because of your divine intervention, I am making my way through.

Thank you God.

CHAPTER 1

August in New York is brutal. The sweltering heat and the staggering humidity, along with the exhaust fumes from the gazillion cars, can make you hate this city. The crowded streets, filled with eight million residents and about two million visitors all vying for a small piece of Manhattan Island, can overwhelm the most ardent New Yorker, including me. I was born and raised here, and there are times when I want to get the hell out of Dodge. Who am I kidding? Where the hell would I go? The problem is, if I ever *did* leave New York, I would expect to do the same things *there* that I do here. 24 hours open. Does that place even exist?

The sound of a car horn disrupts my thoughts, letting me know that the light had turned green. I proceed up 5th Avenue, people-watching as I go. Traffic is unusually slow today. I smile to myself—what I am saying? It's like this every damn day of the year. I would have driven my car if my parents didn't have to borrow mine for their weekend getaway. Why my dad doesn't get rid of his broken-down jalopy, I'll never know. That thing is always in the shop. Memories; he says that car holds great memories. Of what? I wonder. Sending his mechanic's children through college? I had to drive to Lynbrook for a briefing on a case that may end up in our lap, so I had to borrow a car from our carpool. Being as fly as I am, of course I was going for one of the newer models just delivered. I was late getting to the carpool, so I had to pick from what was left. Cars we typically use when we are trying not to say 'HEY, OVER HERE, FEDERAL LAW ENFORCEMENT AT YOUR SERVICE.' The one I got stuck with is a beauty. This old car has no air, makes this godawful noise, and is the color of burnt toast. Still, it beats walking in this heat. You know what humidity does to your hair. I guess I should be happy that the car got me to Lynbrook and back to the city safely.

As I slow for another light, a call comes over the radio requesting all available units to proceed to 135th and 5th Ave. Reports of a street fight that turned violent with said gunfire. I am only five blocks away. I floor the gas, siren blaring as I try to get through the parking lot of cars with no place to go. As I approach the scene, I see a swarm of uniformed police officers running in all directions. People are screaming that someone had been shot and needed an ambulance, all the while cursing and screaming about how slow the police are in responding to their neighborhood. True or not, this is the presumption of most of the residents in this area. In this neighborhood, that's nothing new; same old story, us versus them in every aspect of city life.

The crowd is growing with people coming out of apartment buildings, barber shops, beauty stores, and the local bodegas. What the hell is going on here? I feel like I stepped into a three-ring circus. Chaos seems to be the order of the day.

All of a sudden shots ring out in the crowd; people are running like roaches when the lights are turned on. The atmosphere is overcome with screams as panic ensues. No one knows for sure where to run for cover. More police arrive on the scene with guns drawn, not sure who or where the bad guys are, but prepared to shoot anyone moving.

As the crowd thins out, I see a young man lying on the ground, covered in blood. A police officer is attempting to stop the bleeding by putting his hand over the wound, using a piece of the victim's shirt. I see he is talking to the victim, but I can't make out what he is saying. At that moment, the ambulance shows up and the paramedics take over. Before they can lift him onto the gurney, they try assessing the severity of the damage. Because there is so much blood, it looks like they are having trouble locating where he had been shot. There was more than one shot fired, so no one is certain how many times he may have been hit. I see his head moving up and down as the paramedics frantically work on him. After a few minutes, they lift him onto the gurney. The attendants barely have the kid inside the cab when the ambulance takes off faster than a speeding bullet—no pun intended. He looks in bad shape, and it's hard to know if he is going to make it.

It's a mess. People are crying as police try to question anyone who will talk to them. Speak of an impossible mission. Everyone here knows that there is no love lost between the people who live in this area and the cops. The history here is not one that would unite residents and the police. Take it from me: in this neighborhood it's not the residents who have the serious PR problem. Ask anyone; police are not to be trusted. There have been too many police shootings of black and brown people, some making national news, and not enough convictions of the police who are charged. People are once again in the streets, frustrated and angry over what they perceive as no justice. Every time something like this happens, it feels like a powder keg about to blow. I would hate to be the Commissioner of Police in this town, or any other, for that matter. It's a big responsibility managing that powder keg so that it doesn't blow. I don't think I could do it.

Another day, another shooting, and it's only one o'clock in the afternoon. If anyone tells me that I should be used to this shit happening almost every day, I will stick my beautiful shoes up their ass. It is hard for a person of color when it comes to police shootings, period. It's worse when you are in law enforcement. You don't know what to feel. It becomes a tug of war between emotions and questions. Are you black first? Or are you a cop first? These are hard questions, and I'm afraid I don't know the answer. Being a federal agent insulates us a bit because we are not directly in the line of fire doing day-to-day policing. That doesn't mean that I don't have feelings that I must control. It can get scary at times, working the streets not looking like your typical special agents are supposed to look, praying that you are not mistaken for God knows what or whom. We always make sure to keep the local authorities abreast of any operations we may have in their jurisdiction so that no feelings get hurt and no dispute erupts over who is in charge. Friendly fire is very much a reality. I was black a long time before I became an agent. It can be a heavy burden, questioning the decision I made that I was so sure of at the beginning. I couldn't wait to save the world, fighting the good fight for the good people of the world. Well, at least the ones in New York. Now I have days when I think, what the fuck is the use. Busting your ass for what? Bag the bad guy one day, the next day someone else is walking in his shoes. Working in any capacity as a law enforcer can be challenging, frustrating, and at times intensely difficult. I knew that coming in; it was my choice to enter into this arena, and I do have a duty to uphold that I take very seriously.

Because this is not an officer-involved shooting, there's not the parade of top brass arriving to pose for the press. There are no TV news trucks here yet, which surprises me; they usually are the first ones at a crime scene, waiting to interview that person seeking their fifteen minutes of fame. I turn around and there they are—spoke too soon. Life as we know it in today's society. Sad commentary.

Things begin to quiet down a bit as the forensic team arrives and the yellow tape is plastered around the crime scene. Police are still trying to question witnesses with no luck. Big Robert "Moose" Hansen pulls up with his K-9 partner Nitro, who immediately goes into police mode after an officer gives him a piece of clothing from the victim. With all the nasty smells on the street, it amazes me that dogs can ever find any useful information, but they do. They are every bit a police officer as the two-legged kind. Curious onlookers are standing around talking among themselves, not being of any help to the police.

I am about to get into my car when Sgt. Matt James yells out, "Hey, Agent Blacque, I don't remember sending for the feds. I think NYPD can handle this situation. We don't need a babysitter."

"Don't get your panties in a knot," I reply. "I was in the neighborhood and wanted to see if I could help. I have full faith that NYPD can handle the situation without Big Brother." It looks to me like things are under control, so I get back in the car and make my way to the office.

CHAPTER 2

Now I know you would like to know who I am. My name is Shalimar Blacque, but everyone calls me Shale. I am a federal agent for FICA (Federal Investigation on Criminal Activities). I work in the midtown office here in New York, but my headquarters is in Washington, DC. I have been working for the feds about eight years now, and I love it. I am keeping a promise I made when I was much younger to think outside the box. I was recruited right out of John Jay College of Criminal Justice and have never looked back. There was a mandate for all federal and state agencies to hire more women and minorities into local and federal policing. FICA, the FBI, and the CIA, along with the NYPD, were actively recruiting at colleges such as JJCCJ. The changing complexion of the country called for diversity in all aspects of law enforcement.

Opening up positions that were once strictly white male dominated allows for more interaction between the communities that are policed and the people doing the policing. I picked FICA because of all the agencies, they had the best track record for advancing women in significant positions within the organization. The best opportunities for advancement were there for you as long as you had the drive to work for what you wanted and to be one of the best. Nothing could stop you but you. Also, they were starting a division of agents who were younger and had street savvy, who did not conform to the old traditional agents. You know, wearing the beige, gray, and black suits. Think Mod Squad from back in the day, only on the federal level.

There are times when it is appropriate for the uniform look, like court appearances, press conferences, and things along those lines. I try hard to let that be few and far between in my normal working life. Working within the urban jungle of New York City, we don't have to dress like we are in the secretarial pool. Nothing says law enforcement like the suit. I had my style and was not going to be hemmed up wearing outfits that made me look more like a man than a woman. Trust me, I am all woman. Having said that, I must admit I do look amazing in a suit.

Training was a beast, but I excelled in it. You go through a grueling regimen of firearms training, and fitness routines that could qualify you for the Marines. Practical self-defense techniques were also taught to help with assertiveness training. Everything is done to help with our professional development which we will need to do our job. It was much harder than I imagined, but I was determined to prove to myself that I could do it. Working on my investigative skills was foreign to me because I had no idea what my skills were.

Honestly, the hardest part for me was the firearms training. I never liked guns; hated them, in fact. There has been too much death and destruction in my neighborhood that is a direct result of gun violence. Learning the proper way to handle firearms gave me a better understanding of them. If I was going to be chasing bad guys with guns, then I had to overcome the fear and misunderstanding of these weapons. Having never been around them, I did very well on the shooting range, much to my surprise.

Self-defense was and still is my all-time favorite. Martial arts training gave me the confidence to know that just because I am a woman did not dictate my ability to defend myself, regardless of the size of my opponent. There is something so compelling about the fact that a woman can overpower a man much larger than herself. I highly recommend it for all women. Eight years later and I am still taking classes. The fact that I grew up surrounded by boys, related and unrelated, made me fearless. I was just one of the guys. Training was just another way of playing with the boys, only they were much bigger and rougher. To say I was a tomboy is a major understatement. Growing up the way I did, I kick ass in basketball; the fact that I was six feet in the 12th grade didn't hurt. I shoot a mean game of pool, and I can run faster and jump higher than most of the boys on my block. I can ride a bike like nobody's business and can swear like a banshee. I was just one of the boys. My dad would always say to me that I was a young lady and needed to act like one. "I don't know why you hate playing with dolls or wearing beautiful dresses. You look so pretty all dressed up; you could be a princess." At the same time I would hear, "Shale, spitting in the street and beating up boys isn't something a young woman would do."

Looking up at my dad with the biggest smile on my face, I would say, "But Dad, it's so much more fun, and I'm so good at it."

Graduating first in my class afforded me the opportunity to pick where I wanted to work. I could choose anywhere in the nation, whichever regional office I wanted. New York has always been my first choice. You've heard that old saying, "Once a New Yorker, always a New Yorker." I did have opportunities to travel, both national and international, on assignments. I took this as my chance to see the world. In the eight years, I have managed to exceed any expectations I might have had. Working hard and the continuation of my studies have elevated me to special agent status. Most of the work I do is routine. You know, the usual: paperwork, making phone calls, spending hours in front of the computer, following up on leads, interviewing witnesses.

Then there is the other side, the more physical side: working the streets, doing surveillance, working undercover, being there at an arrest. I like the mixture of the two. However, if I am honest, I would have to say that I am at my happiest working the streets and being in the middle of all the action. Never knowing the outcome of any situation is what keeps the job interesting. I can honestly say not many things surprise me anymore. I was told by a prisoner once that he did not want to be handcuffed by a woman and a nigger. This from a guy who killed three people. Needless to say, I won that fight. I won't say what I told him; let's just say he never heard the word "fuck" used so poetically. I admit that I can be a little gung-ho at times, but it's because I love my job so much.

I am an only child. My older brother died when I was two and he was five from sickle cell anemia. So you can imagine how thrilled my parents were when I told them that not only did I want to be a cop, but a federal agent. My mother had a harder time with this decision, as you will learn later. The thought of his little girl running around with a gun chasing criminals...well, my dad was fit to be tied. But now he is my biggest champion. I have worked a couple of high-profile cases, one that made the national news. My father has a scrapbook filled with the goings-on of his special agent daughter, just ask him if you can take a look. No, wait, you won't have to. The book is on the coffee table in the living room. I am my daddy's daughter.

My family is everything to me. My immediate family is small, but my family overall is a zoo. My father is one of twelve children. My grandparents were married at fifteen and had a baby almost every year after. My youngest aunt is only nine years older than I, and my oldest uncle is only sixteen years younger than my grandmother. She had seven boys and five girls in all. I have 25 cousins (16 are boys) and a couple of aunts and uncles who are crazy as hell and should be in a mental institution. No, seriously, they are off the chain. You name it, we got it. Let's see, we got drinking problems, drug problems, babies and more babies, men problems, women problems, financial problems, legal problems. When you grow up in such a large family, you get to see all sides, the good and the bad. I have some cousins who made the decision at a young age that they were allergic to working a nine-to-five and found other ways to make money. Petty things here and there—number running, dealing illegal cigarettes, if you know what I mean. I have an uncle who is very proud of the fact that he ONLY went to jail three times for the same thing. He calls himself a small businessman just helping out the community. The police call it peddling stolen goods. You would think that having police in the family would deter any illegal activities. Not in my family. I was told it's good to have someone on the inside, just in case.

Growing up in all this insanity, I often wonder how I was able to stay sane. All the credit goes to my mother. She was the one who made sure I knew that there are consequences for my actions. I should always be kind, work hard for what I wanted, and most importantly, to fear God. God, I was told, has the last word. Scared the shit out of me; still does. My dad gave me the love of music. By the time I was three, I was singing along with Aretha Franklin and Gladys Knight. My dad and I would sing together to his favorite James Brown. In my neighborhood, music was always playing. There would be R&B playing throughout the week up until Saturday night. On Sunday morning Gospel would take over. No matter how much or how little money a family had, music was the great equalizer. It has always been a big part of our life. Our apartment was the place where everybody came to party. Except on Sunday, that's the Lord's day.

My parents and their friends would throw rent parties for people facing eviction. Charging an entrance fee, then handing the money over to the people who needed it, is a tradition that goes way back in the black community here in New York, and my parents' circle of friends are continuing the tradition. I would stay up late, dancing behind my bedroom door, listening to the local gossip, smelling cigarette smoke (smoking wasn't considered hazardous to your health back then). I would sneak out to steal some food, not knowing that my parents were watching me the whole time. Once in a while my dad would allow me to stay up so he could show off our dancing and singing skills, taking my last bow of the night to applause and "do it, baby" or "work it, little mama." My mother would be the one who would say, "It is time to go to bed." Falling asleep to the sounds of blue light in the basement music is something I have never fully outgrown. I still fall asleep to music. I have been all over the world, and I never have the same feelings I get when I come home.

My mother's side of the family is much smaller. She and her brother, Maurice, are the only children that their parents had. We lived in the second-floor apartment in an old brownstone building on 125th Street in Harlem, USA. My grandparents lived in the basement apartment (my mother's parents), and my aunt and uncle lived in the top-floor apartment (my father's brother). I wanted to become a cop for one reason: my beloved Uncle Maurice. My mother's brother was this big teddy bear of a man who could make me laugh so hard, I would pee my pants. He always made me feel safe and loved. We had our own mutual love society, and we would vote on who could join this most exclusive club. Because of him, I discovered New York City. He was a Gothamite. He loved this town. He showed me all the possibilities that were right outside my front door. He wanted me to take advantage of everything the city offered. From Manhattan to Staten Island and every borough in between, this is the city that never sleeps, after all. He was one of only a handful of black officers at the time who made it to the rank of lieutenant. Everyone knew who he was. He had a strong sense of right and wrong, and he made sure I knew it too. I loved him almost as much as my dad. He never had any children of his own. I guess that was one reason we were so close. He was married twice, both ending in divorce. Besides his family, the police were all he had, and he died because of it.

He was always trying to help out young people (especially the young boys) in the neighborhood. Knowing how many of them were growing up without a father, he made it his business to be a surrogate dad to anyone who needed a man in his or her life. He was the first to volunteer for whatever new program or opportunity came his way. He wanted to make a difference in not only their lives but for the sake of the community. It was nothing to see him on the basketball court at one o'clock in the morning; if a game was going on, he was there. He always preached about self-respect, having common sense, learning to take pride in where you lived.

It was in the eighties when a new drug scourge, crack cocaine, hit, and it has been particularly devastating for African-American communities. Harlem was no exception. Several of my family members became shells of their former selves. They became the walking dead because of crack. It seemed like everyone had or knew someone on this poison, and just like the music, it didn't matter how much or how little money you had; no one was immune. He spent the next 25 years of his life trying to fight this cancer which affected so many of our families and friends. The community as a whole was under attack.

He would become frustrated at times because it seemed like he was losing the fight, but he would say, "Pray; prayer changes things." There would be small glimmers of hope in an otherwise gloomy situation when someone would say to him, "Because you cared, I am still here." Hearing this was all he needed to motivate him never to stop trying. My uncle was in the thick of trying to eradicate this poison when he was shot and killed by someone high on crack—a neighborhood boy who lived eight houses down from us, someone he had known all his life.

To say I was devastated is an understatement. It was the first time in my life that death came from violence, and I cannot explain the grief that I felt. Not my Uncle Maurice. I just closed up. I felt like there was no reason for living. My mother and I would just sit and cry and hold on to each other for hours. He was killed in June, a month away from his birthday and two months before he was to retire. His funeral was something out of a movie. Seeing all these policemen and women, not just from New York but from all over the country, laid the framework for my decision, whether I knew it or not.

I had a moment to sit with him alone and told him that I was going to follow in his footsteps. A solemn promise was made to do whatever was necessary to make a difference the way he did. I swore on his casket that I was going to be the best damn cop ever, just as he had been. He would be proud knowing that the call to justice didn't end with him. I know I am not crazy, but I could swear I heard him say, "Don't just follow in my footsteps, baby, make your own. Think outside of the box, don't limit yourself. Reach higher, Shalimar. Dream bigger. I have confidence in you to know that whatever you decide, you will be the best at it. Live up to the standards you were raised on. Listen to that moral compass and keep God first. Always remember I got your back, and I will always love you." I went home and started researching.

There have been pivotal moments in my life where destruction has occurred. The top two are (1) the murder of my beloved uncle and (2) September 11, 2001. Some events are so tragic that you never really get over them; you just learn to share space with their memories. I was in school on that particular September morning that started out like any other ordinary September morning when the first plane hit the tower. Everyone around me assumed that it was a freak accident or pilot error, but when the second plane hit, panic set in. New York City was under attack, and no one was prepared for the aftermath. The streets were filled with the walking wounded. Blank looks and sheer confusion along with tearstained faces greeted you as you wandered aimlessly, not sure where to go or what to do. The images of the twin towers with big black holes going through them and the sight of people jumping to their death will be something I will take to my grave.

We were in the city but totally disconnected from family and friends because there was no kind of reception at all, cell phone or otherwise. I knew my parents were freaking out, wondering where I was in all this madness. With no way to communicate and in a total daze, I just started walking along with all the other walking wounded. I had been walking for about 45 minutes, and as I passed this small bodega, this heavy-set man came running out, shouting, "They are down, they are gone." People were asking, "What is down?" "The twin towers," he was scream-ing, "the towers are down." As many of us as could fit in that little store watched a small TV, barely working with hangers as antennas, watching our world collapse around us.

The sight of those buildings coming down and the black smoke that hovered over lower Manhattan; I will never be able to express how we felt on that day. Strangers were holding onto people they would never have any contact with otherwise, crying and sobbing uncontrollably. I felt like I was going to pass out. I honestly don't remember much after that. A woman was holding me up; we just started hugging and crying, joined by most people in the store. My world at that point was a fog, and all I wanted to do was wake up from this nightmare.

I started walking again, not sure how long I had been walking or where I was. It was pitch black when I turned the corner and saw my parents running to me, crying and laughing at the same time. I collapsed in my father's arms as I remembered that my cousin Eric worked in

Tower One. All at once I thought of my aunt and uncle. They were living a different kind of hell, not knowing if their son was alive or dead. I just started praying, "God, please wake me from this nightmare so that things can go back to the way they were. Please, God, save my city. Please, God, let my cousin be alive." All I could say was, "Eric, what happened to Eric?"

"Shalimar," my mother was screaming, "Eric is alive. He is hurt but he managed to escape the building before it went down. He is in the hospital."

By the end of that day, my eyes were the color of ruby-red pomegranate from all the crying. The next few days are a blur, but one of the most touching memories I have is walking down 5th Avenue and seeing all the different police and fire personnel from all around the world attending services at St. Patrick's Cathedral, dressed in their formal dress. It was incredible. I was watching as they were getting into formation when one of the policewomen came over and gave me a hug. The tears started all over again.

Anytime there is a disaster, natural or otherwise, the news reports always talk about how resilient the people are, how they rally around each other to bring back as much normalcy as possible. Well, New Yorkers are no different. We came together to bring our city back to life. We were determined not to allow terrorists to stop our way of living. New York is the city with the fuck-you attitude, after all. We will bounce back from this horror, and we did. It took some time, but the rebuilding has begun. The new towers are up; people are moving back to Lower Manhattan. We got our hustle and bustle back. This experience only strengthens my resolve to become the best agent I can be. In memory of the greatest cop there ever was in my book: my Uncle Maurice. I think of him often, and in a way, I am glad he is dead because 9/11 would have killed him. Life goes on, time moves us toward tomorrow. The pain lessens a little each day, but the memory will never fade away. New York is back and me with it.

Now in my early thirties, standing over six feet in my stocking feet, most people would say I am attractive. I say I am fine. Cocoa-colored skin with a body most women would kill to have. I wear my hair natural, which means I can braid my hair, wear it in an afro the size of Angela Davis back in the day, blow it straight with some curls, or just let it be. Due to my high standards, I have to look fabulous at all times, so you know a sister knows how to hook a look up. When in Europe I always have people come up to me and ask if I am a model. "No," is my answer, "but thank you for the compliment." Only in Paris is this question ever asked. I wonder why? Being so tall can cause a problem when it comes to buying clothes; thank God I live in NYC because tall women have it easier here than most places when it comes to size and fit.

I love beautiful things but am not extravagant. The one thing I do have a passion for is shoes. I am obsessed with anything that goes on your feet: shoes, boots, sandals, sneakers, flats. The higher the heel, the better. I have over 150 pairs, and it still is not enough. You name them, I have them—Gucci, Jimmy Choo, Manolo Blahnik, Prada. On a vacation trip to Florence, Italy, I discovered this new shoe designer, Giovanni Lombardi. When I tell you I died and saw the stilettos, I mean it. I brought back four pairs of the most amazing shoes I have ever seen. Mark my words, he is about to take over the States, and this sister was the first to say his name. I have two pairs of boots that were made especially for me that have a little something embedded inside them. They are only to be worn in case of an emergency.

I live in Greenwich Village in a small building with only five apartments. My apartment is the size of a closet, but I do have space for my shoes. My neighbors are all gay, which contributed to my awesome style. (Every woman needs a gay friend.) I share my place with my cats, Ochie and his mother, Sophie. When I'm on the road, my next-door neighbors, Gary and Rob, care for my babies and act as surrogate parents until I return. They have a small Jack Russell terrier named Miss Amelia Earhart who thinks she is a cat, so the three of them are thick as thieves. I love my apartment; I love the area, the style, the people, and the energy of the Village.

This small section below 14th Street is like a world within itself. I am always amazed at the sights and sounds of this little piece of Manhattan

Island. "24 crazy" is the best way to describe it, and it makes me feel alive. The bohemian vibe, along with the funky shops, restaurants, clubs, and the people, make this, in my opinion, one of the most amazing sections of the city. Everyone in my building has been here for years; no one wants to leave. There is talk that the building is going condo, so I will be forced to make a decision as to my living arrangements one way or the other. I find myself in a family building situation, the same but different as when I was growing up in Harlem. Everything I could want is here. My neighbor Gary's famous saying is that he doesn't have to go above 28th Street in Chelsea, we have everything in the world we need right here.

CHAPTER 3

I am back in my office, having stopped at my favorite deli for a cup of coffee and a sandwich. I am setting up my computer when the phone rings. Sergeant Peter Mason of the 32nd Precinct, which covers the area where the shooting took place, is calling to inform me that the victim from this morning died on the operating table. It is now officially a homicide. He is calling me because he heard that I was there this afternoon and wanted to know why. Why were the feds investigating a local crime scene? How did I get there that fast? Was there something he should be aware of concerning the victim? Were the feds working a case and neglected to notify his office? "NO to all your questions. I was in the neighborhood and wanted to see if I could be of any help." I ask if he has information on the victim. He says nothing. I say again, "I was in the area." He doesn't sound like he is convinced. "Check with my boss if you don't believe me," I say. He hangs up the phone. What the hell?

I don't know what the problem is. You would think after 9/11 we would all be on the same team—you know, chasing bad guys and making this country safe again. The only difference is we go after bigger fish. It could be jealousy or an inferiority complex on the part of the NYPD. Who knows.

As I sit pondering the situation, I hear my boss coming out of his office, cursing as he makes his way to my desk. My boss is Conrad Reese, and from the look on his face, he doesn't look happy. Before I can say hello, he screams, "WHAT THE HELL HAPPENED OUT THERE TODAY? WHY IS THE CHIEF OF POLICE CHEWING MY ASS OFF ABOUT ONE OF MY AGENTS SHOWING UP AT A LOCAL CRIME SCENE? WHAT, ARE WE SPYING ON THE POLICE NOW?"

I try to explain that I was in the area when the call for help came in and went to see if I could be of any help. "Conrad, I was not there to step on anybody's toes. They had things under control, so I left. What the HELL is the problem? It's not like I took over the investigation. The chief needs to take it down a notch. Every time they see the feds, they feel inadequate."

"Listen," he shouts, "they are not my problem—you are. NYPD is a pain in my ass as it is. I don't need you adding fuel to the fire. If they need our help, they will ask for it. I don't need you riding in like the cavalry rescuing damsels in distress. If you don't have enough to keep you busy, believe me, I can find something for you to do."

He storms back to his office, still cursing under his breath. I turn to see the whole room staring at me, waiting to see what I will do next. I walk out of there like I am walking on a runway dressed in mad as hell from head to toe. It takes me all afternoon to cool down.

I am still trying to wrap my mind around what happened today. None of it makes any sense. I keep reliving the events of this afternoon, checking my brain to see if there is something I overlooked, because I am so confused right now. Why did Conrad bust me out like that in front of everybody? Why did the chief of police call him almost as soon as I had left the scene? Come to think of it, why has my partner not returned my call? I had called him as I was cooling off in the car. Something is amiss; I smell a rat.

As if on cue, my cell phone rings. "Hey, beautiful, what's going on? Sorry I missed your call. I was busy, and no, I was not alone."

I have to smile because I know he is telling me the truth. "Listen, Bozo, I don't need to know about your sex life. I need to talk to you. It's real important."

"WHAT IS GOING ON? ARE YOU ALRIGHT?" he wants to know.

"I'll tell you when you get here. Meet me in Washington Square Park in 30 minutes."

"OK, I'll be there."

It is still hot but the humidity isn't as bad as it was earlier. The more I start to cool down, the more I begin to realize that this is a beautiful sunny day. The wind has picked up some; we have a nice breeze flowing now. I am sitting on a bench facing the dog park, watching the dogs enjoy this time of the day. Going over the events of today, it still makes no sense. Why all this fuss over a random kid who looks like a lot of other kids shot in this city?

I am trying to contact my CI (confidential informant). If anyone knows what is going on, he would know.

Side note: For those of you who don't know what a CI is, let me explain. A confidential informant is someone who supplies law enforcement with information about a current or future investigation. It is done on the down low so no one will know who is providing information to the law. Not everyone looks at this situation as being positive. Lives have been lost due to snitching, as it is called in the street. Depending on the relationship and if the information proves to be correct, in return for their help, monetary gains can be made. I have several CI's, but Muffin is the one I use the most. Everyone knows that he talks to me; it's like the best-kept secret that everybody knows. (Question: What kind of name is Muffin for a grown-ass man?)

I hear a car drive up and out steps my partner, Roosevelt Jenkins—Rosie for short—looking every bit a male model posing for the perfect shot in the park. He is one good-looking man. He walks over, smiling that smile. NO, WE ARE ONLY PARTNERS. He is too much of a dog for my taste. Besides, mixing business with pleasure is never a good idea. The thought of happily-ever-after with one woman would give him nightmares. I love him because he knows what he is and admits to it readily. On top of that, he is one of the best agents in our organization. We have been partners for five years now. He has taught me a lot, and I have mellowed him out (maybe not so much).

Roosevelt Jenkins is a man's man. He is six feet six inches and is fine as hell. Forty-five with the ripped muscular physique of someone in his twenties. His coffee-colored skin, along with the gray streaks in his hair, makes him look very distinguished, but he is a fool. He exudes this aura of manly confidence. Women adore this man, and he knows it. He knows how to treat a woman, and believe me, he has a lot of them. I have seen women almost come to blows over him, and the next thing you know they are all laughing and acting like nothing happened.

He was married once to the love of his life and made a vow to make this marriage work. However, if it didn't work, all bets were off, and he was never going back down that road again. Some women don't realize a good man when they have one, and she didn't. True to his word, he is on the loose and loving it. I call him Idris Elba's older brother by a different mother, only better-looking. He is smart, he knows his job and is damn good at it. He is one hell of an agent, and I am lucky that he is not only my partner but also my mentor. He was not put off when he was assigned this young, stubborn, and headstrong I-know-what-I-am-doing me. He had to let me fall a couple of times, and I do mean fall HARD. Believe me, I learned. I can count on him always having my back and teaching me every day to get better at my job. I love that he is true to himself. Take him or leave him, he will never change, and I wouldn't want him to.

"What's shaking, beautiful?" he says as he comes and sits down beside me. "How come we couldn't talk at the office? I was on my way in when you called."

"Something is going on, Rosie. Remember how you said always listen to that rumble in your stomach? Well, mine is doing a salsa right now. I didn't want to talk in the office. Have you heard about anything crazy going on through the grapevine? Any of your informants said anything out of the norm?"

"No, Shale, they haven't. You know if I heard anything, I would have told you. Oh, I did hear about that kid getting shot who later died. Did whatever happened this afternoon have anything to with the shooting?"

"I don't know." I relate what happened at the office, and he agrees that something stinks.

Adjusting his shades, he asks, "Have you tried to get ahold of Muffin?"

"Yeah, I called that little shit five times, but he hasn't called me back. He better call me soon or his ass will rot in jail."

"He'll call. You know how scared he is of going to prison."

At that precise time my phone rings. "Ms. Blacque, what's going on? You rang?"

"Muffin, you no-ass Negro, where the hell you been? I have been calling you all morning."

"Hold up, Ms. Blacque, I was busy. I'm calling you back now. See what I'm saying?"

If I could, I would have pulled his ass through the phone. "Nigger, this ain't no joke." I hate using the N word, but sometimes it just fits. "When I call you the next time, you better call me back ASAP, or you will be somebody's muffin bitch in Rikers." I hang up the phone. Why the hell is everybody getting on my damn nerves today?

I look at Rosie, who is doubled over with laughter. "What the fuck is so funny?"

"You are."

I can't help but smile because we both know Muffin is scared shitless of being locked up. He would sell his mother to stay out of jail.

"Shale, are you going back to the office?"

"No, I have had it for today. I am going home. What about you?"

"I have to stop by the office and pick up the box of files on the Johnson case. I volunteered to return the records to the Putnam County sheriff's office. I promised the sheriff a bottle of bourbon when that case was wrapped up. I am a man of my word."

"That's the only reason?"

Smiling, he says, "I might stop by to see an old friend on my way back to the city."

Laughing, I say, "That's the Rosie I know." We agree to keep our ears to the streets in case something else jumps off.

Rosie's cell phone rings as we are walking to our cars. "Hey, what's up? What? Are you sure? OK then, thanks for the info, Kojac, I'll settle up with you later." Staring at his phone, he says, "Shale, we need to go now."

"Go where? I thought you were heading up to Putnam County"

"Change of plans. That was one of my informants. Guess who is back in town?"

"Who?"

"None other than Blackfish Charlie."

The look on my face says it all—what the hell? "Rosie, are you sure?"

"Yeah, my CI saw him last night and again this morning."

Before I know it, I am screaming, "Son of a bitch. I wonder what made him come back to New York?"

"Word on the street is that his mother is very ill. You know how much he loves his mother. She's the only thing that bastard ever loved in his life," Rosie says with this blank look on his face.

Watching his face has me worried about what he will do next. Walking to the car, never taking my eyes off him, I say out loud, "I wonder if NYPD knows he's back yet."

Rosie looks at me. "Shale, we need to catch that son of a bitch before they do."

"Did your CI tell you where?"

"Kojac said not far from his mother's apartment in Washington Heights."

We leave my car; I will call my dad to pick it up for me. Rosie is on the phone with the sheriff, explaining that he will bring the files up later in the week.

As we drive up to the Heights, we go over all we know on Blackfish Charlie. He is 35 and about six-two. The last time we saw him, he had to be well over 300 pounds. Black as a night with no stars, his nose is big and full; it sort of fans out, taking up the whole middle of his face. He has this huge mouth that could swallow a watermelon whole. He got his nickname because he is the color of soot and has a mouth that resembles a large-mouth bass. Some people say he is as ugly as a gorilla, but being the animal lover that I am, I would not insult the gorilla by making such a comparison. I saw a contest once in the newspaper that listed the ugliest animals, and the winner was this godawful fish called the blobfish. This thing is ugly as hell. Well, think of this fish in human form, black as the ace of spades, and you have Blackfish Charlie. It's not just him. His whole family missed the boat in the looks department. I guess that's why they are so mean.

The Williams family is big; I think there are 14 children, and God only knows how many cousins, aunts, and uncles. They are well-known uptown, and not at all for their charitable contributions. Half of the boys are either dead or in prison. The girls fare no better. Two of the sisters died from drugs. Two are prostituting and are on drugs. His father has been in and out of prison so much, they keep a welcome mat in front of his jail cell. His mother ran numbers for a long time; she never had a real job. She was always pregnant. She is a mean and nasty woman. She would fight anyone at the drop of a hat, men included. If she thought that you were looking at her the wrong way, baby, it was on and popping. God forbid if she had been drinking, she became like Godzilla on steroids. Welfare seems to be the only steady means of support. The other way is hustling in whatever way that means.

Blackfish is a wannabe. What does that mean? Well, I'll tell you. He wanted to be a drug dealer; didn't work out, he was using more than he was selling. After that he decided he wanted to be a pimp, pimping out young girls, including his sisters. Real pimps had a serious problem with this career choice. They let him know in no uncertain terms he was not welcome and took his girls away from him, including his sisters. They almost killed him. Then he wanted to be a loan shark; again not a great choice. He was ordered to quit or he would face the consequences. End of loan sharking. Next was fencing stolen property; that didn't work out for him either. None of his career choices worked out for him until he figured that if he stopped working for himself and joined forces with organized crime partners, things would go better for him in the long run. We heard that he was working with one of the gangs in Harlem and was moving up in the organization, but again he fucked up. He became fixated on this young woman who did not reciprocate his feelings. Word has it that he repeatedly raped her and kept her locked up with him for a week. He did not know that she was the niece of a police sergeant. NYPD has an APB on his ass, so he left New York with the help of his family.

He was somewhere in the South, we just didn't know where. As big as this family is, he could be hiding in clear sight and still not be found.

We do know that he was in Tampa, Florida, for a while because he was involved in a drug-related shootout with local police. He was fleeing with some of his crew and got caught between the police and a couple of agents from our agency who happened to be at the scene. There was a brief period of pandemonium and when it was over, two of his crew were dead. Blackfish managed to escape without a scratch. One of the cops was severely wounded, and one of our agents will spend the rest of his life in a wheelchair. The other agent was lucky; she was injured but was able to escape with minor injuries. Rosie took this hard because the wounded agent is a friend and classmate of his. Fred Thomason worked with Rosie after training in New York for three years before relocating to Florida with his wife and two children. He did not die, but he will never be able to work again. Just like the rest of us, he loved his job, and Rosie took this incident to heart.

Blackfish Charlie is now number one with a bullet on our top-ten list. If we don't get to him before NYPD does, he will be dead by tomorrow. We have jurisdiction over NYPD; those were federal agents he shot, and I'll be damned if I am going to sit back and wait for the city to decide their case first. They can have him after we're done with his sorry ass.

Rosie is ranting. Conrad calls and is on the phone with Rosie. "Everyone and his mother knows that bastard is back in town, but Rosie, we do this by the book. I know you are taking this personally, but we have to play by the rules." He is still talking when Rosie hangs up the phone.

I am on the phone with Muffin. "Did you know that Blackfish Charlie is back in town?"

"No, I didn't."

"Muffin, you are the worst liar. We are on our way uptown, and by the time we get there, you better know something."

As soon as we reach the Heights, we are greeted by a squadron of New York's finest. "Shit," Rosie says, "they know he's back in town too. I don't care how many cops are here. He is mine."

"No, Rosie, he's *ours*. His crimes affect all of us."

Conrad calls me and lets me know that we have agents in the area. "Watch out for your partner; he is not thinking straight."

"I know, Conrad, I have his back."

We park around the corner from Blackfish Charlie's mother's apartment, and as we get out of the car, one of the officers is walking toward us, shouting, "He is ours. You fucking feds will have to wait."

"No way in hell," Rosie says, "will we take a backseat. He is ours."

"Like hell he is," the officer says.

"Do you know what that bastard did?"

"Everyone in the city knows what that fucker did, and I hope his ass roasts in hell."

Rosie is screaming, "That son of a bitch shot two federal agents. After we are finished with him, NYPD can have him."

As they are shouting at one another, they are moving closer and closer to each other. I am trying to stop Rosie, and he is taking me along for the ride. "Stop, Rosie, we are on the same team, remember? We need to work together to catch this bastard. Fighting among ourselves serves no purpose."

Just as they are about to come to blows, cops are spilling out of the building. "He is not here. Repeat, the suspect is not in the building. We need to start combing the area. We know he is in the city because he was here this morning when his mother died."

Police begin dispersing throughout the Heights while I am talking Rosie down from the ledge. "Are you OK?"

"Yeah, thanks for that, Shale. If you were not here, I don't know how far we would have gone."

"I know, Rosie. That's what partners are for, we help each other."

We are joined by some of our fellow agents as NYPD is giving us the evil eye. We need to keep our heads on straight from now on. One mistake and NYPD will hang our asses on meat hooks. Let them do most of the work for us. They know we have jurisdiction; it's our ballgame. That's why all the hate is thrown our way. You wouldn't know it to look at it, but we are on the same team. Yeah, but the big difference is we are in the major league, and they are in the minor league.

We decide to ride around for a while and see what happens next. The sun is starting to go down, but you can't miss the presence of the NYPD. They are everywhere. Rosie hasn't spoken a word since he got back in the car. He looks like he is in a trance. I am behind the wheel now to give him a chance to cool off.

My cell phone rings. "Hey, beautiful, it's me, Muffin."

"I can barely hear you, where are you?"

"I am looking at Blackfish Charlie. He is about to split."

"Where are you?"

"I'm in East Harlem. Blackfish is traveling with people who from here look like they could be family. Damn, talk about ugly."

"Muffin, we all know they are ugly. Where in East Harlem?"

"Wait, I'll call you back."

"Muffin, don't you hang up." Dial tone. I swear I'm going to kill his skinny ass.

"Shale, what did he say?"

"He said he was in East Harlem somewhere looking at Blackfish."

"Let's go, why the hell are we sitting here?"

"Rosie, he didn't say where he is."

"Give me the phone, I'll call his ass back." He calls his number, but the line is busy. "Son of a bitch, you mean we are this close to this low-life, and we don't know where the hell he is?"

A few minutes later Muffin calls back. "Muffin, what the fuck?"

"Listen, I had to hang up. I told you I was with Blackfish."

"You said you were looking at him, not that you were with him."

"You say tomato, I say tomahto. Do you want me to tell you what I heard or not?"

"So help me, Muffin, when I get my hands on you—"

"Listen, big mouth, he is leaving tonight, going back down south. He will be riding in an suv with Texas plates. His cousin will be driving. They will stop off in Jersey so he can pick up some money, then on to Texas. He is planning to slip into Mexico. He said now that his mother is gone, there is no reason for him ever to come back to New York."

"Do you know the plate number?"

"No, but the car is dark blue. They should be in Jersey within the next half-hour."

"Can you find out where in Jersey?"

"No, they left already. That is all I could find out. I will expect a lot more moola the next time I see you for all the——"

Click. This time I hang up on him.

We put out a call to be on the lookout for a dark-blue suv with Texas plates. "We don't know how they will enter New Jersey. They can come through the tunnels, the Holland or the Lincoln, or they could take the George Washington Bridge. Please do not notify NYPD that we have this info. We don't want to start a turf war."

About 15 minutes later we get a call that a dark-blue suv with Texas plates just hit the New Jersey Turnpike in Fort Lee. They took the GW Bridge after all. We now have the plate number along with the name Theodore Williams. Bingo, that's our car. Our agents are told, "Follow at a safe distance but do not, repeat, do not apprehend." We are on our way. It is dark now, which works to our advantage.

We pick up the trail in Teaneck Township and take over as the lead car. The car is being driven within the speed limit as not to attract attention. We drive at a consistent speed until we get to a rest stop. The driver of the suv looks like he is having a hard time making up his mind about stopping. The car changes lanes as if they are going to drive up to the rest area but at the last minute they continue.

We have four unmarked cars, always changing positions, riding beside, behind, and in front of the suv, trying to anticipate their next move. We are in constant contact with each other to ensure that nothing is left to chance. We are playing this by the book so that there is no possibility of jeopardizing our case down the road. We have to be very careful; traffic is not super heavy this time at night, but this being the Jersey Turnpike, it is always busy.

We drive until we reach the next rest area, and this time the car does make a pit stop. The lead car with agents pulls up next to the suv, and I take the gas pump behind. Sonia, the agent driving the lead car, pops her hood and tells the attendant that along with the gas, she would like him to check her coolant level, the light keeps coming on. Standing beside the attendant, she is trying to see how many people are in the suv. She can clearly see two individuals in the car, but no Blackfish.

One of the men gets out of the car and walks inside the building housing restaurants, public restrooms, newspaper stands. Two of our agents from the Jersey office go inside after him. Sonia signals that she can now see another person in the car and after getting a better look, she can make out it is a woman. The agents follow the man out of the building as he is juggling food and drinks. One of the agents runs to give him a hand before he drops everything on the ground. "Thanks, brother," he says.

"Not a problem. Glad I was here to help before you lost your load."

"Thanks, brother, good looking out. Have a good night."

"Yeah, you too."

He pays the attendant and gets back in the car. Sonia closes the hood and gets back in the car. The last car with agents moves into lead position ahead of the Texas car, and we all head back to the turnpike.

Back on the turnpike, the suv is driving under the speed limit, which is 55 miles an hour in this area. We fall back so another car can get in front of us. "What the hell are they doing?" Rosie asks.

"I don't know."

The car in front says, "Something is going on. Sonia, didn't you say there were three people in the car?"

"Yeah, that's right. Why?"

"Because we are counting four heads, not three."

"I knew his black ass was in that car."

"Yeah, we all knew."

All of a sudden the car takes off like a bat out of hell. "What the fuck, what spooked them?"

"I don't know."

We look up and see the flashing red lights, then the sirens of the New Jersey state troopers. "Oh hell, somebody let the cat out of the bag." It looks like a police parade with New Jersey and New York police racing down the turnpike.

The Texas car is flying. "Shale, don't let the troopers pass you."

"Not a chance." I floor the gas pedal. Our lead car is on their tail as they go right, then left, then right. We are zig-zagging all along the turnpike, trying to miss the cars that have come to a standstill, flying past motorists with horrified looks on their faces as they watch this caravan of police cars racing after this lone SUV. I manage to get ahead of our lead car, and I am close enough that I can bump the back of the Texas car.

All of a sudden the back window explodes with the sound of bullets coming from inside the back of the car. "Keep your head down," Rosie yells as I am trying to drive with my head bent almost past the steering wheel, trying to dodge the bullets as they whiz past us. Rosie has his gun and is firing back at the car.

We hear over the car radio, "We have gunfire, repeat, we have gunfire." Whoever is at the wheel is driving the hell out of the car, but I'm no slouch either. I am on his ass. Gunfire is being returned, but we have to be careful not to hit one of the many civilian cars in the line of fire. Thank God the other drivers have stopped driving and are making a way for us to get through.

Rosie says, "Slow down, I want to aim for the tires." He leans out of the window and starts shooting a round of bullets at the back tires. Bull's-eye: we hear the sound of the tires being blown. The car is spinning out of control. The SUV hits one car, then another. The next thing you know, he is heading for this bus filled with people coming from New York. I hold my breath because I know the car is going to slam into the bus.

I don't know how he manages, but he is able to miss the bus and is heading down one of the off ramps. We hear another loud pop and the car is all over the place. Rosie says, "One of the front tires just blew." The car is going 90 miles an hour with this long line of law enforcement agencies from two states and the federal government hot on their ass.

All of a sudden the car flips over and over again, hitting construction equipment stored on the side of the road. There is this loud explosion and a big black cloud of smoke. That suv turns into a fireball that I know you could see for miles. Traffic is a nightmare of police cars, fire engines, and undercover police, along with the thousands of motorists, some who were taking pictures with their phones.

We are all standing around watching; there is nothing anyone could have done. Blackfish Charlie is living up to his nickname. Everything in that car is now burnt toast. We are talking with the troopers. "How did you know what was going on?"

"NYPD called for assistance as they were crossing into our jurisdiction. The suspects were wanted by New York and the feds. We heard he was a nasty piece of work."

"One of the worst," I said.

"Happy to know he won't hurt anyone else."

Life was not kind to Blackfish Charlie; let's hope hell will treat him better.

It is morning before we call it a night. Two states and three agencies were involved, which means triple the paperwork. I am so tired I could sleep in the car, but I want to go home. "Rosie, how are you doing?"

"I feel great." He drops me back at my apartment. "Have I told you lately how proud of you I am?" he asks me.

"No, you haven't."

"Well, I am. You were driving this car like you were in the Indy 500."

"I have a great teacher. Paperwork up the ass in the morning, but for now I just want to close my eyes."

"I know it's late, but I think I will call Fred and tell him the good news. See you in the morning, partner."

"It *is* morning. Sleep tight."

My babies greet me at the door, happier more about eating than seeing me. My beautiful neighbor left me some food. Bless you, Gary. I am starving. I feed my babies, take a shower; pour a glass of wine, and heat up the food. I am exhausted but hungry, so while the food is heating up, I start going through the mail. I notice that the answering machine light is blinking. I have four messages. One is from a friend living in Miami; one is from my cousin, asking to borrow money; one is a wrong number. I am about to delete the last message when a voice I never heard before is giving me a phone number to call back, saying it's important.

I play the message a few times, trying to see if I recognize the voice. I don't. I quickly dial the number he left, but no one answers. I hang up and redial the number about six times. No one ever picks up the phone. The area code is in Brooklyn. I have family and friends in Brooklyn, but this is not a number I recognize. Please, God, tell me tomorrow will not be as crazy as today was.

Just as I turn on the television, they are reporting on everything that happened yesterday and tonight. The reporter starts with the Wild West shootout on the New Jersey Turnpike. "All occupants in the suv were killed after leading police on a two-state pursuit." The other big news story is the shooting of the young man earlier yesterday. As the reporter is explaining the crime scene, a scroll happens across the bottom of the television with the age and name of the murder victim: Tony Mazda, 20 years old. "Police are saying that he was killed with a small-caliber handgun. He was shot three times—twice in the chest, once in the leg."

As I stare at the screen, my mind is asking me: Why do I know that name?

CHAPTER 4

decide to go to bed. My brain hurts and I don't want to think anymore. I get in bed and look around the room. I don't like sleeping alone, but my honey is out of town. I'm batting a thousand today. I look at the cats as they join me in the bed. Sophia takes her spot next me on the other pillow. Ochie lies down at the foot of the bed. I was wrong; I am not alone. The light goes out.

A ringing phone wakes me from a sound sleep. I stumble to answer it. What time is it? "Hello?"

"Hey, baby, sorry to wake you up but I wanted to hear your voice. I am watching everything that took place yesterday on the television. My God, Shale, are you alright?"

I smile a sleepy smile. "What time is it?"

"It is one p.m. Time to get up."

"Negro, if you don't get off my phone... It may be one p.m. in Paris, but that makes it seven a.m. here in New York." Yawning, I say, "I just went to sleep less than two hours ago."

"I know, but what's time between lovers? Do you miss me?"

I start to say no, but he would know I am lying. "Of course I miss you, baby. Because you are not here, I had to call my backup."

He laughs. "Your backup better have four paws and a big head, or shit will fly when I get my hands on him."

We both laugh as Ochie lets out the loudest meow I have ever heard. That just makes us laugh even harder. God, I miss him.

"You didn't answer my question."

"Jonathan, you are talking to me, baby. I promise you I am okay."

"Shale, I don't—"

"Please, Jonathan, don't start with the 'I hate your job' thing, not now." I'm too tired for this fight, so I change the subject. "How is your trip going?"

"Good. Things are moving faster than anticipated, so I should be home by the end of the week. How are you?"

I tell him about my weird day: the shooting, my boss going off, and about the message that was left. I ask him if the name Tony Mazda means anything to him. He says not that he can remember. We continue with a general conversation about this and that. All the while I imagine him here with me, lights out, candles glowing, wine flowing, and jazz in the background. Love is all around. Every time I think of him, I thank God, his mama, and his daddy.

Jonathan Kennedy is the love of my life, besides my father and my late uncle. We have been together three years, and love is good. He is a jazz man, the youngest tenured professor of music at NYU. He travels the world planning jazz festivals where jazz is appreciated. He is passionate about preserving the history of America's original music and passing on that passion to his students, and the world as a whole. Handsome and smart—I hit the jackpot.

He was married before to the sister of the wicked witch of the east. Thank God he came to his senses and divorced 'Broom Hilda' before we met. Now don't get me wrong: from everything I know about her, she is stunning, tall, intelligent, and a bitch. Why he married her in the first place, I will never understand. He told me she married him because she saw dollar signs and knew that he was on the fast track at NYU. He married her because he was young and she looked good on his arm. He told me he never really loved her. Being young and stupid sums it up nicely.

She couldn't understand that he was in this for the passion and not the money. The funny thing is that after they divorced, he did start making money and was able to keep his passion as well. Now I got the man, the passion, and when it comes to the money, I have my own, thank you very much. My mother from a very young age taught me the benefits of saving money. My uncle, God bless his soul, made sure that money was not one of my worries. I would give it all up just to have him back in my life. I miss him more than I care to admit. All in all, I still have to say GOD IS GOOD.

By the time we finish saying our 'I love you's,' three hours have come and gone. It is now 10 a.m. I hang up, missing him even more.

The cats are up and hungry and I have to go the bathroom, so I get up to feed the babies, and as I am leaving the bathroom, the phone rings again. "I know you love me," I say as I pick up the phone, but the voice on the phone is not Jonathan; it is the voice from the message. He starts to say something but goes quiet. "Who is this?" The phone goes dead. It's too damn early in the morning for this bullshit. I get dressed and am out the door.

Everyone is talking about the events of yesterday. "Great work, everybody." Conrad is walking around sounding very like a proud papa. I was mesmerized watching things unfold. "The result will cool things down a bit between our agency and NYPD. I got a call this morning from the commissioner, and he was saying some very nice things for a change. It will take about a week for all paperwork to be completed, and he said he would consider it a big favor if our agents can have their paperwork done in two days." Rosie says that won't be a problem. "Great," Conrad says. "You may need to go down to One Police Plaza, but they will let you know." Turning to go back to his office, he says to me, "Shale, I didn't know that was you driving the car. All I can say is you were driving the hell out of that car last night."

"Thanks, boss. I have an excellent teacher."

Rosie smiles. "I have an excellent student."

The next week is quiet. We finish our paperwork and are interviewed by NYPD. "Blackfish and his cousins were incinerated in the explosion. There was nothing left but we did find several guns and semi-automatics in the rubble."

We are told by one of the police officers that when the family was told that Blackfish was now dust, one of his brothers said, "Great, we won't have to bury the sorry son of a bitch." What a warm and caring family, and what a sad and pathetic life.

Jonathan ends up having to stay in Paris for another week, lucky bastard. I am in serious need of some downtime. I want to do something where I don't have to think. I call my cousins Nelly and Dee for a girls' night out. We are all around the same age, and we don't see each other as much as we like.

I am pleasantly surprised when Dee's daughter Joy joins us. She is in college out of state. What a beautiful young lady. She has her head on straight, is smart, and has always known that she wanted to be an architect. She is on her way, staying on the dean's list for two years. See, this is the other side of my family. We have smart and crazy. Just your all-American family.

We go to a movie and have dinner afterward. It is so much fun catching up with family and each other's lives. Everyone wants the real 411 on what happened with Blackfish Charlie. Nelly says, "Girl, you know we live vicariously through you." Joy is giving us what life is like on college campuses these days.

The topic of the night, of course, turns to when will Jonathan and I get married. "When we decide, you all will know. My mother will be beating the hell out of her drum. We are quite happy with the way things are. If we got married now, it would be for other people and not us. That is not a reason to get married." We spend the rest of the night talking husbands, babies, boyfriends, and jobs. We have a very good time.

I love my cousins. Each one is a real dynamo in her own right. They are more like the sisters I never had than cousins. We make a promise to make time to see each other more often for a cousins' night out. For years, we have been saying we want to do a weekend getaway, just us girls. Well, now it's time to stop talking about doing it and plan the damn thing already. It is agreed that by the fall, we will have something planned. Joy says she will make sure we do.

CHAPTER 5

Another weekend has come and gone. Monday morning Sophie and Ochie are up early, wanting to be fed. They have this uncanny ability to know just when my alarm is about to go off. I lie there for fifteen minutes more until I had no choice; they want to eat now.

I am eating breakfast and watching the morning news when my phone rings. The number isn't showing up on my Caller ID, and before I can say anything, the voice from a week ago gives me an address in East Brooklyn, and hangs up the phone. I still don't know the voice, but I quickly get dressed, running out the door.

I call Rosie and tell him about the phone call. He will meet me in Brooklyn. "Wait for me, Shale. I mean it. You don't know what the hell is going on here. Don't take any unnecessary chances, especially when you are by yourself. Promise me."

"Rosie, I won't do anything stupid."

"That's not exactly a promise, Shale."

"OK, partner, see you when you get here. Hurry, Rosie."

The address is that of an old, burned-out building from the 70's that hasn't changed since the fire. I arrive a few minutes before he does, and as I look around, I pull out my gun, not knowing what I will find.

I don't venture into the building, waiting for Rosie to show up. God only knows what the hell is in there. I take a look around outside. If the inside is anything like the outside, I don't want to go in. As far as I can tell, there doesn't seem to be anyone else here but me. I hear a car pull up and run over to Rosie. "Listen, it is so dark in there, I don't think a flashlight alone is going to work."

Rosie thinks for a minute. "I have an idea." He turns his car around so that he can turn his headlights into the building. He turns his high beams on and a stream of light floods the place.

We enter with pistols drawn in one hand and flashlights in the other. As we enter I am walking ever so lightly. I am not taking any chances; just my luck I will fall on my ass and break something. What the hell was I thinking to wear a new pair of boots? They are hot, though.

The only light in the place besides the headlights and the flashlights is from where the windows and doors used to be. All the windows are at the top of the building, so all of the natural light is shining at the roof line. I hate this shit. Even with the car lights and the two flashlights, it's still black as night. The smell is greeting us at the door. As we enter, we can hear rats running around. Following the beam of a flashlight, we see rats the size of fat cats running for cover. The stench hits me in the face, and I feel like I am going to throw up. We can tell that this is a perfect place for a shooting gallery. We can see used needles and drug paraphernalia on the floor.

Rosie slips but is able to catch himself before he hits the ground. "Are you OK?"

"Yeah. I don't want to know what the hell I just stepped in."

This building seems to go on forever. It's not very wide, but it is very long and narrow. The lights from the car can't reach the back of the building. With a look of frustration and confusion, I turn to Rosie. "Why in the world was I told to come here? I don't see anything here worth our time, and I have never been in this area before today. Do you think it's a setup?"

"I don't know, Shale, but I believe we need to get the hell out of Dodge."

We head to the nearest door opening when Rosie suddenly slips and this time, he can't stop himself from falling. "Fuck!"

"Partner, are you OK?"

"Yeah, Shale, I'm having the time of my life. Whatever this crap is, I just hope it's not shit. I have on a new pair of pants."

"Rosie, does it matter if it's shit or not? It's nasty, whatever the hell it is. You can always buy new pants, fool. There's only one of you."

"Thanks, Boots."

As he tries to stand up again, he slips and falls. This time his foot hits a pole that was holding up part of the rotted roof, and the roof collapses down on us. Light comes streaming in the building as we dig ourselves out from under the debris. We can now see what we couldn't see in the dark. In the corner are four bodies lying on top of each other. The rats had been having a banquet with the bodies as pieces are missing. We cannot move, looking at the sight in front of us. I try to run but my feet feel like they are planted in cement.

Rosie pulls out his phone and calls for backup. Within minutes the whole borough of Brooklyn sounds like one big siren. By the time the units arrive, we have made our way out of the building. Cops are covering the area like ants at a picnic. There are patrol cars, police helicopters flying above. Reporters from the different news channels and newspapers are flooding the area, all competing to be the first to let the city know about the murders. The chief of police arrives with his entourage.

Conrad shows up and walks straight to Rosie and me. "Why did I know the two of you were involved?"

"Don't give us any shit, Conrad, you were the first person we called," Rosie says.

"Tell me what happened. Start from the beginning and don't skip anything."

I tell him about the phone calls, about the last message giving me this address. He asks me if I recognized the voice. I say I didn't. The puzzled look Conrad has on his face matches what I am feeling inside. "I wonder why you were called and not the local police?"

"I have no idea," I say.

The chief of police comes over to question us about the murders. He wants to know how come it was the feds who discovered the bodies and not NYPD. Why were we the first ones on the scene? Did we know something that they didn't know? What was our connection to the bodies? I repeat about the phone calls. He has the same question that Conrad had: "Why call you?" As we are talking, the coroner's assistants started bringing out the bodies.

One by one the bodies are brought out of the building. The bodies are of one Hispanic or Italian male about 25 years old, two African American men, one about the age of 27; the other looks around 35. The last one is a Caucasian male of about 45 who is wearing a suit, unlike the other three, who are wearing jeans and tee shirts.

The medical examiner walks by with this look on her face that has all of us worried. Conrad asks what had caused that look. She hands him a small bag that contains a badge. The man in the suit was a cop. Not only was he a cop, but a detective with the 75th Precinct, which covers this part of Brooklyn. The medical examiner is asked to put a rush on the results of the autopsies, but could she give a guess on how they were killed. It appears that they all had been hit with a blunt object, and then shot in the head. The cop had the most trauma to his body. He had been shot four times and both his hands were cut off. She would know more after the autopsies. As she is leaving, she turns and says, "By the way, they have been dead for about a week."

The news travels fast among the police on the scene that a detective from their precinct is one of the dead. Disbelief and a look of shock is on all the faces, especially when they find out that the detective was Ben Cannon. Ben Cannon was a decorated detective on the force who had his eyes on being a captain. He was well liked by the rank and file and had been on the force for a long time. There are more questions than answers, and everybody wants answers. What was he doing in that burned-out building? What was his connection with the other bodies? Everybody has their own opinions, and the most logical answer is that he was working undercover. If he was, it was news to his boss.

For some reason, I am not buying that. I don't know why. Whoever killed him wanted it known that he was a cop. Otherwise they would have taken his badge and ID. Something is rotten here, but I can tell you this: I would never say what I am thinking out loud, not in this company. Every cop in the city will be working this case, not resting until they know why Ben was killed and who killed him.

The building is under 24-hour surveillance as the crime scene will be turned upside down. The forensic division will be working around the clock. If more help is needed, they can just say the word: support from the rest of the city, as well as any federal forensic team, is at their service. These murders will force our agencies to pull together to solve this case.

The next day we are called in for a special briefing to form a task force which will work with local authorities. Normally this would be a local matter with only NYPD involved. However, until we know what my connection is to this case, we are now part of the investigation. Conrad will be the point of contact for our agency and Captain Raymond Smith of the 75th Precinct for NYPD.

By the time of the meeting, we have the names of the dead: Terrence Mazda, 25; William Gates, 27; James Reed, 29. They all have criminal lengthy records, ranging from larceny, arson, aggravated assault, robbery, and rape to drugs. Princes, every last one of them. I am working at my desk, going over the information that has come in concerning our deceased. It has been nonstop since we discovered the bodies, so it takes a minute before I realize that I had seen or heard one of the names before. I find the news video from a week ago, when the name Mazda appeared on the bottom of the screen. Mazda was the name of the young man who had been shot and killed. I call the medical examiner's office to check if they will run tests on both Mazdas. I want to know if they could be related.

CHAPTER 6

The medical examiner calls back with the results: they are brothers. Our first big break in the case, thank you, God. It's been a couple of days since the discovery of the dead bodies and about a week since I spoke to that little fuck Muffin. I have been trying to reach him with no luck. I guess I will need to go looking for his skinny ass. Why he continues to try my patience, I don't know. We have been doing this dance for years now. He knows that I know how to hurt him and can, and yet he persists on racking my nerves. If the information I get from him wasn't on point, his ass would be in jail now. I know his usual hangouts, so I go from the bar to the barbershop to the pool hall. As I pass the liquor store, guess who I see coming out of the liquor store holding a 40-ounce? My little prey.

For a man of such a small and skinny stature, he sure can drink a lot. If the liquor doesn't kill him, I will. As I pull up to the curb, he spots me, and it's show time. "Hey, Shale baby, long time no see." I grab him by his shirt and throw him against the car. His 40 hits the ground, "WHOA, Shale, what the fuck?"

"Where the hell have you been, you little shit? I have been calling you for over a week." Before he can answer, I throw him in the back seat of the car. Steam is coming out of my ears as I jump in the front seat. We drive off to Muffin's stooges laughing their asses off.

Looking in the rearview mirror, I start to laugh at the sight of this mess in my car. This grown-ass man is lying almost in a fetal position, crying like a little boy who just got spanked by his mother. I stop the car and turn to Muffin, who is still crying. "Shut up, fool, before I slap the shit out of you. Why are you crying? I didn't even hit you."

"I know, Shale, but I dropped my forty ounces, and it was my first one of the day."

I shake my head; what a royal fuck-up. "I'll tell you what: if you talk, I will buy you another forty."

He stops crying and says in a pissed-off tone, "*Is that all?* What about my usual? Do you know how much you embarrassed me in front of my homies? Do you? And what about all the info I gave you on Blackfish Charlie? I'm still waiting for you to show your gratitude on that bit of info. Do I get a simple thank-you? NO, I get treated like I'm some fucking criminal!"

"SHUT UP, IDIOT, BEFORE I SHOOT YOU BETWEEN THE EYES. You are in no position to bargain or ask for anything, and you are a little criminal. I told you before when I call you, I expect you to answer before I hang up the phone." Muffin has tears in his eyes and starts to say something. I hold up my hand. "If what you are about to say has nothing to do with the murders, you are dead meat. Start talking."

"What murders?" he asks. "Come on, Shale, you know if I heard anything, you would be the first to know."

I am looking at this fool, fighting back the urge to slap him silly. "Muffin, I don't have the time to play these games with you. Now talk."

He can see I am in no mood for his foolishness, so he says, "The word on the street is that the detective was on the take. He had his hands in everything and was shaking down the criminal elements. It was either pay or go to jail. He considered himself a big man around town. He never acted like he was afraid of getting caught. He did what he wanted and with whom he wanted. He had a thing for prostitutes of color, and I heard he had a coke habit."

Looking at him through the rearview mirror, I ask, "How the hell was he able to get away with all this, and nobody noticed?"

"Shale, you can't be that naïve. Do you honestly believe that he was the only dirty cop in all of the NYPD? They look out for each other. You

heard the old saying, one hand washes another? Well, there is a shitload
of hand-washing going on in the NYPD."

"Muffin, you can't condemn a whole department on the actions of
a few. Not all cops are bad."

"I didn't say that all cops are bad, but the ones who *are* bad are
treacherous. Not only was he protected by his own, but he also had
protection from the streets. He was in bed with some appalling people."

"What people, Muffin? Who are these people? Give me something
to work with here. Give me some names, anything. Do you know who
his partners are?"

"No, I don't. But I'll tell you this: he has to have friends in high
places for him to carry on the way he did. I bet now his bosses are acting
surprised that he is dead. They all knew he was crooked, and nobody
gave a damn because he was in with the lowlifes of this world. Watch, I
bet the next news reports will say what a great cop he was, working to
rid the community of crime, making the streets a safer place. They can
all kiss my ass. They are all a bunch of crooks."

He pauses. "I know he was NYPD, but with all the shit he was into,
I'm surprised that he didn't land on the feds' radar. Maybe someone
who works for Uncle Sam is in on it too," Muffin says.

I say, "That's not possible," but to myself, I wonder.

I drive Muffin to the other side of town, pay him, and repeat myself:
"If I call you and you don't call me back, I will hunt you down." He gets
out of the car and runs down into the subway.

My mind is going a thousand miles a minute. Could anyone I know
be involved in this shit? Cops and federal agents in bed with the devil? I
guess at this point we can't rule anyone out. Everyone is suspect.

I am tense and need to let off steam. I call ahead to see if I can
get some time in with Hanshi Akihiko Yamamoto. He says to come on
over, it's been a while. He will make room for me. I have been taking martial arts since I joined the feds. I am going for my second-
degree black belt in karate. I should be farther along than I am, but
with work, I can't always train the way I should. I find this is one of
the best ways for me to release. There are better ways to release, but

I digress. Hanshi Yamamoto is a master of the arts, and he is especially good with women.

His classes are always full, so I was happy he was able to see me. We greet each other, and right away he tells me he can feel how stressed-out and tense I am. He designs a routine for me and after warming up, he puts me through the wringer. We start with karate, then judo. He puts me through the wringer of jujitsu, aikido. After that we start using melee weapons and polearms. I work out for $2\frac{1}{2}$ hours, wet to the core.

I feel like a new woman after taking a very long and hot shower. I decide to stop by and see my parents. As I drive up, I see my father sitting on the steps of the brownstone with my uncle who lives on the third floor. Our two German Shepherds, Duke and Missy, are keeping them company. I walk over and the dogs greet me with sloppy wet kisses and more kisses. There is nothing like the sight of dogs wagging their tails, happy to see you. I kiss my dad and my uncle and sit down between the two of them, catching up. My mother drives up with bags full of groceries. My father takes the bags, and I give her a big kiss. After putting away the food, she joins us on the steps. My cousin Junior walks up and kisses Mommy and me on his way home. I tell them all that I can about the investigation. I see the look on my mother's face, so I change the subject quickly. "So Junior, how's your love life?"

My cell phone rings. It's Jonathan, who is back in the city. I excuse myself and drive over to his place, excited to see him. He is standing in the doorway when I get to the apartment. I almost knock him down. As we walk to his bedroom, articles of clothing are dropped almost in a straight line. By the time we get to the bedroom, we are completely naked. Miss-you sex with the man I love, my second-best workout of today.

We sleep in very late. I wake up to the smell of fresh coffee, which he brings to the bed. I tell him about the case. He tells me about his trip and reminds me how wonderful Paris is and how much better it is when I'm there with him.

I look at this amazing man and count my blessings that we are together. Everyone wants to know when we are getting married. Who knows? Everything with us is great right now. The only sore spot is my job. He hates it. He is not the kind of man who wants his woman home, barefoot, and pregnant; however, he doesn't want his wife running around with a gun, shooting and being shot at by criminals who wouldn't give a shit if the cop was a woman. I actually understand, but I love my job, and children are not on the top of my list, so here we are.

We take a long, lingering shower, and afterward go out to our favorite place to eat. We both live in the area, so after eating we walk through the Village, stopping to do a little shopping. We end up at my apartment to drop off some of my purchases, pick up the mail, and check on my babies. Jonathan does not come up with me because he runs into one of his students. The cats are not in the apartment, so that means Gary has them.

There is a knock on the door. Gary sticks his head in. "Hey, babe, the children are with us. I came home and all I could hear was the cats meowing. What kind of mother are you, leaving the babies to starve?"

"I know," I say. "Ochie only weighs a ton."

Laughing, he says, "Girl, some people like a little meat on the bone, just saying."

"Get out," I shout. I can hear him singing in the hallway, "Girls just want to have fun."

I put the mail on the table and check for any phone messages. I have a message to call the headquarters in DC. That's weird; why didn't they call my cell or call me at work? I go through my mail, and there is an envelope with no return address. I open it and inside is a plain white sheet of paper with the letters cut out, saying: WATCH YOURSELF, YOU DON'T KNOW WHAT YOU ARE GETTING YOURSELF INTO. DON'T BE STUPID. I put the letter in my purse and head downstairs. I don't let Jonathan see the letter; this would be the kind of thing that would push him over the edge, and if I showed it to him, I would never hear the end of it.

We leave to go back to his apartment. While he goes into the wine bar, I text Rosie about the letter, saying *I need to see you now*. I tell Jonathan that I have a meeting to go to, so I would meet up him later.

Driving to meet Rosie, my mind is going a thousand miles a minute. The phone calls and now this letter. What the hell does all this mean, and what is my connection? Could this be tied up with one of my old cases? No, that can't be it. If that was the case, why was Rosie not involved? He was the man in charge; I was only the rookie. Besides, all our cases are sewn up tight. No, that can't be it. There has to be another reason. I just hope I find out what that is before I go crazy.

Rosie is at one of our meeting places in Central Park. He is talking to a beautiful young woman dressed like she is going or coming from the gym. Sitting in my car, watching him do his thing, I can't help but smile. This man has a way with women. He is handing her his card as I approach.

Smiling, he looks at me. "What? I was minding my own business when this young lady asked me how to get to the Boathouse Restaurant. Being the gracious New Yorker that I am, I had to talk to her and make sure she had the right direction."

Laughing, I say, "We New Yorkers thank you for all you do on behalf of the city."

"I was going to ask you how was your night, but that won't be necessary. I know Jonathan is back in town."

"What can I tell you, Rosie. When you're right, you're right."

I show him the letter and he stops laughing. The look on his face is that of brotherly concern. "Was this letter delivered to your apartment?"

"Yeah, it was with the rest of my mail. The stamp shows that the letter was sent from Manhattan."

"I think someone is trying to tell you something," he says.

"YOU THINK?." "But why me? Why the phone calls? And now this. I'm just glad that Jonathan didn't come with me upstairs, because if he knew about this letter, he would have freaked the fuck out."

Rosie says, "I'm not sure why you, but there has to be a good reason."

"Well, when you think of that reason, please let me know. Conrad is on my ass because he thinks I am not telling him everything I know about this case. What the hell am I supposed to say to him when I don't know what my connection is? Oh, by the way, I had a message from headquarters."

"Why?"

"I don't know."

"Why would they call you at home when they could have called you at the office or on your cell?"

"They just said to call back when I had a chance." The silence is palpable. "I don't know what to do or who to trust—except you, that is. I can trust you, right?"

"Every day of my life," he says.

"Rosie, we need to find out the connection of the Mazda brothers to Ben Cannon. Muffin told me the streets protected him, and he wasn't the only dirty cop on the take. I wonder how far up the ladder this thing goes."

Rosie says, "I want to know who on the streets he was in bed with, and how come we are only hearing this shit now. Listen, I will check with my sources, and you need to talk to Muffin again. I think he is holding out on you. Also, Shale, you need to be careful; we don't know what the hell we have stepped into here."

"I know," I say.

I call Muffin as I leave the park. Of course it goes to his voicemail. Why is this nigger testing me?

As I am leaving the park, I notice that I am being followed. Approaching a light that is about to turn red, I floor the gas and go through the light; the car does the same. I call Rosie and tell him I am being followed. He says to head back to the park and he will double back. The car is still following me, only closer. I drive until I come to an area where there is construction going on. The road is blocked with equipment, so I have to drive like a stunt driver to avoid all the shit that is in my way.

As I turn the car around a bulldozer, Rosie is on the other side. The car that is following me is in between both our cars and the bulldozer. We jump out of the cars with guns drawn. "FEDERAL AGENTS, get out of the car!" I shout.

"NOW!" screams Rosie.

The doors open and two plainclothes police officers get out with their guns drawn. "NYPD, drop your weapons."

"NO, you drop yours," I scream. It looks like a scene out of an old western movie. The four of us are still standing there with guns drawn; nobody is moving. "You put your weapons down; we will do the same."

"How about you put your weapons down, and we will talk," one of the detectives says. "We will all lay down our guns at the same time."

"NO," says Rosie. "You first."

Once they see we are not backing down, they withdraw their weapons. We slowly put down our weapons, making sure not to take our eyes off the cops.

"Why are you following me?"

"The murders in Brooklyn."

"Why the hell didn't you let me know who you are? I was ready to blow your brains out."

"We didn't want to alert you in case..."

"In case of what?"

"We were not sure how you are connected to the murders."

"I don't know myself. Someone has involved me without my knowledge, and I'm mad as hell. Before the phone calls, I was never in that section of Brooklyn. I don't even know how they got my home phone number. The only connection I know of is Muffin. I know that little shit knows more than he maintains."

Rosie asks, "Why don't you tell us what is going on, since you obviously know more than we do."

One of the cops introduces himself as Victor Ramirez, and the other man is Brad Shaughnessy. Both are Internal Affairs (IA) officers. "How did you pick up on me?"

"You crashed our surveillance we have on Muffin, and we weren't sure how much he told you."

"Why would you be investing Muffin? He is not a cop."

"No, he is not, but he is in this up to his ass. He is only one of a handful of persons of interest that we are investigating. We wanted to know how much you feds know about a local case that should only involve NYPD."

"I will not repeat myself again: I told you I have no idea why I was singled out."

"Well, we are involved now, whether we like it or not," Rosie says, "so why don't you investigate dirty cops, and we will handle the rest. From where I'm sitting, this is well beyond NYPD. It has reached the federal level, so it is no longer a local matter."

Victor responds, "We need to know what Muffin told Shalimar."

"Like?"

"How many more cops are involved? If he could name names? Whatever else he could tell us to help with our end of the investigation."

"All Muffin said was that Ben Cannon was being protected by the streets and that he wasn't the only cop on the take. He was up to his neck in all kinds of bad shit. He made out like he was a big man around town without fear of being caught. That makes me think someone higher up had his back. Someone maybe in NYPD. From what I heard, you guys should start talking to some of the working girls on the street. He had a thing for prostitutes of color, and a serious coke habit. Do you know that to be true?"

"Yes," Brad answers. "That's why we had him under surveillance."

Rosie smiles and says, "You guys are lousy at your jobs, since he ended up dead."

"Someone tipped him off about the investigation. We now know that Ben and his crew were using that burned-out building to hide some of their take." Brad continues, "The building is being razed by sections because we are finding bundles of cash hidden throughout the ground. Our forensic accountants are still working on what has been found so far. I think it is well over five million dollars and counting. We don't know who was hiding the money, and unfortunately, the only one alive to tell us is Muffin."

Smiling, I say, "I know Muffin didn't have anything to do with the murders. He may be involved with the money, but his ass is scared of his own shadow. I don't think he has ever held a gun. I honestly believe he knows nothing about buried money. Trust me, he would have let that slip by now."

Victor says, "Maybe Ben killed the others because he was afraid that someone would talk if the higher-ups got wind that money was going missing. Over five million dollars so far, you bet your ass someone knew something was going on. Ben was spiraling out of control, and a decision was made to cut ties."

Rosie asks, "If Ben killed the others, then who killed Ben?"

"I don't know if I believe Ben killed the others," I say. "My gut is saying they were killed together, and Ben's hands were cut off because he was the one stealing the money."

Victor says, "Whoever killed them either didn't know about all the hiding places or didn't have time to dig up everything."

"Does IA have anyone else under suspicion, cop or no cop?" I ask.

"We are not ready to release that information yet, but I can tell you that this operation is getting bigger than first thought."

Brad starts to say, "We think someone who works——"

Victor finishes by saying, "——in your office."

Rosie and I look at each other, not believing what we are hearing. "In our office? Why not the FBI or CIA? Why does it have to be our office? Are you sure? Where's your proof? Everyone who works in our office has been vetted and has been there for years," I say.

"Ben was a cop for years and look at him," Brad says.

My mind goes back to my conversation with Muffin, who said the same thing. There is a long silence when Brad says, "We should work together. Dirty cops give both our agencies a bad name. We want to weed out the bad seeds. What do you think?"

Before I can answer him, my cell phone goes off at the same time Rosie's phone goes off. I answer and it's Pookie, Muffin's girlfriend, crying on the phone that two men took Muffin and threw him in a car. She isn't making much sense, and I am trying to comprehend what she is saying. "Do you know who took him?"

"No," she says, "but he was bleeding, and Bullets Morgan stated that they beat him before they threw him in the car. Nobody did anything because they were cops." Rosie is getting the same information. "HELP HIM, PLEASE," she cries.

We tell Victor and Brad what is happening. They both get on their phones. Rosie and I have no other recourse but to trust them. Right now finding Muffin is top priority. I call Pookie back to see if she has calmed down enough to answer questions, and she says yes. I ask her to tell me everything that went down, no matter how small she may think it is. I want everything she knows. "And don't lie. We need to find him. Something he told you could help us. I don't want to hear from you that you don't know anything, because I know you know."

As I am talking to Pookie, Rosie says one of his contacts has information. Muffin was last seen in Queens. There are a number of abandoned buildings near the river, and the informant says he saw two men getting out of a dark-blue sedan and Muffin was with them. He also says it didn't look like Muffin was walking on his own.

Victor is on the phone and comes back with information that he knows where Muffin is: one of the cops they have under surveillance has a GPS on the car, and the car is in Queens. Victor tells his team, "Don't call this in; we will take care of this ourselves." 'Can't take any chance' is the theme song. Trust no one at this point. He gives us the address and we all jump in our cars.

As I am racing to Queens, all I can think about is Muffin. As much of a pain in the ass as he can be, if anything happens to him, I will never forgive myself. He doesn't deserve to go out like this. I know that he is way over his head, and it will get him killed.

The three cars are in constant contact as we approach the area. We turn off the sirens as we get closer to the building. We see a sedan parked in the front of the building, so we go around to the back. We get out of the car with guns drawn. Rosie goes to the left of the building, I go to the right, and IA is standing straight in the back.

Rosie is closer than the rest of us, so he looks through a broken window pane with most of the glass gone. He motions for me to get closer and as I get closer, I can hear Muffin crying. It sounds like they are beating the shit of him. We synchronize our movements and on three,

Rosie says in a loud voice, "FEDERAL AGENTS, COME OUT WITH YOUR HANDS UP." We get the answer back with a barrage of bullets coming in our direction.

We didn't want to just open fire because Muffin might be in the way. Rosie starts shooting because he has a clearer view of the inside. Victor and Brad jump in their car and drive the vehicle into the building while I run in behind the car, gun blazing.

Muffin is in a chair with his hands tied behind his back; his face is swollen three times its normal size. There are five men with guns running in different directions, shooting at the same time. Victor and Brad are shooting from the car windows. Rosie, shooting from my left, is able to nail two of the men, Brad another one, and Victor is able to get one who is trying to escape out the back.

I run to Muffin, trying to untie him, when I am hit from behind and grabbed around my neck. He picks me up like I am a rag doll, and I am over six feet tall without heels. This tells you how big this bastard is. I am fighting for my life as he pulls me to the back. Rosie, Brad, and Victor are yelling at him to let me go. He holds his gun to my head, saying stay back or he would blow my head off. They can't get a clear shot without the chance of hitting me. I am trying to free myself, but the grip he has on me is too tight. I suddenly stop struggling and go limp; this move allows me to flip this bitch over. He lands on his back, hitting the floor hard. The gun falls out of his reach, which gives me time to settle myself.

He jumps up and runs toward the crumpled remains of what at one time were stairs leading up to the top floor. Most of the steps are missing so he is literally jumping up to land on what few steps are left. I take off after him, repeating his actions. The floor is like walking on quicksand. It will not take much for this whole thing to fall out beneath us. The little light that is coming through is not much help, but he is not a little man, so he cannot just disappear. "You stupid slut, I can't believe you were dumb enough to come after me without your backup. I'm going to enjoy killing your black ass."

"Bring it on, big boy." He charges toward me but falls due to weak flooring. "Too late to beg for your sorry ass," I say. The small stream of light coming from holes in the roof makes it appear as if he has steam coming out of his nostrils.

By the time I get close to him, he is standing up. He reaches into his pocket and pulls out a small-caliber gun. I do a spin around so fast that the gun is flying out of his hand before he can get off a shot. "You nigger bitch," he is seething.

"Nigger bitch? Is that all you got? Too bad the last person you will see is this nigger bitch smiling as you take your last breath." He is coming at me like a locomotive, but he falls again because of all the debris on the floor. He lands on his back near my foot and tries to grab my ankle.

Jumping out of his way, lifting my right leg, I come down hard on his right eye; the heel of my boot goes all the way through, my foot resting on his face. Blood is coming out of that eye in all directions. He is screaming and at the same time trying to lift my foot. It is as if he is having a violent grand mal seizure. The way his body is jerking back and forth, he did manage to throw me off balance. He is trying to hold his eye and at the same time stand up, but he doesn't get far. There is nothing for him to hold onto, and because he is so disoriented, he can't see the hole in the floor. I back away until I am near one of the only poles still standing. As he is thrusting around the floor, it starts shaking and rumbling, and in a split second the floor gives way and he goes down hard, landing on his back.

Rosie is screaming, "Shale, where the hell are you?"

"I'm OK, but I can't say the same for Left Eye." I look through the hole and can see he is not moving, and for good reason: there is a long rebar wire that has pierced his neck.

The guys have to help me down, the flooring is that unstable. "Is everyone OK?" I ask once I am on solid ground.

"Yeah, we heard the roof and knew it was about to come down, so we had time to move."

I am covered in blood, standing over this dead body, looking down at his neck with this long metal rod sticking straight out. "Son of a bitch, I bet that hurt," Brad says, looking at this mess. His left eye is wide open, the right eye is gone. He looks like something out of a Frankenstein movie.

Victor, laughing, says, "Damn, girl, you have a lot of guts. Glad you're on our side."

"It's all that Kung Fu shit she's into," Rosie says, smiling. He is next to Muffin, untying him as Victor is calling for backup and an ambulance.

I run over to Muffin, who is not breathing. Rosie starts CPR. "Come on, Muffin, hang in there." Victor and Brad are going around, looking at the men lying dead on the ground. Victor is on the phone, explaining to his superiors what just went down. He also contacts our office and leaves word for Conrad.

Only two of the five men have ID on them, and they both turn out to be cops: William Brown and Rome Kind, both from the 104th Precinct in Queens. One of the other men we think is a cop but he doesn't have any ID on him. "We need to find out now," Brad says.

Victor looks at us and says, "Damn, how many cops are involved in this shit?"

Muffin is not moving and his eyes are beaten shut. "Muffin, can you hear me?" Nothing. Just then we hear the sirens pulling up and police spilling into the building.

The paramedics rush in. "Over here," Rosie says. "He's the only one still breathing. The rest are dead."

They start working on Muffin, attempting to get some kind of sound or movement out of him. Conrad rushes over to me. "ARE YOU OK? JESUS, WHAT HAPPENED? YOU LOOK LIKE SHIT."

I say, "You should see the other guy," as he goes over to the dead man with the big hole in his neck and looks at me, smiling.

"I see that judo shit works."

Looking down at Muffin, I ask, "Is he going to be alright?"

"I don't know," says the paramedic. "It looks like he was drugged with something before they beat the cramp out of him." Muffin is taken away in the ambulance as we start telling the events of what happened to the same group of top brass as when the four bodies were discovered.

We start at the part where we were surrounding the building. "Wait," the chief of police says. "How did you know they were here?"

The four of us look at each other and before we could say anything, Brad says, "We got a tip from one of our informants." (Remember, we can't trust anybody; they can't know about the surveillance.)

The chief doesn't look like he believes him but says nothing more. We continue with the story as the five bodies are being removed. "Get cleaned up and meet us back at the station this afternoon. Be there."

As we make our way back to our cars, we are blinded by the press. "Damn, these people have radar that the army should borrow." I look at Rosie and see blood on his arm. "Oh my God, Rosie, you were hit."

He looks down. "It's not too bad," he says, "I'm only grazed."

"Why didn't you have the paramedics take a look at you while they were here?"

"I'm OK," he says. "Besides, I have my private nurse who will take care of me."

We all start laughing. My partner: even when he is shot, he still has women on the brain.

CHAPTER 7

On the way home to get cleaned up, I check my cell phone to see if anyone had called. There were three messages: one from Pookie, still hysterical and ranting about Muffin; another from my father, who was watching things as they unfolded on the television; the third from Jonathan, who heard from my dad to quickly turn on the local news. Fuck, how am I ever going to explain this to the men in my life? I am not looking forward to having this conversation with Jonathan. He already wants me to quit my job.

I decide I will call back my dad. First, I let him know that I am OK, I was not hurt. He is thankful that I wasn't hurt, but he has to let me know how concerned he is about me. I tell him I appreciate his concern and how much I love him. "Where are you now?" he asks.

"On my way home to shower. I have a meeting back at the office. Give my mother a kiss."

"I will," he says.

As I approach my door, I see that it is slightly ajar. I take out my gun and get closer. I slowly push the door open, ready to blow up somebody's ass. I saunter into the apartment as quietly as I can. Ochie comes running over to me, meowing as he rubs up against me. I keep moving, looking over my shoulder as I move in closer to the living room, I hear the TV. I'm thinking to myself, the son of a bitch is watching my TV. I jump out. "HANDS UP, MOTHERFUCKER," gun pointed and ready to shoot, when Jonathan jumps up and says, "Don't shoot, it's me."

"JESUS, Jonathan, you scared the shit out of me." My heart is beating so fast I have to sit down.

"I'm sorry I scared you. I thought you would have seen my car outside and know I was here. You scared the hell out of me, rushing in here with that damn gun pointing at me."

The only sound outside of our heavy breathing is silence. Sophie jumps up in my lap, rubbing her head against my chin, looking for her *hello, you are home* rub. After a while, I notice that I still have my gun in my hand, so I get up and put the gun in the box where I keep it. I head straight to my small bar and pour myself the biggest glass of vodka that I can put my hands on, and while I'm at it, I pour one for Jonathan. The look of concern is all over his face.

"I was at school, and everybody was watching and/or listening to the special report on the shooting in Queens. That is when your dad called me. I almost broke my neck getting to the nearest television. Who is the first person I see coming out of the hellhole of a building but YOU? The reporter was saying that you were almost killed. I started freaking out and left school. I wanted to be here when you got home. Shale, you cannot keep doing this shit. It is way too dangerous and one day you will be killed. How the hell am I supposed to handle that?"

"Listen," I say. "Look at me. I am OK. You know I know how to handle myself." I try to hide my neck so he can't see the bruises. He is pacing back and forth, not letting me get a word in. My eyes start to burn because of the tears that I didn't know had started falling.

He looks at me with tears in his eyes and says, "I need to not see you right now. I don't know how much more of this shit I can take." As he leaves the apartment, he slams the door so hard both Sophie and I jump.

I have a good cry, hugging Sophie, still sitting in the chair, not moving. I don't know how much time passes before I try to get up from the chair. Every part of my body is aching. I stand under the shower with the water as hot as I can stand it. My heart is breaking, and I can't stop crying. How the hell am I going to be able to fix this? I have no idea. I really want to go to bed and pull the covers over my head, but we have that meeting back at the office that I can't miss. I start to call Conrad and tell him I can't make it, but he will have a fit, and I don't want to hear his big mouth, so I slowly get dressed and out the door I go.

The office is buzzing when I return. People are running around like crazy. "What's going on?" I ask.

Conrad says, "You guys were right about the man without ID; he was a cop. Not only a cop but a federal agent out of the Buffalo office."

"Shit, Buffalo? All the way from Buffalo?" I say.

"Yeah, his name was Edward King, and he was on the force nine years. They are sending us his records now."

Donald, one of the agents who was not at the scene earlier, says, "Hey, we heard what went down today. Are you OK?"

"Yeah," I say, "I'm OK."

Rosie is on the phone when I get to my desk. "Hey, partner, you kicked ass today. I'm proud of you."

I smile. "Thanks, partner."

"Your shooting is getting a lot better, and you remembered all that I taught you," he laughs.

As we enter the conference room, the chief from NYPD and the regional director of the FBI have already started the meeting. Conrad felt it was time for inter-departments to work together, at least until we know what the hell we are dealing with. It is all hands on deck. It's sad, but we are at war with some of our people.

Everyone is trying to talk at once when the door opens and in steps our boss from Washington. This shit is serious if Buzz Macintyre is here from DC. He comes over to where Rosie and I are sitting. "How are you two doing? I heard what went down today; glad to see you both made it."

"We're alive," Rosie says.

"This is a fucked-up situation. We need this now like a hole in the head."

Conrad comes over and the two of them shake hands. "Buzz, we were not expecting you," Conrad says. "We have things under control; there was no reason for you to come from Washington."

"Let me be the judge of that," he says.

The meeting starts and Buzz addresses the group, saying, "We are under a microscope. This shit has gone national and international. Every step we take will be scrutinized by the press. Everyone will have their opinion on whether we are doing the job that needs to be done or covering up for bad cops. I don't know about you, but this makes my ass hurt. We don't know how far this corruption goes, but the public doesn't give a damn if it's only a few bad cops. All of us suffer under the illusion that we are all in the same boat. That the apple is rotten down to its core.

"We need to map out our plan using only the people who are in this room. You were chosen because of your commitment to law enforcement, and I know that all of you hate dirty cops, local or federal, as much as I do. It gives all of us a black eye, and public opinion goes in the toilet. I don't need to tell you how important it is to contain as much of this operation as possible. No telling how many more dirty cops are involved in this mess. They now know that IA is involved so they will be in a hurry to cover their tracks.

"We will appoint a task force that will only report to me, Conrad, IA chief Melody Chin, and Chief Marvin Harp, NYPD. The FBI will be used on a when-we-need-them basis. They are working on their own investigation that may tie into what we are dealing with."

We go over some of the things he wants to be done immediately. Buzz breaks down the task force, saying since Rosie, Victor, Brad, and I have gone this far, we should follow it to the end. We agree.

As the meeting breaks and I am about to leave, Buzz tells me to stay in the room; he needs to talk to me in private. Rosie is giving me the evil eye as I close the door. "What's up, Buzz?"

"I left a message on your phone at home because I didn't know if you were with Rosie or not, and I want this to be a private conversation between you and me."

"Buzz, what the fuck are you talking about? Why not Rosie?"

He sits down and says, "Listen, we now know that we have a mole somewhere in this operation. Things are happening that could only be done with prior knowledge. We think that someone in this department is involved, and we want to be careful not to play our hand until we know who we are dealing with."

I know what he is saying is right, and it does make sense not to lay all our cards on the table. I am about to say something when it hits me why he wanted to talk to me alone.

"YOU ARE OUT OF YOUR FUCKING MIND IF YOU THINK ROSIE HAS ANYTHING TO DO WITH THIS. HE IS AS TRUE BLUE AS YOU AND ME. HE HAS BEEN AN AGENT LONGER THAN I HAVE. I TRUST THAT MAN WITH MY LIFE." I am screaming at him at the top of my lungs. "HOW COULD YOU EVEN THINK THAT THE TRAITOR IS ROSIE? WHAT PROOF DO YOU HAVE? SHOW ME YOUR PROOF RIGHT NOW!"

"Keep your voice down," he says. "I wanted this to be a private conversation, remember?"

I am steaming right now. How the hell does he expect me to calm down when he is accusing My PARTNER of stabbing us in the back? Calm down my ass.

"I didn't say it was him. We are trying to cover our asses for when this shit breaks. I know I can trust you. That is why I called YOU."

I look at him long and hard before I turn and walk to the door. "You are so full of shit, Buzz. You want me to spy on my partner. That I will NOT DO." I almost break the glass in the door as I storm out of the room. Rosie is looking at me like, what the hell. I keep walking and don't stop until I reach my car.

I am sitting in my car, crying. How could Buzz think Rosie has something to do with this mess? This on top of Jonathan being mad at me and Muffin half dead. I say a silent prayer for God to give me strength. I wish I was a little girl again so that my daddy could make things better. But I'm not a little girl and the problems I face now, Daddy can't make better, so God, I need all the help I can get. I get myself together and make my way to the hospital and check on Muffin.

I am on the elevator, and as I get closer to his floor, I hear this commotion coming from the waiting room. I step out of the elevator, and there is Pookie, big as a house, about seven months pregnant (*who knew he had it in him?*), trying to get to this young girl whose blonde wig is on the floor. The girl is struggling to get her earrings off, calling Pookie all kind of bitches and whores. Pookie is telling her that she is in the right place to die because she was going to kill her when she gets her hands on her skinny skank ass. Muffin's mother is in between them, trying to make Pookie sit down, at the same time trying to hold this crazy woman back. All the while she is trying to keep her balance so she won't fall on her ass.

Hospital security has been called and is trying to separate the two of them and rescue Muffin's mother. I don't know if I am crying because I am laughing so hard, or I am really crying. It takes four security guards to pry them apart. Everyone on this floor stops to witness ghetto buffoonery in all its glory. I am standing by the nurses' station along with a couple of nurses, making a bet on who could whip whose ass. Since Pookie is seven months pregnant, the one nurse places her bet on the young girl. I don't know; Pookie is in for the kill. I wouldn't bet against her. She is cussing as she is made to sit down.

Muffin's mother has this look of relief on her face as she sits down, saying, "I can't handle this shit." Before anyone can stop her, she reaches inside her pocketbook and pulls out a pint of ghetto blast wine, the cheapest and most horrible-tasting crap money can buy. She turns that bottle to her lips and drinks the whole damn thing. That bottle doesn't leave her lips till it is bone dry. The looks on everyone's faces are priceless. She puts the top back on the bottle and places the bottle back in her pocketbook like nothing happened. Now I know where Muffin gets it from. Could this be any more ghetto?

Pookie sees me and tells me she wants me to arrest this skinny bitch for attacking her in her delicate condition. The young girl is telling her to kiss her ass. I tell both of them to shut the fuck up, or I would arrest the both of them for behavior unbecoming to idiots. I go over to the young girl to find out who she is. "I am Muffin's woman," she says.

"Like hell you are." Pookie struggles to get up but can't quite make it.

"Stop it, both of you. You do know they have a prison wing in this hospital, don't you? This will be the last time I tell either one of you to stop all this foolishness. My next move will be to handcuff both of you. *Together.*"

One of the security guards yells, "Lock both of their crazy asses up."

I look over at Muffin's mother—she is fast asleep. Lord help me. Now that it is quiet, I ask the young girl her name and what is her relationship to Muffin. She tells me her name is Taqweeshea, and she is Muffin's woman, but I could call her Twee. She says that she and Muffin had been together four months cause he is tired of Pookie's old ass and wants a young thing who knows how to put it down. As she is saying "put it down," she is slowly going down like she is about to squat. Then she starts lifting her no-ass up and down. "Like this. This is what my man love about his Twee."

Pookie jumps up. "Bitch, I will show you what this old ass can do. You think I can't—"

"SHUT UP, PLEASE," I scream. "Pookie, if you don't sit your big ass down. Can we please act like grown folks for a minute?" I almost forget why I am here. "How is Muffin?" I quickly remember. Nobody answers. "Did he die?"

"No," says Pookie. "He is in surgery right now. We've been waiting over two hours, and we haven't heard anything. Shale, I want this whore out of this hospital right now. I don't care what she says, Muffin is MINE, and in two months there will be another little Muffin to go with the six we have at home now."

Taqweeshea looks like she was hit in the face with a nine iron. "That son of a bitch got *seven kids?* That nigger told me this was the only one he had, lying motherfucker. Nobody makes a fool out of Queen Taqweeshea. If I had known this shit before, I could've been Long Tooth's woman instead of this skinny-ass pole stick."

Still cussing, she gets up to leave, and as she walks past Muffin's mother, she trips over her pocketbook and falls flat on her face. Pookie is laughing so hard, I think she may go into labor right then. As Twee is leaving, Pookie picks up her blonde wig and throws it at her. "Take your nasty-ass bush with you, ho."

CHAPTER 8

We wait a little while longer. Since Taqweeshea left, things are much quieter than before. Muffin's mother wakes up just as the doctor comes out and says that Muffin came out of surgery just fine. "He has a lot of internal injuries. We managed to stop the bleeding, but time will tell. We will keep him sedated for now, and we should know more in the morning."

I leave those crazy people at the hospital. I have been riding around for a long time because I don't want to go home. I call Gary to look after my babies. I pick up the phone to call Jonathan, but I don't call. He is still upset, or he would have called me by now. I call my parents and leave a message. I haven't felt like this in such a long time, I'm not sure how to handle everything that is going on.

Rosie calls. "What's up?"

"Nothing, just driving around."

"I am at the Cage bar, meet me for a drink."

"Give me ten minutes."

He is sitting at the bar, nursing a drink. "Hey, partner," he says as I sit down. "Why the long face?" He orders another drink for himself and, for me, a vodka and cranberry, which I drink down as soon as I touch the glass. "Problems?" he asks. I look at him but don't say anything.

The questions start. "Why did Buzz want to talk to you alone? And why did he call you at home and not on your cell? I want to know what the hell is going on, Shale, talk to me."

"Rosie, we have been partners for over five years, and we don't keep secrets from one another. I don't know what is wrong with Buzz, and I don't know why he wanted to talk to me. He was talking crazy, so I left the room. I think he is paranoid about this whole situation and is frustrated that we have no real leads so far in this investigation. I think he is worried that there are more of our agents involved. You know how he feels about this agency. It's a matter of pride in the work we do. To think more agents may be involved, he is having a hard time with that."

We are on our second round of drinks when a woman comes up to Rosie, kissing his ear, making her way around to his mouth. The entire time she is kissing him, her eyes never leave me. Rosie introduces us, but she has no interest other than Rosie. She asks him to buy her a drink and takes a seat next to him on the other side. He orders the drink as she begins to whisper in his ear and runs her hand up and down the inside of his leg. She tries kissing him again, but he says no, now is not the time or place. She is not happy. She turns up the glass and doesn't put it down until it is empty.

Looking at the mirror that is behind the bar, I see her rolling her eyes, mumbling to herself. I lean over and ask her if she has a problem. She is about to say something, but Rosie, seeing the look on my face, gets up and takes her outside. "Good looking out, Rosie," I say to myself, because I wanted her to say something smart. It would have been a better scene than the one at the hospital.

He comes in and says he will see me tomorrow; we need to set up a meeting with Brad and Victor to see where we stand. "OK, I will call Victor. See you tomorrow."

I am driving home when my phone rings. It's my mommy. She and my dad had a date night, so they were out when I called. "Did you have a good time?"

"Absolutely," she says. "I always enjoy myself when I am with the love of my life." She tells me more about their date. We talk about Muffin and what went down at the hospital, which gives us both a good laugh. Before we hang up, she says, "Baby, please be careful. We are so worried about you, especially after your father spoke to Jonathan. He is a good man, Shale. Don't lose him over this job. Good men are hard to find these days, and I don't want you to be lonely and end up on your own. I want grandbabies someday."

"I know, Mommy. I don't want to lose him either, but he has to see my side of this too. I was a cop when he met me. This is who I am."

"I pray that things work out, baby."

"Me too, Mommy. I love you and give my daddy a kiss."

I decide to call Jonathan, but he doesn't answer. I am tired and I need to soak in a hot bath with a drink and let today go. A little kitty time will help me to unwind; I miss my babies. I sit in my car for a while, going over what happened today.

I look up suddenly because I think I see someone in my rearview mirror watching me. God, I am so uneasy. I know I need sleep. Taking no chances, I make sure that I can feel my gun as I park the car.

The next few days are quiet, which I welcome. I need the downtime. Jonathan is still MIA, which means he is still very upset. I pray this is not the end of us. Not talking to him is breaking my heart. I miss the hell out of him. I did end up calling him again; he has not returned any of my calls.

Work is a great distraction during the day. Nighttime is when I feel the emptiness the most. On top of all this shit, I still can't shake the feeling that I am being watched. Every night I go home, I make sure I can reach my gun. I have been feeling like this over a week now. I know I am not crazy.

Walking from my car into my building looking over my shoulder, paranoid or not, my gut is telling me that something is off. I get to my apartment and check the door. It is locked but I take my gun out of my purse and open the door slowly. My lights are on timers, so the living room is lit. I move about the apartment, still checking things out. The cats are not here so they must be at Gary's.

Just as I think everything is alright and I start to relax a little, some-one jumps me from behind and knocks me to the floor. My face hits the corner of a small glass table as my gun flies out of my hand. Blood springs from my nose as he reaches down and turns me on my back. I feel the weight of his body as he jumps on top of me, placing both hands around my neck. I am trying to fight him, but he begins choking me. *Shit, not this again.*

I can't see his face because of the knitted ski cap he is wearing, and the way he is sitting on top of me is blocking my view of where my gun landed. He is applying more pressure when suddenly I go limp. He loosens his grip just a bit; it's enough for me to push him off of me. I try to crawl over to where I thought my gun fell, but he grabs my leg and is pulling me toward him.

I make myself turn on my back so that I can have a clear shot of his face. I start kicking as hard as I can, aiming for his face. One of my kicks connects with his nose; blood is running like a faucet.

He gets up and tries to punch me in the face, but I throw the first punch, and it knocks him into my glass coffee table, breaking the thing in two. I reach down to grab him but he is quick on his feet, and before I can stop him, he hits me again. I can feel he is hitting me with the full force of his body, so I know that I have to be quicker than he is.

I move as far away as I can from him and with everything in me, I proceed to run directly into his stomach. For all the times I didn't want to train with Hanshi Yamamoto, I appreciate him more now than ever before. In my head I hear him saying to me, *You are in control of this fucked-up situation. Don't be discouraged by his size. Concentrate. You can overcome his might if you remember all that you have learned. Now kick his ass.*

As he is trying to stand up, with my right leg I kick him as hard as I can in the face, knocking him off balance. Before he hits the floor, I kick him again. He hits the floor, crying out in pain. "You son of a bitch, you don't know what pain is yet." I stagger over to him and with everything in me, I come down hard on his balls, making sure my stiletto heel crushes his dick on impact. He lets go of his face, and both hands are holding his crotch as he is screaming. I go for my gun, face bloodied, lip swollen, nose feeling like it is broken. I should shoot his ass, but I pick up my phone and call 911.

As I am waiting for the police, the Betty Crocker Patrol comes charging through the front door, waving rolling pins, dumbbells, umbrellas, whatever they could get their hands on. "Oh my God, Shale, are you OK? We came as soon as we heard the noise, but we had to make sure we were prepared for battle. We didn't know how much help you needed," Gary says. "Oh my," he adds, looking down at the hooded man moaning and crying on the floor, holding his crotch. "Girl, what were you trying to do, stomp it off? By the way, fierce boots."

Lamont says, "Oh God, Shale, look at your apartment. You had such a nice apartment. Now not so much."

I try to smile, but my face is in pain. Looking at this group of men who were coming to my rescue makes me love them that much more. Gary looks like he is about to cry. "Honey, look at your face, your beautiful face."

By the time the police come, I have taken off the knitted ski cap from my attacker. I am trying to get a good look at his face, but he is still doubled over, and blood is all over his face and mine. I have never seen this man before in my life. I ask him why he was trying to kill me, but I guess it's hard to answer questions when you're in that much pain.

The Betty Crocker Patrol has formed a circle around him, daring him to move. Miss Amelia Earhart, Gary's Jack Russell terrier, is barking her head off. I guess she is standing guard too.

Rob wants to start cleaning the apartment, but it is now a crime scene, and we will have to wait until the forensic team gives the OK. Conrad and Rosie arrive at the same time that the ambulance pulls up. Officers and paramedics are attending to my assailant, who is still on the floor, and the attendant is trying to clean my face when they walk in. "Jesus, Shale, your face is a mess," Rosie says.

"Thanks, friend."

The cops had handcuffed the bastard and are taking him out of my apartment, limping. Conrad can't believe his eyes at the sight of the

Betty Crocker Patrol with their homemade armor. This is the Village, after all. "Do you know who this bastard is?" Conrad asks.

"No, I never saw him before," I say. "He was waiting for me when I got home. We had a party, as you can see." My apartment looks like Afghanistan after a bomb blast. I feel like shit and look worse.

The attendant asks me if I want to go to the hospital. I say no. "Please put ice on your face to help with the swelling and take these pain pills. You are going to need them soon."

I give my report, and one by one everyone leaves my apartment except Rosie and Conrad. Every part of my body hurts and I can barely move. I sit on my couch while Rosie gets some ice for drinks and my face. Conrad, looking all fatherly, says, "You are off the case as of now."

"No," I say.

"Yes," he says. "You could have been killed tonight. You are in too deep, and we still don't know what the connection is between you and whatever the hell is going on. I want you to take some time off until we get a better handle on this situation. That is an order."

Rosie and I are alone after Conrad leaves. "Pour me another drink, will you, Rosie?" God, every time I move a new pain goes off in my body.

Rosie says, "You need to sit in a tub of very hot water. But I don't want you to stay here; maybe you should go to your parents' tonight."

"No," I say, "I don't want them to see me the way I look right now. It will freak them out. Right now I need sleep. The attendant told me to take these little green pills and it's lights out."

"Do you want me to call Jonathan?"

"NO. I just want to be alone tonight. I am in no mood for 'I told you so.' GO. I will talk to you in the morning."

He doesn't want to leave, but he does, only after I promise to call him if I need him.

I look around my apartment and start to cry. No matter how strong I think I am, right now I feel like a frightened little girl.

There is a knock at the door; it's Gary. As soon as I see him, I break down. He holds me and tells me he doesn't want me in this apartment tonight by myself. I am so tired at this point, I can't argue. I go to his apartment, and his partner, Rob, has a bath all ready for me. I soak in the hottest water I can stand and go over tonight in my head. I am so confused about my part in this case, but I can't think right now.

CHAPTER 9

ob brings me a drink and as he leaves the bathroom, I look up. Both Sophie and Ochie are looking at me like *who the hell are you?* I am fucked up so badly, my cats don't recognize me. I start crying all over.

After my bath and a rubdown, I take the little green pill. It doesn't matter that I had been drinking, I don't give a shit. In about two seconds the world is lost to me.

When I do wake up, both my parents and Jonathan are in the room. I can see that my parents have been crying, and Jonathan has murder in his eyes. I try to move but I am still stiff and in pain.

My father comes over to the bed to help me sit up. "You look like shit," he says.

"I love you too, Pops. How long have you been here?" I ask.

"Two days," my mother says.

"I've been out two days?"

"Yes."

It takes me a minute to remember that I am at Gary and Rob's.

"Shale, you should have gone to the hospital and been seen by a doctor."

"Mom, I wasn't hurt that bad. Ooh..." I try again to get up, but my dad is holding me still. Jonathan hasn't said a word. I look over at him, but he walks out of the room.

"Shale, you could have been killed this time. This has to stop. How long do you think we can go on holding our breath every time the phone rings? You are our only child, and we don't want to lose you."

"I know, Dad. I'm not going anywhere soon. I don't want to worry you and Mom. Listen, I have been working this job for years. I've been through some crazy shit before, but nothing like this. It's this case, and I need to see it through. If I am going to die, I want to know why."

My mother starts crying. "Don't say things like that."

On the third day I go back to my apartment, and the place is spotless. While I was out, the boys came and cleaned up everything for me. They even replaced my broken table.

I haven't talked to Jonathan since he left the other day. How come he acts like he is the one hurt when it's my black ass in pain?

Rosie and Conrad have been calling to see how I was coming along. My nurses would take messages. "She needs to rest, no exceptions."

I call Rosie. "Welcome back to the living," he says. "How do you feel?"

"Getting there," I say. "What's going on? Do you know who this bastard is who attacked me?"

"Yeah, hired gun out of Philly. Name is Roger 'The Goon' Beaver. Do you know him?"

"No, I never heard of him."

"He has a record longer than my dick, a real piece of crap. His rap sheet reads like a novel—assault, kidnapping, extortion, drugs. He spent jail time in New Jersey and Pennsylvania."

"Rosie, is he mob related?"

"Can't say for sure. He is suspected of being a hit man for the mob. Circumstantial evidence at best. I think he works for the highest bidder." I am about to hang up when Rosie says, "You fucked up his groin area pretty good. From now on I think he will be a bottom." We both laugh.

"If I was able to get to my gun, his ass would be a singing soprano. I would have tried to blow it off." I hang up, searching my brain, trying to see if his name rings a bell. Nothing.

I don't come out of my apartment until three days later. My face has gone down, and I move more easily now, with a little less pain. My parents have almost moved in my apartment, and I am told that my crazy boy cousins are beating the street, looking for who knows what. It's the thought that counts.

Victor and Brad call to check up on me, and we make arrangements for the four of us to meet in my apartment later on this afternoon.

I make my parents go home. And *no*, I have not spoken to Jonathan since the attack. He needs his space, and so do I.

I call Hanshi Yamamoto to schedule a training session. He asks if it's too soon. "No, not at all," I say. "It saved my life, the training I received from you." He suggests that we wait another week to see how I'm doing.

I venture outside with my bodyguard (Rob) and go the grocery store. I need to feel the sun on my face. I get back in time to see Brad, Victor, and Rosie pull up in front of my building. "I don't care what anybody says, you still look pretty good to me," Victor says with a smile.

"I can still kick ass. Ask Beaver Booty." I arrange some snacks on a tray along with drinks. "OK, boys, what do you want to drink? I have soda, beer, water, iced tea."

"Nothing stronger?" asks Rosie.

"I didn't think you were drinking. Aren't you all on duty?"

"Yeah, right. Here in your place, you don't tell, we won't either."

I break out the booze, and we get down to business. "Oh, by the way, Mr. Beaver fell in the shower and is in the prison hospital, the poor thing. Shale, seems you have friends in Rikers."

"Yay for friends, God love 'em." We all smile.

"They said he still has his dick in a sling."

That makes me laugh, belly-aching laughter.

We go over the files they brought with them, trying to connect the dots. I still have no idea who this Beaver person is and who would hire him to off me. We look at evidence IA has collected, along with photos. We listen to wiretap tapes. We each give a scenario of what we think happened. We are trying very hard to connect the dots between the attack and this case.

Victor is about to say something but pauses. "What is it?" I ask.

"Is it possible that the attack is somehow connected to one of your other cases?"

"I don't know; it could be, but which one? Rosie and I both worked the previous cases, and no one is attacking him. Besides, all our other cases are sewn up tight."

"I only asked," Victor says, "because we can't find a connection between the murders and the attack. Somehow this seems different, more personal. I really don't think it has anything to do with what is going on now."

I look at Rosie. "Do you think the same thing?"

"I don't know what to think. We still can't figure out where you fit in this whole thing. Why you for the phone calls and letter?"

I tell them since I have been home, my mind keeps going back to Muffin. "I know this little shit, and I don't think he has told me everything. I don't know how he connects to the shooting of the Mazda kid, or the four bodies in Brooklyn, but my gut is telling me I need to question him again."

Rosie calls the hospital and is told Muffin is off the critical list, so now would be a good time to talk to him. I tell them I think it would be better if I talk to him alone. I know where to hurt him the best. It is agreed that I would go to the hospital and see how my little baby is doing.

Victor and Brad leave for a meeting. Rosie stays and finishes his drink. "How are you, really?"

"I am doing great. I am starting to feel like my old self again." I smile. "I have all the protection I need; the boys will not let me go anywhere by myself. I have to wait for them to check the apartment before I can come in. I'm in a good place. I thank God every day that I am still here."

"What about Jonathan?"

"He called and we talked. He had to go to California for work. He feels like we need time, and I agree. We will talk when he comes back. I honestly don't know, Rosie, what will happen. I love him, but he has to accept my job. I don't want to give it up just like that. Rosie, what the hell am I supposed to do, stay at home and be the dutiful little wife? Or get a job sitting behind a desk from nine to five? That would kill me." I start to cry again.

Rosie gives me a hug. "Shale, if it was meant to be, it will." As he leaves, he looks at me. "This is why I don't fall in love." We both smile.

Gary and I go up to the hospital to see Muffin. Gary wants to know if he is gay with a name like Muffin. "Take it from me, HE IS NOT GAY." On the way up to his room, I tell Gary about the last time I was here. Laughing, he says, "Girl, that should have been a taping for a ghetto reality show." He waits for me as I go to Muffin's room.

Muffin is sitting up in his bed. "SHALE," he says, "oh my God, I heard what happened to you. I prayed to God that you were OK."

"Thank you," I say, "but you look worse than me. How are you?"

"OK, I guess. They removed some of the tubes from me this morning. Listen, I just want to thank you for rescuing me. If it were not for you, I would be dead. Thank you," he says again as he starts to cry.

I go over and give him a big hug. "Where would I get all my information if you were gone? There is only one Muffin. I need you to stick around and help me fight crime, you little criminal." We both laugh. I sit down beside his bed and say, "I know you haven't told me everything, Muffin. Too much shit has happened. I need you to not lie to me anymore and start telling me the truth. I know you are involved in this shit up to your neck. I just don't know in what way. Now I want to know why you were almost killed." He is softly crying. "Muffin, think of your unborn baby who is on the way. How is Pookie going to care for this baby and your other six children? Damn, Muffin, seven kids? I didn't know you had it in you."

He stops crying and then, laughing, he says, "Looks can be deceiving." I smile. "I didn't tell you everything because I was scared. I knew if I told you everything, they would kill me."

"You almost died now, Muffin, and I don't know everything. Stop dragging this shit out and tell me what I want to know. Now."

He looks me in my eyes. "Listen, Shale, we were stealing money."

"Who are 'we,' Muffin?"

"Terrence, William, and Jimmie."

"Wait, before you go on, I want to know how you met Terrence."

"We had the same dealer."

"OK, go ahead. Who were you stealing from?"

"At first, we didn't know. OK, this is the truth. We were using that building to do drugs. One night we go there, and we see this man in a suit digging into the back of the building. We were only going to rob him, but Terrence said to wait, let's see what he was digging for. He goes to his car and brings out a bag, drops it in the hole, covers the hole, and leaves. We wait for a little while and go and dig up the bag, thinking that drugs were in there. Terrence opens the bag, and it was filled with money, more money than we have ever seen. We couldn't even count it all. We thought we had died and gone to heaven. We were trying to decide if we should take it all or leave some for next time. We were high, Shale. We didn't think about whose money it could be."

"Where does Ben Cannon come in?" I ask.

"We decided that we would stake out this place on the same night each week. He showed up every time. The first time we each took about fifteen hundred dollars, give or take. After that a little more each week. I didn't know when he started watching us or even if it was him, but a month in we were about to leave when he shows up, holding a gun. We didn't know what to do; I was so scared I started shitting my pants. We just knew we were dead. At that point, we knew he was a cop. He told us that if we wanted to live, we had to work for him."

"Doing what?"

"He wanted us to do collections for him from some of the smaller businesses in Harlem, Brooklyn, and Queens. He didn't give us a choice: do it or suffer the consequences. We needed to repay the money we stole, or our families would pay the price. Shale, he claims he knew to the penny how much we took and about our criminal record. We would be looking at spending the rest of our lives in jail if we didn't do as he said, or he would make us dig our own grave. William told him to go to hell; he shot him in the leg. Aiming the gun at his dick and pulling the trigger made all of us cry like babies. We had no choice but to do what he wanted."

I asked him how long they had been doing his dirty work. He said for over a year. "Muffin, how much did you take?"

"Shale, I don't know. But Ben said over 75,000.00. I don't know if that is true, that's what he told us."

"75,000.00 each or collectively?"

"Total for all of us. I don't think it was that much, but who was going to argue with this deranged man with a gun and a badge? He also said that we were being watched, and if we said anything to anybody, he would make sure that the cops found our bodies floating in the East River. They would then kill our families. He looked at me and said, 'I personally will kill your momma.' Shale, you know how much I love my momma."

"In all this time, did you meet anyone else?"

"No, but we would hear Ben on the phone talking to someone he called the boss. Whoever 'boss' is, he speaks Spanish. Ben would try and say a few words here and there, like he could really speak the language. The boss was not impressed because I heard him shouting, 'Speak English, you dumb fuck,' through the cell phone."

"Did you know that Terrence had a brother who was killed a month ago?"

"Yeah, we met him a couple of times at the hangout. They both were crazy as hell. They told us that their father was some kind of killer and was serving a life sentence. Terrence said his father was his hero. We didn't believe them because we thought that they were pulling our leg. I told Terrence to stop bullshitting us, and he had this crazy look in his eyes. Made me want to believe him after that. Now it all makes sense; they were nuts. The young one had a mouth on him. He started mouthing off to his brother this one time, and Terrence hit him in the mouth with his fist, and they started fighting each other like they were mortal enemies. We were standing around, laughing our asses off. Ben was like, they are brothers, right? Too bad his mouth got him killed."

"What?"

He looks at me. "Ben killed him."

"Ben?"

"Yeah, he was there that day, but he was wearing his uniform. He bragged how he shot the kid and was surrounded by his fellow cops. Nobody was the wiser. He used the same gun he shot William in the leg with. With all the shit he was into, getting a gun was a piece of cake. He was not dumb enough to use his own service pistol."

"Why did he kill him?"

"Because he started complaining about the money, the fact that there was none. He said that his brother was getting the shaft, doing all the dirty work, and Ben was the one pocketing the money. He said he found out where his long-lost mother or sister was living, I can't remember which one, but he said he told her of the situation. She told him to just say the word, and she would have some friends take a trip to New York to handle the situation. Ben told the boss and was told to take out the little shit. Ben had some of his goon friends start the fight in the street with Tony. They could have killed him at any time, but Ben wanted to do it himself. He was flying high on coke, and the thrill of killing this punk kid in the middle of all those police made him feel like he was king of the world."

"Did Terrence know that Ben killed his brother?"

"Hell yeah, he knew. Ben bragged about it to anyone who would listen. What the shit could Terrence do? Ben told him if he had a problem with the fact that he iced his brother, he'd better keep it to himself. Killing him would be just as easy."

"So, Muffin, if this was going on for over a year, why did this arrangement end? Why were they killed?"

"Ben got greedy. He started keeping the money we collected. He said that since he was the one taking the most chances, he should keep more of the money. If anyone asked, he would say that we were the ones stealing the loot. Then we would be somebody else's problem. He didn't give a shit; we were losers anyway. We later found out it was drug money coming in from all five boroughs. I was supposed to meet them that night to turn in the money I collected, but Pookie thought she was in labor, so I had to take her to the hospital. I called Ben and told him that I was going to be late about an hour. I was on my way there when

I heard about the murders. I know now that the plan was to kill all of us; I guess Ben forgot that whoever was watching us was watching him."

"Greed will put blinders over your eyes, and you forget common sense," I say. "They had a party for one in your honor the other day. We need to keep you under wraps until we get to the bottom of this. I will make sure there is a cop outside your door twenty-four hours until you can go home. Is there someplace that your family can go in the meantime?"

"My mother's sister lives in Mississippi; we can go there."

"As soon as possible," I say. I get up to leave when I ask him if he knew who THEY were.

"No, I never had the pleasure."

I make sure he has protection and head to the office.

CHAPTER 10

Gary walks me to my office and makes sure I am in the door before he leaves to go walk Miss Amelia Earhart and feed my babies. As I walk to my desk, I get a standing ovation from the room. "Nice going, Shalimar, heard you kicked ass. Kung Fu, baby, black samurai."

I take my bow. "It's nice to be home," I say.

Rosie and Conrad are at my desk with a welcome-back hug. Conrad asks if the doctor gave me the OK to be back at work. I never answer, just change the subject. "Anything new to report?" I ask.

"I have a meeting," says Conrad. "We will talk later."

Rosie tells me not to sit down but come with him for a ride. He asks me how Muffin is doing. "Fine. The little shit is scared out of his mind. He has every right to be. They tried to kill him once before. Something tells me they will try again."

"Ever since you were attacked, I have been on my informants' backs to find me some answers. I've called in almost every favor owed me. I started from scratch and went through most of our past cases. I found out something. You will need to sit down for this."

"What the hell, Rosie, you are scaring me."

"Tony and Terrence are the offspring of..."

"Who, Rosie?"

"Thomas B. Wolf."

It takes a minute for this to sink in. "Thomas Wolf? THE Thomas Wolf?" I say.

"One and the same," Rosie says.

"OH MY GOD, I haven't heard that name in, what, four years? That slimy son of a bitch is rotting in prison, isn't he?"

"No, he died about two months ago. He had stomach cancer really bad, ate him up. I heard he was in severe pain; last few months he was in a semi-coma."

"There is a God," I say. "Saved the taxpayers of New York State money not having to keep this devil alive for the rest of his life. I should have killed him when I had the chance."

Thomas Wolf was one sick motherfucker. This was one of the first cases that I worked. The agency had been working on this case three years before I joined. Rosie was assigned to be my partner, and I had to learn as I went along. This was a hard case for a newbie to be assigned, but it was all hands on deck to catch this son of a bitch. Thomas Wolf had abducted ten women and four children, all girls; the youngest was three. He raped, tortured, and mutilated their bodies for his sick pleasure.

He had the State of New York in a sheer panic for years. His victims were from all over the state, so there was no real pattern to his behavior. Most serial killers will usually kill people of their own race. Not Thomas; this psychopath killed anybody he wanted to. The only survivor was the last one, a little girl of five from Ithaca. We don't know why he didn't kill her. He never said. She will need medical and psychological help the rest of her life, but at least she is alive.

Working with agency profilers, we finally caught a break and found his killing ground. It was located in a wooded area in upstate New York. A childhood friend's family had a small scrap metal recycling business that went under years ago. The place had been condemned, but nothing was ever done to the buildings on the property. The property line extended back into a wooded area, and there was a small shed-like structure that he had turned into his own personal torture chamber. It took a lot of blood, sweat, and tears, along with many sleepless nights, but we finally caught the bastard. When we had him in custody, we were able to do a thorough search of the entire property.

For the first time in my life, I was looking into the eyes of pure evil. It took an act of God for any one of us not to just blow his fucking brains out. As he was led away in handcuffs, he had the most demonic smile on his face. Walking into that room, we knew we were walking into hell. The smell of death was in every inch of that room. I immediately started throwing up. Realizing what took place here, imagining the screams of the women and children screaming for their lives, made all of us sick.

Big strong federal agents were crying like little babies. The place was like the scene out of a horror movie. There was a large table in the middle of the room surrounded by pails and buckets. Every step you took left a shoeprint in blood. On the walls were chains that were bolted to the walls. He had concealed the entire room in double cement and took out all the windows. Bloodied mattresses were in one corner of the room, and on a small table next to the larger one were knives of all shapes and sizes. There was video equipment set up so he could tape and watch himself later as he masturbated to his sick fantasy.

After all the evidence had been collected, the entire property was razed. Nothing there now but an empty lot. We always thought that he had an accomplice, but it was never proven until we found the body of his childhood friend Leaf Brunson. He was butchered, and his body parts were buried throughout the property. We also found buried in the evidence pictures of Thomas and Leaf with a couple of the victims. Two psychopaths bent on evil so vile it cannot be put in words.

The State of New York was breathing a little bit easier after his capture. Too bad we no longer had the death penalty, because he would have had a state full of people lining up to off this piece of shit. The doctors were happy to have him alive so he could be studied, to try and find out why he was the way he was. Bullshit—kill the son of a bitch. Study his bones, I say.

That was one of the happiest days of my life. It made me realize the good I could do and how much I loved being an agent. There was no turning back after that. I had found my career, and I knew I had made my uncle proud.

I can't believe what I am now hearing: the Mazda brothers were the sons of Thomas Wolf. "Why is this the first time we are hearing about this, Rosie?"

"It appears the mother left him before the killings started and moved to Oregon. We knew he was married but were told the wife died. We did not know about the boys. She was always a party girl who never wanted to be a mother, so she gave up the boys to her cousin to raise. They were not part of her idea of how she wanted to live her life. You can't party with two brats in tow. The cousin's surname is Mazda. Since she had custody of the boys at such a young age, they took her last name."

"But how is this possible? We investigated the hell out of that case. Why didn't any of this show up?"

"The information we are now getting is that she faked their deaths because she was afraid of Thomas. I guess she had some idea of how insane he was and ran. Everything in our records showed that they had died in a car accident out west. Turns out her cousin's husband was a sheriff and was instrumental in carrying out this ruse. The boys turned out to be too much for the cousin, so she put them out, and they were on their own for a long time. Sometime in the last two years, they came back to New York."

"What about their mother? Is she still alive?"

"Don't know. We are still checking."

"Wait, Muffin said that Terrance told him he found his mother, or was it his sister? I need to ask him. What was her first name?"

"MACY," Rosie shouts out. "We now know that Macy is not her real name. Her real name is Marsha. Marsha Honeywell."

We sit in silence. "Damn. I was finally at a place that I didn't have nightmares about Thomas Wolf, and now we have his demon seeds doing God knows what in New York. Now all three are dead. Like I said before, there is a God. Rosie, we need to find out if their mother is living. Hearing all of this smells of revenge."

"Victor was right when he said the attack on you seemed personal. The more I thought about it, the more I came to believe he was right."

"But why? I wasn't the only agent who was there when Thomas was arrested."

"No, but you were the one in his sight. You were young, beautiful, and he could see how much you were affected by what he had done. He probably fantasized about you while he was in prison. I think we are right, Shale. This attack has something to do with that sicko, and it's just a coincidence that his boys are wrapped in our other case."

I say to myself, *I know we are right.*

We head back to the office, find Conrad, and tell him what we suspect. He agrees that we need to find Mrs. Wolf. We send out an APB (all points bulletin) for Marsha Honeywell Wolf. I am on the phone most of the day, phoning and emailing contacts, texting our DC office; we need all the help we can get.

Rosie and I are going for something to eat when we get a message that Roger Beaver wants to talk. We head over to Rikers.

Roger is sitting in a chair in the middle of the room, bandages still visible, with his arms and legs cuffed. His lawyer is sitting next to him, writing something on a pad lying on a long table. As I walk in, he doesn't seem as big as he did when he attacked me. As soon as he sees me, he tries to cover his groin area, which makes me smile. Rosie says, "You wanted to talk, so talk."

"What will my client get in return if he tells you what he knows?"

"Nothing," I said. "He attacked a federal agent. What the hell does he want, dinner and a movie?"

Roger is squirming in his chair. He starts to say something, but his lawyer tells him to shut up. "Listen, my client called you because he wants to make a deal. He is looking at a long prison sentence here, and Pennsylvania has the death penalty."

Rosie says, "The way I see it, we win either way. We don't need to deal with this sack of shit. He is going down. We got word that our counterparts in PA are happy we found you. They have several warrants with your name on them: murder, extortion, drugs. Seems you've been a busy little bee. You will face the death penalty."

As this scene is being played out, I am sitting there saying nothing. All I can do is sit and listen, hoping the bastard will give us information on where we can find Macy/Marsha whatever her name is. Rosie says, "Let's go, he ain't got nothing to say."

As we get up to leave, he says, "I will tell you who hired me to kill you."

I turn and look him in his one good eye. "WHO!"

He thinks for a minute. "MARSHA WOLF."

"After all this time, why would she want me dead?"

"Because she is still in love with Thomas. She is terrified of him, but at the same time she couldn't stay away. She was able to stay in touch with him while he was in prison through a friend of theirs who lives in Jersey. She is as crazy as he was. He made her believe that you were the reason he was in prison and that they could never be a family again. He told her he was in love with you and that as long as you are alive, he could only love you. She became obsessed with the idea that they could be a family again if you were gone."

"How the hell could they be a family? That devil is DEAD. What a bunch of freaks," I am shouting.

"How did she find you?" Rosie asks.

"We go back a long way. Thomas and I were in prison together a long time ago. He introduced me to Marsha; we became the three amigos. We were inseparable, we did everything together." Before we can ask, he says, "Sex included. Marsha is a freak and Thomas loved watching her have sex. With me or anybody else. You name it; we did it."

"How do we know that you were not part of his killing spree, since you were part of the amigos?"

"No way was I part of that shit. No way."

"Why not?"

"Because Thomas started getting more mental. He was no longer satisfied with the things we were doing together. He wanted to include more people—women—and he didn't care if they wanted to go along with it or not. His temper became more violent the more drugs we were using. If we didn't want to go along with his fantasies, there was hell to pay. Whenever we went out and he saw a female that he liked, he would always talk about all the things he wanted to do to her. I asked him one time, what if she wasn't interested or into the things he wanted to do. He smiled and said, 'Like she would have a choice.'

"I could see where this was going, so I decided it was time to leave. I told Marsha that I was going to leave, and she told Thomas. The next thing I know he has a gun in my mouth, rambling on and on about how nobody leaves him. All the shit I have done in my life, this was the first time I thought I was going to die. Marsha started sweet-talking him and rubbing up on him. He started smiling and dropped the gun. They started having sex, and I ran to the bathroom. Later, after drugging and drinking, they fell asleep. I grabbed some money and got the hell out of town."

"Where did you go?" Rosie asked.

"I had friends in Vegas, so that's where I went."

"When did she get pregnant?"

"I don't know. That happened after I left."

"How do you know that you are not the father of one or both of those demon seeds?"

"I took care of that a long time ago. I had a vasectomy when I was in my early twenties. Never wanted brats."

"You son of a bitch," I say. "You knew about the abductions and murders. Why didn't you notify the police?"

"Why the hell would I want to help the police? Besides, he was no longer my problem. I was doing my own thing in Vegas. I moved back to Philly last year, and that's when I ran into Marsha. We picked up where we left off, if you know what I mean."

"What a sick bunch of idiots. Where is she now?" I ask.

"I don't know. The last time I saw her, we were driving from Philly to come to New York."

"Where does her friend live in Jersey?"

"I don't know, she never said."

"You are a liar," I say. "You are full of shit. What was the purpose of this meeting if all you are going to do is lie to us?"

"I am not lying. Everything I told you is the truth."

"Why this conscience turn of events?" Rosie asks.

Roger says softly, "I know I'm going to die in prison. What have I got to lose? I will never see Marsha again, so what's the point. I'm not an old man, and I will die the way I lived—fast and furious."

After a few moments of silence, I say, "I hope that you get forgiveness from God, because my wish for you is that you end up with your partners, Thomas and Marsha, the three amigos roasting in hell."

Rosie and I high-five each other as we leave the jail. We were right. The next order of business is to find this crazy bitch.

I call the Philadelphia office and let them know what we just found out. They will coordinate with us any information they come up with. I call my parents and speak to my daddy. I tell him that I feel like things are finally getting back to the way they were before all this craziness started. "Does that include Jonathan?" he asks.

"I don't know, Dad. He will need to make that call."

Bringing up his name hurts, but right now I have more pressing things on my mind: get Marsha before she gets me. I call and check up on Muffin, who is being released from the hospital. He will be joining his family in Mississippi. Everything is arranged for him to leave New York tonight.

We go back to the office to pick up some of the records and files from the Thomas Wolf case. We need to comb through the information to see what we missed the first time. The key to finding Marsha is to find this friend in Jersey. I pick up a box to take home with me.

As I pull up to the apartment, Rob is sitting on the steps. He helps me with the box. "Gary has cooked dinner, and a glass of wine has your name on it." Dinner is delicious and the wine wonderful. I am surprised with a dessert of strawberry shortcake. It is a nice end of this crazy day.

I go home to my cats. I get myself comfortable, finish off the bottle of wine I had started yesterday, sit in the middle of my floor, and start going over all the evidence in the Thomas Wolf case. This was one sick bastard. Going through the files brings back all the horror he inflicted on his victims and their families. Seeing the pictures of what he had done makes me want to throw up my dinner. I put them aside because I can't bear to look at them anymore. I start from the beginning, looking for any information concerning New Jersey. I don't see how we could have missed anything, we were so thorough—but we missed Marsha and the boys. I know it has to be here.

I fall asleep on the floor. I am running for my life. The figures are gaining on me because of the shoes. I am running and trying to get out of my shoes at the same time. I keep running, they keep gaining on me. I turn and run into an old rundown house in the woods. As I enter the house, the door closes and Thomas Wolf is guarding the door, so I can't leave. I turn to run and Marsha is coming toward me with a knife. She is faceless, with only fangs in place of teeth. I have nowhere to run.

I wake up screaming with Gary and Rob knocking my door down. I let them know I am OK, that I had a nightmare. They won't leave until I let them in. I have to put away the pictures because I don't want them to see the horror.

They ask if they can help me and I figure that six eyes are better than two, so the three of us begin to go through the reports, not sure what we would find. We had been looking for about two hours when I start getting sleepy and decide to call it a night. I assure the boys that I will be alright and that they can leave me alone.

I am putting the files back in order when the cats come over for their nightly tummy rub. As I love on my babies, Ochie jumps up in my lap and as he does so, he tips over the glass with a drop of wine still in it. The wine spills on some of the paperwork. As I am cleaning up the wine, I notice a small Post-It note that was stuck in between a report about twelve pages long. There was something written in pencil that had faded with time. I can't believe my eyes, but to be sure it isn't the combination of wine and sleep, I run to my desk, looking for the magnifying glass that belonged to my grandfather, and go back to the file. Using the magnifying glass, I look at what is written on the note, and the biggest smile comes on my face. There is our connection to Jersey, an address in Camden.

I call Rosie. "Get up, partner; we are going to Jersey."

CHAPTER 11

On the way to Camden, I call our Jersey Bureau to inform them of the investigation. By the time we arrive in Camden, they have agents and the local police at the address. The house is a dilapidated row home that is showing its deterioration very well. No one answers from the knocking, and it doesn't seem like anyone is home.

We have a warrant, so we enter. That is a big mistake. This place looks like it has been hit by an inside tornado that decided to stay awhile. How anyone can live in a shithole like this is out of my realm of understanding. As soon as we come through the door, the stench hits us in the face like a one-two punch of a prizefighter. Immediately our eyes start tearing, the smell is that strong. We look like we are all peeling onions. Rosie flips the switch but of course, there is no electricity.

Covering my face with my hand, I look in the kitchen and can't go in. There are roaches running everywhere, and you know somewhere rats are running wild. Dirty dishes are piled up in the sink. A pile of dirty clothes lies by the back door. There is a small bathroom in the corner of the kitchen with just a sink and a toilet, which is filled with old shit and vomit. The living room floor is covered with empty liquor bottles. Beer cans everywhere and cigarettes butts floating in yellow-colored liquid in a big plant-like pot minus the plant. Drug use is very evident as we can see used crack pipes and broken needles on a long coffee table pulled to one side of the living room.

There are small traces of a white powdery substance on the table. One of the officers says, "The residue looks like cocaine." Because there is no electricity, there are candles in every part of the downstairs. Some are used, some are brand new. Next to the large coffee table sit two extra-tall giant candles that stand just below the window still, extra light for when the drugs are being used and or mixed.

"Rosie, I am trying to understand why they would have open flames burning from the candles if they are cooking up drugs in the same space. It's a wonder this place didn't blow."

"Beats me," he says. "Lucky, I guess."

A couple of the agents go upstairs and yell down not to come up; it is as bad as the downstairs. We open every window in the house and still have to leave to escape the smell. We call in for reinforcements as well as the hazmat unit. There is no telling what is causing all those nasty smells, besides the shit we can see. We don't want to take a chance that there are hazardous materials somewhere in the house, especially if drugs were being cooked here. The strong odor could also be linked to the other abandoned houses on either side of this dump. Boarded up by the city, you can see that some of the boards had been removed—perfect drug dens.

All of the occupied homes, the few that are here, are all on the other side of the street. It is decided that the police should clear the area until we know what is going on. No one answers the knocks on the doors; either they are not at home or they just don't give a damn.

We wait outside while the hazmat unit goes through the house. We are informed that some of the smells are from dead animals. There are a couple of dogs and cats that look like they may have starved to death. It makes me more determined to catch this bitch, being the animal lover that I am.

We are finally able to go back into the house, not that we are in a hurry to. We find out that the owner of the house is Tom Lloyd, a local man who is well known to the police. He has a record going back to his teenage years. The police have been looking for him for about six months. He is wanted for the murder of a local drug dealer he was fighting with for control of the city's drug trade.

Rosie asks if he is married. We are told not that the police are aware of. Women are not a problem for him. He has a woman for every day of the week, mostly known prostitutes. The local police are looking for Mr. Lloyd; now so are we. I just know he is our link to psycho bitch.

Just as we are leaving, a car pulls up across the street. An elderly man and woman get out of the car, yelling, "It's about time you showed up." They have been complaining about this house for years. They claim nothing was ever done. Local police tell a different story.

As the couple approaches us, I ask, "You are?"

"We are the Randalls, Marshall and Emma Randall. Who are you?" Mrs. Randall asks.

"We are federal agents," I reply.

"About time some real cops showed up. These sorry-ass rookies we have here couldn't shoot a hole in a donut even if the damn thing had a hole already in it. A bunch of good-for-nothings. They don't have to live in this hellhole so why should they give a damn. If you ask me, they all are on the take." Looking at Rosie, she says, "I watch a lot of cop shows on television, that how I know the lingo."

The sergeant is about to say something, but he doesn't stand a chance. "Don't try showing up now that the feds are here. You had your shot. This used to be a great street to live on. You knew who your neighbors were. We always looked out for each other. We used to have block parties all up and down the street. Remember, Marshall?"

"Sho do," he replies.

"Not anymore, not for a long time now. Drugs and gangs have killed the good times. People don't feel safe in their own home. This place turned into a ghetto almost overnight. You can't sit on your porch without a bullet flying past your head. One of our neighbors, Mr. Roland, was shot and killed in broad daylight trying to help his nephew, who was in a fight with a gang member trying to rob him. In broad daylight, can you believe that? People started moving just to get away from this hellhole."

Mr. Randall finally joins in. "We are out of here too. Can't wait." Shaking his head, he says softly, "Can't wait."

"I'm sorry to hear about your friend," Rosie says, "but can we get back to Tom Lloyd? Can you tell us the last time you saw anyone at the house?"

"It's been about two months," Mrs. Randall says.

Rosie turns to the police sergeant. "You have been looking for him for how long? And he has been right here under your nose. Did you ever think to keep his home under surveillance?"

"What the hell is wrong with you fuckin feds? Of course we were watching the house. We want this son of a bitch more than you do. I don't know what the hell these people are talking about. Everyone is out to get the police. This ain't no fuckin cakewalk out here. We are at war with the criminals and the community who feels like we don't do enough. Stop complaining and try helping us out more. You see more than we do, and yet you live by the code don't snitch, don't tell. What kind of fuckin sense does that make? You are killing each other, and nobody gives a damn. Yet you want the police to clean up your dirty laundry."

Mrs. Randall jumps in. "You got some fuckin nerve. You expect the community to come forward for what? We've been complaining for years and not a damn thing has been done. Why should we help you do your job when the police are doing nothing about the dirt in your own house? Crooked cops been doing what the hell they want in this neighborhood for years and nothing has ever been done. Talk about not snitching. That blue wall of silence speaks volumes. It works both ways. You cover up for one another until the shits hits the fan. I know that not every cop is dirty, but why aren't more good cops speaking up for the ones that are shit? Maybe then you would have more people trust that something would be done."

The silence is so heavy you could cut it with a knife.

"We can all agree that work needs to be done on both sides," Rosie says. "This problem is bigger than just this three-block radius. Throwing darts at each other is not the answer and screaming has never worked. We face the same thing in New York, and until we can agree to sit and talk like grown folks, we will never reach any type of understanding.

Now we are here only because we believe this bastard is our connection to a case we are working on. That is the only reason we are here. We need both sides to help us catch a psycho."

Smiling, I am saying inside, *That's my Rosie, always the diplomat.*

He is about to continue when one of the cops says under his breath, "Sorry-ass fed."

"Excuse me, son, is there something you want to say out loud?" The cop just stands there with this dumb look on his face. "That's what I thought," Rosie says. Again the tension is rock solid.

"Now, boys, "we have guests. Mr. Randall, what can you tell us about Mr. Lloyd?"

Clearing his throat, he says, "Parties would go on all night long. Drug use was in the open, known prostitutes and hoodlums coming and going in and out that house like it was a revolving door. Someone would get drunk or high and the next thing you knew, a fight would break out and the next thing you knew, guns would be going off. Houses broken into, people robbed at gunpoint. Loud music while people are trying to sleep. Some of the most disgusting words in a song I have ever heard in my life."

Mrs. Randall joins in. "Except that one song, Marshall, you know the one, 'swing lower.' That's it, we like that one, don't we, baby?" They begin to sing and dance, making up the words as they go. Makes me smile. I know love like this—my parents.

"Sorry," Mrs. Randall says, "we tend to get carried away with ourselves. Where were we?"

"The house across the street."

"I don't what the hell they were doing in that house, but the stench would travel across the street to our side of the street. I think they were cooking crystal meth," winking at Rosie. "Made us want to throw up."

"We know the feeling."

Looking at each other, she says, "We have had it. We are moving to Florida to be closer to friends. No more snow, no more coats, no more Keystone cops, no more hell."

"Getting back to Mr. Lloyd, we know he is not married, but do you know if he has a steady woman in his life?" Rosie asks.

"Hoes mostly, but there is this crazy woman who is always around the house." Mrs. Randall says she had been cussed out by this nut for no good reason a number of times. "One time I asked her if she could pick up the trash that was in front of their porch, and she picked up an empty beer bottle and threw it at me."

Rosie and I look at each other and say at the same time, "Marsha." I ask if they have any more information about the family, friends? They say no and start to leave when the wife turns and says she met this man one time who said he was Tom's cousin from Baltimore. "Thank you so much," I say as we headed south to Baltimore.

Conrad is called from the car, updating him on the information we learned. "Good job," he says. "I will notify the authorities in Baltimore. This is one time we will need the cooperation of the BPD. I will also see to it that some of our people are there as well."

Mrs. Randall was more help than she realized. She kept a record of the goings-on of that house and was able to give us the license plate number of the Maryland car. We find out that the car is registered to a man named Maurice Brown. He is very well known to BPD. It is decided that we will meet at a staging area outside of the city limits. We need to see what we are up against and strategize over what our options are.

Police Chief Raymond Pope is briefing us on the situation. He starts with Maurice Brown. "Maurice Brown, again a known felon with a long record. He has been in and out of jail for the last thirty years. You name it, he has had his hands in it. Right now he considers himself a Mack Daddy Pimp of the Year and an up-and-coming drug dealer. Never had a permanent residence, just drifts from one sleazy motel to another. With the type of women he pimps out, sleazy motels is the best they can do. Most of them are on drugs and look like it. The most recent info we received from our CI's is that he is staying with some friends over in the Northeast projects. This is one of the last standing high-rise projects in Baltimore. Most have been torn down."

Taking a deep breath, he continues, "This causes a bigger problem for us than you could imagine. One of the most violent gangs in the city operates from those projects. They are called 'Lost Religion' and they run most of the drug traffic within the city. They wouldn't care if we were there for them or not; if we go charging in, we will have a fight on our hands and people will get hurt. Maurice and Marsha are not aware that you are after them. Believe me, all hell would break loose."

"Do you have any idea how many gang members there are?" Rosie asks.

"Not exactly," he says. "We know who the key players are, but there is no telling how many eyes and ears they have. Remember, not all people think they are scum. They have a lot of people on their payroll. Anyone tipping them off would be well rewarded, even if they are not in the gang."

Going through the paperwork they had with them, we compare the picture of Marsha we got from the Camden police to the one they have. "Yeah, that's psycho bitch."

I ask, "How do you know her?"

"Prostitution and drugs. The last time she was arrested, she was causing a scene in a hotel room. Police were called and when they entered the room, she was trying to cut the dick off her john. She claimed he didn't want to pay her after he damn near fucked her to death. He didn't want to pay, so she was going to take a piece of him or kill him, whichever came first. She started screaming at the top of her lungs all the shit she had done to him, all the while waving that big-ass knife. The john was so scared, he shit the bed. The police had to Taser her before she dropped the knife.

"When she was booked, she claimed that Maurice was her husband and her pimp. He is a big man, and she was threatened with violence if she didn't go out and make him some money. She claims she had a quota to fulfill every night or there was hell to pay. I would consider him dangerous just due to his sheer size and unpredictable behavior. We are looking at him for the disappearance of one of his girls, who has not been seen in about ten months. We don't have the evidence to prove he had something to do with her vanishing act, but it is a well-known secret he had something to do with her. If he didn't do it himself, then he had someone else take care of her. Knowing him, he wouldn't want to share the kill. Make her an example, then the other girls are too afraid to talk. Keeps them in line that way. Marsha made sure to let the judge know all about his violent tendencies and the supposed abuse she went through as a young girl. She got away with being sent to a mental ward instead of jail time. We know she was lying about the abuse."

"How?" I ask.

"Her cellmate came forward and said that they concocted the story so that she could avoid jail time. Marsha is a freak. No one has to force her to do anything she doesn't want to do. The judge didn't believe the cellmate, saying she was trying to get her sentence reduced, so her judgment stood. I have to tell you I believed the cellmate and I still do."

"The way I see it," Conrad says, "no matter how we play this, we will be noticed. There are far too many ears and eyes for us not to be. We just need to make sure we are well covered and just go for it."

Rosie says, "I agree. What choice do we have?"

"We need more players on our side," Chief Pope says.

Conrad chimes in, "Let me make some phone calls."

Within half an hour we have agents from the FBI and the DEA as well as half of the BPD. It is decided that our best chance of less interference from civilians and having the element of surprise on our side would be to strike in the early morning.

We regroup at 4:30 a.m., and after briefing everyone on what is about to go down, we head over to the projects. The Baltimore agents had contacted their CI's and were told Maurice was holed up in the Northeast projects with this woman who said she is his wife. To their knowledge, he had never been married.

We head over to the projects, which are these two massive high-rise buildings. Each building is twelve floors high. The buildings are part of a complex which includes small family houses with an enormous play area filled with a basketball court, swings, sliding boards. On one side is an area that at one time was a garden; now it is a junk pile. The buildings are labeled Tower 1 & 2. We want Tower 1.

There are ten cars and vans of federal and local police. We had predetermined, based on the makeup of the complex, how we would cover the area, so that we had people surrounding the buildings as well as the single-family homes. Police helicopters will be our eyes in the sky. The outside area is completely cleared except for the few people hanging out and those on their way to work. Trying to contain the people just hanging out is difficult if they think they are about to witness the gun-fight of the century. Even though it is early in the morning, we always keep in the back of our minds how the press can smell a story, and as large as this operation is, you can bet they won't be far away.

Not knowing all the players in the gang and where they are located, believe me, we are armed and on heightened alert. All of this for that no-good bitch and her freakazoid boyfriend or whatever he is to her. We are not here to start a war with this damn gang; they are not who we are after this time. Always be prepared for the unexpected, my uncle used to say. Boy, was he ever right. I say a silent prayer: please be with us. Both God and my uncle.

The lobby is big and gray. There is trash scattered around the floor. Erased graffiti blankets one side of a wall; the other side is taken up almost entirely by mailboxes. There are two small elevators and a door leading to a stairwell. There is an *Out of Order* sign on the door leading to the laundry room and a smaller door with the words *Utility Room* written across it in big bold letters rounding out the lobby. The laundry room has a door leading to the outside but is blocked by machine parts so no one can enter or exit. In total, there are three stairwells: the one in the lobby and the other two leading to the outside—one in the back of the building, the other on the far right side of the building.

Both elevators are on the ninth floor, not moving. We had already decided to walk up the stairs. Why give an advantage to anyone by tak-ing the elevator. Leaving agents in the lobby, we split into three groups, each taking one of the stairwells. Someone yells out, "What floor are you going to?"

Chief Pope answers by walkie-talkie, "The ninth-floor, apartment 903."

"We know that apartment well. It is where Devil Eyes lives. He is one of the leaders of the gang. We heard that Maurice was supplying girls to the gang; I didn't know they were that tight. This is a fuckin nightmare. Devil Eyes is so paranoid, he would shoot his own mother if he thought she was staring at him too long. Please be extra careful. This crazy son of a bitch is a loose cannon."

"Damn," I say, "you mean we have to walk up nine flights of stairs?" (Figures it couldn't be on the second floor.) Why did I have to have on my new three-inch Lombardis? You can't imagine how hard it is running upstairs in three-inch shoes. Of course I run up the stairs because if this bitch is here, I want to meet her face to face.

We finally reach the ninth floor, adrenaline pumping. Agent Ballios, laughing, says, "Shale, I can't believe how fast you ran up the stairs wearing these heels."

I say, "I couldn't believe we didn't pass your hair lying on the steps back there."

"HA-HA, not very funny," he says.

"I thought it was," I say, smiling.

My group comes up stairwell one because we were told it was closest to the apartment. The floor has three hallways with four apartments in each hallway. There are three doors leading into the stairwells and a big door with the words *Utility Room* written across the front located between two of the hallways. There is an unusually large lock at the top and bottom of the door. They are checked to see if they are locked; they are. There is a garbage chute next to the elevator bank with a bag full of garbage just sitting there. Too damn lazy to open the chute door. Damn shame. The walls are painted this ruddy yellow color with (again) erased spots where graffiti had been and where new graffiti has taken its place. The tile floors look like they have not had a bath in a very long time.

Even at 4:30 in the morning, music is playing loud enough that we don't have to worry about anyone inside hearing us. One of the agents asks how people can sleep with all this racket going on. "Too afraid to complain," Rosie says.

Making sure that everyone is in position, guns drawn, vests on, we put the agent with the ballistic shield in front as well as the battering ram, just in case it is needed. Armed with a search warrant, one of the agents knocks on the door. "FEDERAL AGENTS. OPEN THE DOOR." We wait; nothing happens. Again he knocks. "FEDERAL AGENTS. OPEN THE FUCKING DOOR." We can hear movement inside, but no one opens the door.

Rosie is in the front of the pack. "Break the damn thing down," he screams.

The ram is used and as soon as the door flies open, someone from inside starts shooting. People never cease to amaze me. All hell is breaking loose, bullets are flying everywhere, and people are sticking their heads out of their apartments, trying to see what is going on.

As we enter the apartment, we are hit with a fog of marijuana smoke so thick we can barely see. The place is not very big, just oddly shaped. There has to be at least eight men in this small apartment. Trying to maneuver in such a tight space with all the commotion between us and the drug dealers is chaotic. Shots are exchanged, and when it is over, three of the eight are dead. One of the dead is identified as Devil Eyes. Another is ID'd as Grave Digger; another one of the ringleaders. The third looks like a baby; he couldn't have been older than 20. Two are wounded and on the way to the hospital, the other three are taken into custody.

Going from room to room in this two-bedroom apartment, we find enough guns to take over a small country. Drugs are everywhere. We find boxes and boxes filled to the brim with bundles and bundles of dollar bills in the closet of one of the bedrooms. One of the other bedroom closets has been turned into an arms dealer's dream. "Look at all this shit, Rosie," I say. "All this from this gang?"

"I don't think so," he says. "My stomach is doing flips right now. This operation looks too big to just have this gang involved, even if they did control most of the drugs in this city. There is no way they could have amassed what is in this apartment on their own. I smell bigger fish in this frying pan."

We are moving around the apartment when one the agents posted in the hallway yells, "We have runners. A man and a woman running down stairwell three. They came out of the apartment closest to three."

We start running toward the agent as he points in the direction they are heading. Rosie yells, "Check that apartment. If anyone is in there, arrest their asses."

We split up so that there are agents going down all three stairwells at the same time. Guns drawn, we are taking steps three and four at a time. As we hit the landing of a floor, we would have an agent search it. Trying to cover all the floors and stairwells means we need everyone possible. We have cops running up all three stairwells as we are running down. Stairwell number three looks like a police convention with uniformed police and agents on every floor. We have people on the landing and searching each floor going down.

The problem is with all the apartments on each floor, we have no idea who they know and who would hide them. "Shit, did anybody see anything?" I am yelling. All I hear is no, nothing, clear. "Where the fuck could they have gone? They weren't that far ahead of us. They had to duck into one of these apartments; there is no way we wouldn't have run into each other with all these cops in the stairwell."

We make it down to the lobby area, and no one has seen them. "Damn it, we were so close," Rosie says. "We might need to do an apartment-to-apartment search."

"God, Rosie, how the hell would that be possible? Twelve floors with twelve apartments on each floor. Can you imagine how fuckin long that would take?"

"Don't worry," he says, "they will not leave this building alive. We have an army surrounding the building and eyes in the sky; we'll find them."

The elevator door opens as agents start bringing the confiscated drugs, firearms, and money from the apartment. We stand and watch as they bring more and more confiscated goods out the building. By this time we not only have the neighborhood watching, the news crew has arrived.

Conrad arrives with Chief Pope to assess the situation. "They are holed up inside one of those apartments, but which one?"

All of a sudden there is a commotion as this woman is trying to get through the police line. "I live here," she is screaming. "I live on the ninth floor, my apartment is on the ninth floor. What is going on? Where is my son?" The police are having a hard time trying to get her to calm down.

A few minutes later this man who says he is a neighbor comes over and pulls her aside to let her know it was her son Justin who was killed. He manages to catch her before she hits the ground. Thank God the paramedics are there. She is taken to the local hospital. The neighbor tells us that her name is Nadine Moore, and she is a good mother. She works a regular job and two nights a week at a part-time job, trying to give her only child what she didn't have growing up, but he wanted the fast life. She did what she could, but the streets had a hold on him, and she recognized that she had lost him. It was just a matter of time. "I feel so sorry for her," he says. "Justin turned nineteen a month ago. Another tragic story of growing up too fast," he says with tears in his eyes. "It's a damn shame," he says, walking out the door.

Watching as the last of the boxes are being brought out, I say to Rosie, "I don't know why, but I want to go back to the apartment."

We leave Conrad and Chief Pope discussing what's next while Rosie and I go back to the ninth floor. We look around but there isn't much to see. The agents did a great job in emptying out the place. There is still a mix of police, agents, and forensic techs still on the scene.

Rosie and I start walking up and down the hallway, checking the doors to the apartments to see if any of the doors are open. As we approach Apartment 909, I notice that the door is slightly ajar, and then it closes slowly. This is the apartment closest to stairwell #2. Rosie signals to take a position, and we slowly move toward the door, guns drawn.

As he reaches to open it, the door flies open, and Maurice and Marsha push past us toward the stairwell. Rosie is on the phone. "We have them. They are running down stairwell number two."

We take off running after them. This time they are in our sight, so we will be able to see if they get off on another floor. I am running like my life depends on it—and it does. Maurice is making Marsha eat his dust, he is so far ahead of her. As we are running down, agents are running up. "FEDERAL AGENTS, STOP," I yell.

"Kiss my ass, bitch," she says.

"Stop and let me show you how I would," I yell back.

I can see that Maurice and the agent are about to collide. Again I hear, "FEDERAL AGENTS—"

Suddenly the sound of a gun going off stops us cold, then rapid gunfire. I hear Marsha screaming. Looking over the banister, I can see Maurice falling in a hail of bullets. "Got him," one of the agents says.

Marsha is screaming and crying at the same time. Just as I reach the level she is on, she turns to me with blood in her eyes. I yell to the agents, "Stand back, this crazy bitch is mine." She has a knife in her hand and lunges at me, but I move so fast that she misses. I turn and kick her in her back, making her hit the wall, which makes her drop the knife. I kick at her again but this time she turns and catches my leg, taking me off balance. My gun goes flying out of my hand. As I start to fall, I grab hold of her pant leg and bring her down with me.

All the while she is screaming that I took her family away from her. I made her husband fall in love with me and out of love with her. That I killed him and turned their sons into criminals. We both fall down a flight of stairs. She manages to get up before I do and raises her leg to kick me. I grab it before it has a chance to connect and push her back as hard as I can. She falls down to the next level and hits her head on one of the steps. Blood is flowing from the back of her head near her neckline, and she is not moving.

I sit, trying to catch my breath. It seems like hours but it is only a couple of minutes before I try to get up. That is when I noticed that my arm is bleeding. The bitch cut me with the knife before I made her drop it. Rosie is screaming at me, asking if I am alright. "Yeah," I say, "she managed to cut my arm with the knife. Other than that, I am OK."

I get up, a little dazed, looking for my gun, when all of a sudden she jumps up and starts coming at me, looking like the walking dead. She does this flying leap thing; I duck and she goes over the railing, landing three floors below. This time, she will not move. The agents who are below us are surrounding her dead body. "Don't ever invite me to your ass again, bitch."

Rosie looks at my arm. "I think you will need stitches."

"I don't think it is that bad."

"Just so you know, I did have your back," he says, "but you looked like you had things under control. Besides, I love to see two women fighting."

"Pig."

The stairwell is now crawling with law enforcement. The coroner and his people are removing the dead bodies, and forensics is going over the place with a fine-tooth comb. I watch as they placed Marsha's body on the stretcher. Looking in her face, you could tell she was beautiful at one time. But the fast living, the men, the drugs had taken a toll on her body. Even in death, she looks crazy.

We hear from one of the agents that they caught the man and woman who first ran past us, making us think they were Maurice and Marsha: Daz Stone and Cathy Blake. They both have warrants out for their arrest, dealing drugs and parole violation. "Don't you just love it when things come together, Shale?"

"Absolutely, Mr. Rosie."

As we walk out of the building, all I see is the flashing of the cameras. Conrad and an army of agents are standing next to Chief Pope. "Great job," the chief says. "We have been after these bastards for a long time. This area needs a rest from all the hell they have been put through. Most of the people who live here are decent, hard-working people, doing the best they can, being held hostage to the few who would kill their own mother for fast money. Drugs are evil, and you can bet unfortunately there is already somebody waiting to take over."

"You would win that bet," Rosie says. "Believe me, this crew was not running this show by themselves. I would stake my life on it."

Conrad says, "We do what we can and keep fighting the good fight."

A paramedic comes over and takes a look at my arm. "You need to go to the hospital so they can sew up that cut."

"I don't need to go."

"She will go," says Conrad. "We will see to it."

We don't get back to New York until the afternoon. By then, I have about 50 messages from my family and friends. I have to stop by my parents' house before I can go home. My mother is crying about her baby, and my dad is saying that it's a good thing that cunt is dead cause he would have killed her himself. My uncle and cousins are ready to go the morgue and kill her again. My family: always ready to kill for me. Now that's love.

I call Gary to let him know that I am OK and head home. When I get home, the crew is waiting for me and gives me a hero's escort to my apartment. They make me wait in the hallway while they give my apartment the once-over. I kiss my babies, make myself a stiff drink, and soak in a tub of hot water. I am now feeling Marsha. Rob has food waiting and offers to heat up something for me, but I'm not in the eating mood. I fix another drink and go through the messages that were on my phones, cell and home.

The last call is from Jonathan. He wanted to make sure I was OK. The sound of his voice makes me cry. I miss the hell out of him, not to mention we haven't made love in a while. It makes me think about our situation. Is all this shit worth losing the love of my life? Why did I have to choose? Why can't I have him and my job? I would never ask him to make a decision between me and his love of music. I was going to call him back, but I can't bring myself to pick up the phone. Sophie and Ochie both come and take their places on the bed while I cry myself to sleep.

The sun is going down when I wake up from a sound sleep. That hot water did wonders for my body. I lie there for a while. The last few months are coming and going in my mind. So much has happened in such a short period of time. The past has a way of interrupting your now life, and you are not always prepared for the end results.

The cats are letting me know they want to eat. I get up, go to the bathroom, and put some water on my face, looking in the mirror to see if there any visible signs that yesterday I was in a fight. My arm hurts a little where the stitches are. I ended up needing 20 stitches. That dead bitch. Oh well, I got the best end of that deal.

Looking at my babies tear into their food makes me realize that I am hungry too. I think I will join them.

The buzzer rings. It's Jonathan. Damn, that man can still make my heart skip a beat. I buzz him in and go to unlock my front door just as he appears at the top of the stairs. I hear him speaking to Rob, who is telling him they are keeping a close eye on me. Jonathan shakes his hand.

As soon as my door closes, Jonathan has me in his arms. I forget all about food. He picks me up and takes me to the bedroom. We make love, long and slow, making up for lost time. At some point I call into the office to tell them I am taking the doctor's advice and taking the day off. We spend the whole day in bed. We don't speak to anyone except my parents, who call to see how I am feeling. I am feeling fine.

Jonathan gets up and fixes us something to eat. I turn on the television to see what is happening in the world, and of course the big story is yesterday's raid and the killing of the three drug dealers, along with Marsha and Maurice.

Why must the reporters interview the most ghetto fabulous among us? I guess everyone wants their fifteen minutes of fame, but seriously. They always get the people with no teeth in their mouth, or the woman who weighs 300 pounds with nine children. Or the man who has a 40-ounce in a brown paper bag, talking Ebonics. They cannot be the only type of people who live in this area. I know I have cousins who grew up and still live in the projects. I have friends who grew up there as well, and they don't fit the stereotype. You never see them being interviewed. It makes me sick.

Jonathan does not say a word as we watch the report, but I know we can't avoid this conversation we must have. Great sex aside, we have real issues, and I don't know how we can reach a compromise if we don't discuss the situation. I start first.

"I know, Jonathan, that you are having a hard time with my job, and I know you don't want me to get hurt, but this is what I signed up for. I love my job, and I am well aware of the dangers, but I was doing this job when I met you. I would never think of asking you to stop something you loved because it makes you who you are. I know my job is more

dangerous than most, but the satisfaction I get knowing I make a difference completes me. It's part of the person you say you love."

He says nothing at first, and then he looks at me and says, "I would
never ask you to quit your job to be a stay-at-home wife. That's not the
kind of woman you are, and not the kind of woman I want either. But
Shale, how can you ask me to go to sleep not knowing if I will get a call
in the middle of the night telling me you were hurt or even killed? Not
knowing from day to day if I would ever see you again. I love you too
much to lose you that way. I don't know how to fix this, but I say we
give it a try. We will take one day at a time. If this was meant to be, it
will work itself out."

He is about to say something else, but before he can, I jump on
him, kissing his words. We land on the floor from the couch, and that is
where we make love again.

The next day I walk into my office with the biggest smile on my
face. Rosie just laughs. "I see that doctor-ordered day off did wonders
for you."

"You have your nurses; I have my doctor." Smiling, I say, "Jealous?"

"Hell yeah," he says. "You were having fun while I spent the night
by myself."

"Good," I say. "Your bed needs the rest. Let it air out." We both start
laughing.

Conrad walks by. "What's so funny?" he asks.

"Nothing, just talking about airing out our mattresses."

"What the hell is so funny about a mattress?"

CHAPTER 12

"**M**eeting in my office now," he says.
The meeting is with the brass from One Police Plaza. We go over everything that happened, making sure that everything was by the book. We don't want any reasonable doubt to derail all our hard work.

We are on the phone with the Baltimore office and Chief Pope finalizing our reports. The drugs that were seized had a street value of $7.5 million, and there was over a million dollars in cash. The weapons seized were everything from handguns to assault rifles to grenade launchers. There were nine semi-automatic shotguns along with ten Tasers. This is no ordinary street gang. Just the power of the weapons alone, then adding in the money, points to bigger players. Every federal law enforcement and local authorities are now involved in this case. We just opened a can of worms. No way in hell is this just a local drug gang.

The killing of Maurice and Marsha, along with the other drug dealers, was ruled justified, so our part in the case was wrapped up. Our Baltimore office will take over, and we will assist if needed. That whole sick family will never be allowed to cause pain and heartache to anyone else. Marsha wanted to be a family again. I pray that they are all roasting in hell TOGETHER as a family. I think about the two boys; they never stood a chance with the parents they had. Who knows how they would have turned out with the right people in their lives. We will never know.

The closing of one case and the continuance of another. There is no way that small-time drug dealers could amass all that money and drugs. The big question now is who it is.

• • •

While that meeting was going on, another meeting is taking place in Brooklyn. There are six men in a room with no windows. The place is filled with smoke and is brightly lit. There is a round table in the middle of the room with a long, narrow table against the wall beside the door. Each man has a gun on his person along with the semi-automatic guns on the long table. On the round table are piles of money and empty bags waiting to be filled, along with boxes of disposable gloves. There are two money-counting machines on the table along with writing pads and pens.

There is a knock on the door. One of the men goes to answer it while the others all draw their guns. "Who is it?"

"Open up the fucking door before I blow a hole through you and it, then you will know who it is." The man enters the room as the others put their guns away and continue counting the money.

"We took a big hit with those fucking feds busting up our Baltimore operation. It's gonna take some time to rebuild that franchise up again. I don't give a fuck about the body count, but our money and drugs—damn, that hurts. We need to tighten up our whole East Coast operation. Those fucking cops now smell blood, and they are not going to stop." He has a bag in his hand that he puts down on the long table. "I know you boys are hungry. Stop for a minute to eat, then get back at it." Moving some of the guns, he takes from the bag sandwiches, bags of chips, cookies.

"What, no beer?"

"Fuck beer," the man says. "Drinking makes you stupid, which causes mistakes. You can drink after we are through. This money has to be counted and bagged before the boss gets in. He's in a meeting."

• • •

Strategic planning in place, our meeting ends with everyone in agreement that we work across agency lines. Conrad and the brass stay in the office while the rest of us are excused. Rosie and I decide to take Brad and Victor out to lunch, since the meeting took place in our office. It's the least we can do.

We head over to our favorite diner and take a booth with me facing a window. We talk about everything that happened in Baltimore, and how we finally have a happy ending to the nightmare of Thomas Wolf and his deranged family. "Yeah," Rosie says, "and the drug dealers were a nice surprise."

We order lunch and as we are eating, I look outside and who do I see walking down the street? MUFFIN. What the hell is he doing in New York? He is supposed to be in Mississippi. I started to shout his name, but something tells me to stay quiet.

I watch him until he turns the corner. I can't believe it. Clearly he is crazy, coming back before it is safe to return. I tell the guys that I have an appointment I forgot about and excuse myself. "Where are you going?" Rosie is saying. "I drove."

"I'll get a cab. See you back at the office."

I hail a taxi just as it is about to turn the corner. I am about to tell the driver what I want him to do when he turns around with this big smile on his face. "What's up, cousin? Where to?"

I cannot believe it—my lazy-ass cousin Tyrone. "What the fuck are you doing driving a cab?"

"Of all the cabs in New York, you had to hail mine," he said. "You look surprised, cousin."

Tyrone is one of my cousins I mentioned earlier who has an allergy to a regular nine-to-five. I don't believe I have ever seen him doing anything constructive. Here he is in living color. He is looking at me in the rearview mirror, grinning from ear to ear. "When? Why? How come?" All these questions come pouring out my mouth.

"Listen," he says, "I had to get a job, or my new old lady was going to kick my ass out in the streets. I had no choice. But you know I was not going to get a real job. I needed something I could do while sitting on my ass."

Yelp, that's my cos. It hurts to laugh right after eating.

He turns serious. "How are you really? After what happened in Baltimore."

"Look at me. Don't I look OK?"

"Watch yourself, cos. I know you can take care of yourself, but you are only a woman, after all."

I try to hit him through the divider. "I bet this woman can kick your lazy ass."

"Hell, I know you can, as much as you used to kick my ass growing up. Why do you think I always picked you to be on my side?"

"Cause I was better at every game we played."

"Damn right you were."

"I want to meet your new old lady. She is alright in my book if she can get you off your ass and make you get a real job."

Laughing, he asks, "Why are you hailing a cab? You don't have your car anymore?"

I explain, "I was having lunch with Rosie, and he drove. I thought I saw Muffin. Have you seen him recently?"

"Yeah, that skinny son of a bitch was at the liquor store down the street earlier. I was surprised to see him; I thought he had to leave town. Why did he come back?"

"I don't know, but believe me I will find out."

We catch up on family matters as he drives around, keeping our eyes open for Muffin. Ten minutes go by before we see the worm coming out of a liquor store. He seems to be talking to himself. I tell my cousin to slow down so I can jump out of the car before he knows I see him.

Just as Muffin is about to cross the street, I am out of the cab and have him by his neck. He drops the bag that is in his hand, and the bottle shatters into a million pieces as the red color of the wine runs down the sidewalk. He smiles and says, "We gotta stop meeting like this."

Muffin sees my cousin sitting in the cab. "Yo, cos Tyrone, what's up?"

He tries to walk over to the cab, but I grab him and push up against the fence. "Why the hell are you back in New York? You are supposed to be picking cotton in Mississippi."

"Listen to me, Shale. I was going crazy down there. My grandmother was on my back about me and Pookie getting married; she had the baby, a girl, by the way. Now we got seven kids living in an old house with my mother, grandmother, aunt, and two cousins. If I didn't leave, I would have killed somebody."

"You coming back to New York may solve that problem for you," I say.

"My boy Stack called and told me the coast was clear to come back to New York. I heard what happened in Baltimore; you got those sons of bitches. And the best part is that I was nowhere to be found, so what's the problem?"

"You idiot, you don't think there is a connection between Baltimore and what happened in Brooklyn? The problem, you little shit, is the people who were killed are the small fries; they didn't have the brains to control an operation of this magnitude. We need the people at the top, and until we know who that is, you are not safe. Because you took it upon yourself to come back, don't think I will be there to protect your skinny ass; you are on your own."

He is looking at me in total disbelief. "How can you tell me some shit like that? You *have* to protect me, you are the fuzz. Not only that, but the *federal* fuzz. It is your civil duty. Didn't you take some kind of oath?"

I look at this idiot, turn, and walk back to the cab as he is cussing me out. As I get into the cab, I turn and see that the fool is crying. What a total asshole. To be honest, I don't know if he is crying because it has hit him that he is still in danger, or that he lost another bottle of wine.

I have my cousin take me back to the office. "Don't forget dinner at my parents' on Sunday; you'll get to meet Vivian."

"I would not miss that for all the tea in China. Later, cos."

Rosie is hanging up the phone as I am coming in. "Where the hell did you run off to without a car?"

I walk over to his desk. "Guess who is back in town? Muffin."

"What the fuck is he doing back in town?"

I tell Rosie what happened and why Muffin said he was back. "You want to know something weird? When I saw him, I was about to shout

out his name, but something stopped me, and I don't know why. It was only the four of us at lunch. Don't you find that strange?"

Rosie says, "There are a lot of things that I find strange about this case, but we never go against our gut feeling."

Rosie's phone rings. It's one of his CI's who says he heard something that Rosie might want to hear. He makes arrangements to meet him while I return phone calls.

One of the calls I return is to my friend in the DC headquarters, Evelyn Lewis. "Hey, girlfriend, sorry I missed your call."

"No problem," she says. "I was calling to say hello, I haven't talked to you for a minute."

We catch up with each other. I ask about her daughter, Gail, who was a little thing when we met. "Girl, she is as tall as you are and is driving now, which is scaring the shit out of her father. She is so proud to say she knows you whenever she sees you on television. You know it's because of you that she wants to be an agent. Her dad is pushing for something safer, like being part of a bomb disposal unit." We shared a good laugh.

"Give her a big kiss for me. Let her know I haven't forgotten my promise that she can come and spend a week with me in New York after all the craziness settles."

She tells me the office went crazy as they watched what unfolded in Newark. "Our office was very involved with the Thomas Wolf case, and to know that all the loose ends have been tied up is a reason to celebrate. I wish we could get a handle on this current case."

She tells me the other reason she called was they got a tip that Muffin was back in New York. How could the DC office know about Muffin? And if they know, then it is common knowledge he is back. I say out loud, "If we know, then everybody will know."

CHAPTER 13

Rosie calls on his way back to the office. "What do you want to eat?" This was going to be a long night. Conrad had left for the night, but not before dumping five boxes of records and files he wants us to go through. The night crew at our office is a little lighter than during the day but with everything that is going on, we have a few more bodies than usual. I look at the clock. It is 10 p.m. Damn, I didn't know it was so late. I call my dad and Jonathan to let them both know I am still at the office and will call them when I get home. I also leave a message for Gary so that the Betty Crocker Patrol won't worry. I have no choice; he called twice.

By 2:30 a.m. we have gone through most of the files. The cleaning people are here, going through their nightly routine. Coming out of the ladies room, I see Rachael Mendoza, who is the supervisor of the cleaning crew. We stop and talk. She has been here since I joined the force; she is one of those people who can make any day brighter. I notice as we talk that there are some new faces that I don't recognize. She says finding people who really want to work is not easy. People are lazy and don't want to get off their asses, so she has a revolving door of people who come and go. This crew has been here for about five months. There are two women and three men. I smile as I pass to go back to my desk.

Rosie says it is time to call it a night. He has plans that he wants to try and salvage. We did not think we would be here so late. "Sounds like a plan, partner. I am so ready to go."

We say goodnight to Rachael and leave when I remember I left my cell phone on my desk. I tell Rosie that I need to go back to get it. "OK, I will wait for you outside."

As I turn the corner, I see one of the men on the cleaning crew going over my desk with a feather duster. He is looking through my papers like he is looking for something in particular. I move so he can't see me, but I can see him opening my drawers, going through some of the files that are on the desk.

He picks up my wastepaper basket and starts looking at the papers I had thrown away. I turn and make my way back to Rosie. I tell him what I saw, and he suggests we go back in and act like we left something.

He is cleaning Rosie's desk when we come back in. When he looks up and sees us, I think he is going to shit his pants. "Sorry if we scared you," I say. "We forgot our keys."

"No problem," he says and quickly moves away. We both go through our desks. The files that were left out are not of importance, so he did not see anything that he shouldn't have. I go to look for Rachael. I want to know who this guy is.

I find her in the small room that houses the cleaning supplies. I ask her who he is and how long he has been with her, because I didn't remember him before tonight. She tells me his name is Jose Mendoza (no relation), and he has been with her about two months.

I know that everyone who works for the government, even contractors, goes through background checks before they are hired. I ask her about his background. "Yes, most of the time a background check is done. I didn't do one for Jose because he worked at One Police Plaza, and had been there over a year. A background check had been done at the time he was hired by the city." Her friend is the supervisor of cleaning there, and so she didn't feel like she had to repeat what was already done. He also was her friend's daughter's new boyfriend, so there was a personal relationship, and she liked him. This was not the first time her friend Rosa recommended someone to her, and there never was a problem.

I ask if she knows why he left that job. She says it was because of the hours. He needed to work nights. Is there a reason I am asking questions about him? I tell her he looks like someone I know.

I tell Rosie what Rachael told me. "Something stinks," Rosie says. "My gut is doing flips."

"Yeah," I say, "shit stinks."

The next day we tell Conrad what happened the night before. He calls over to One Police Plaza and talks with his friend Benny. Benny is like Conrad: he has been a cop for years, and there is nothing that happens there he doesn't know about. Conrad tells him what happened and how Jose ended up at our office. "We need to verify his story, and we need more info on this cleaning supervisor who recommended him to Rachael." He tells Conrad he would get back in touch.

In the meantime we check every database we can get our hands on, looking for any information we could find on Jose. I call Rachael to get an address on him, but she doesn't answer, so I leave her a message.

Benny calls back in about five minutes. He is talking very fast, and we can hear commotion in the background. "They just found the cleaning supervisor dead in the cleaning closet. She had been strangled. Her name was Rosa Castillo, and she has worked at One Police Plaza for eleven years."

The manhunt is now on for one Jose Mendoza. This probably is not his real name, but it's all we have for now. The last place we saw him was here in the office. An APB is issued for his arrest as a suspect in the murder of Rosa. I tell Conrad that I had been trying to contact Rachael with no success; he orders a car to go to her home. Just in case.

Conrad wants the office torn apart. We don't know what we are looking for, but that doesn't stop us from looking. We turn the entire office upside down when one of the agents signals that he found something. Under the coffee station setup is a small bug. We continue searching the rooms looking for more bugs; there has to be more than the one that was found. Sure enough, we find two more—one in a coat closet, the other in-between Rosie's and my desks. We found our mole. That son of a bitch had the perfect cover to be able to plant these bugs. The rest of the building is on lockdown as an investigation gets underway to see if there are any more devices planted.

We are still trying to contact Rachael when we get a call from the agents sent to Rachael's. They found her; she had been strangled. She is not dead, but it doesn't look good. She is on the way to the hospital right now. We don't know why he didn't kill her, but we are happy he didn't. Jose is trying to sew up loose ends. We need to find him ASAP. We are on the warpath after hearing about Rachael; she is well liked here, so we are taking this very personally.

There is a dragnet along the eastern seaboard. The city is under tight security. We have every cop in NYC looking for this bastard. Every airport, train station, car rentals, every mode of transportation is being watched. Our tech team is going over the bugs, trying to get as much info as possible.

I call the hospital to check on Rachael. She is in intensive care; her family had just arrived to be with her. I am glad she is not alone. I feel like my mind is about to explode. I go to the ladies room just to have some quiet time and think. My heart goes out to Rachael. She doesn't deserve this. I say a quiet prayer that she gets through this.

I am washing my hands when someone grabs me from behind. He grabs my hair and pushes my face into the mirror. It takes me a minute to grasp what is happening. I try to get my balance so I can make him release his hold on my hair. I am able to use my body to push him against the stall door; this gives me a chance to turn and face him. I don't give him a chance before I do a running jump and kick him in his face. Blood squirts out of his mouth and nose. He falls in the toilet, and I am able to land a kick to his groin. He lets out a loud yell as the door to the ladies room bursts open with six agents, including Rosie, all holding their guns ready to shoot.

"I'm OK," I say. "Can't say the same for him. Gentlemen, meet Jose Mendoza. What balls he has to have the whole city looking for him. He was here all the time, right under our noses."

The agents grab him and start to beat the shit out of him before Rosie shouts, "Stop, we don't want to give this son of a bitch a reason to walk." Jose looks like he was in jail riot. He is still trying to hold his balls as he is being handcuffed.

As we leave the bathroom, more agents, along with Conrad, are standing in the hallway with guns drawn. We hear cheers as the word gets out that we have him. He is still wearing the uniform that the cleaning crew wears.

We put him in interview #2, read him his Miranda rights, and get some Band-aids on his face.

"I wish I could have used my gun; I would have blown your head off your body." He starts to say "bitch" when I see that two of his teeth are missing.

I start laughing. "You are right," I say. "I'm a bitch with a badge and a gun, and I still have all my teeth."

We interrogate him for hours. All we are getting from him are bullshit answers. "Why did you attack me?"

"I didn't attack you. I was fighting for my life; you attacked me."

Laughing, I say, "I attacked you in the ladies room?"

Looking up with this dumb look on his face, he says, "I didn't know I was in the ladies room. I thought someone was after me and just ducked into the first door I saw."

Rosie says, "I take it you don't know anything about the murder of Rosa Castillo or the attempted murder of Rachael Mendoza?"

"Who?"

"Your supervisor, dickhead."

"Oh, that Rosa and Rachael. No, I didn't. WAIT, Rosa is dead?" He starts speaking in Spanish and making the sign of the cross. "Did you say someone also tried to kill Rachael?" Again the sign of the cross. "What is this world coming to? People can't even go to work nowadays."

"Shut the fuck up," I say. "You're giving me one son of a bitch of a headache."

We get word that Rachael has a great chance for recovery, but she will remain in the hospital for about a week, depending on how well she responds to treatment. She was found unconscious, so the doctors want to run more tests to see if there are any lingering effects to her brain due to oxygen deprivation. Her family is strong believers in prayer, so she will come out of this without question. She will be well taken care of; she comes from a large family. This news is the only other bright spot in our night.

Jose has his one phone call as he waits in the pen. NYPD wants his ass, but if we release him now, he will not see the morning, and he is better to us alive than dead. We need to get as much information from him as we can. The first question is WHO? We need to know who is behind this.

When he is taken for his mug shot and to be fingerprinted, we learn that he has tried to erase his fingerprints with acid. It slows things down a little in ID-ing him, but it isn't foolproof. He didn't do a very good job. We are still able to get his true identity. His real name is Miguel Hernandez, and he has a rap sheet that is taller than he is. He is wanted for murder and drug trafficking in his native Mexico. What is he doing in New York and how was he able to enter the U.S.?

Time has gone by so fast, before we know it it's 6:00 in the morning. We have been running since the attack, and we are all tired. We are all running on adrenaline and very strong coffee, couldn't stop if we wanted to. "How many cups have you had?" Rosie asks.

"I can't remember. I have been going over and over these files, and I still don't know what I am looking for. But I know it's here."

Rosie looks like he is ready to drop as he sits at his desk. I get up to get another cup, but it's all gone. I make another pot. "Fresh coffee is ready."

"Hit me," Rosie says.

Agents from the DEA are interrogating Miguel, who has not said a word after he had his phone call. I walk into the room with the one-way mirror, watching Miguel sitting at the table with this smirk on his face. He is staring into the mirror as if he could see me on the other side.

There is a knock on the door leading into the interrogation room and in walks David Levin, lawyer to the criminal population of the tri-state area. "I need a minute alone with my client. Please leave. Oh, and tell the agents on the other side of the mirror to leave the room. I want to speak to him in private."

We all step out into the hallway. "What the fuck? What the hell is David Levin doing representing this piece of shit?"

"Haven't you heard?" Rosie says. "All he ever represents is shitbags."

Conrad asks how he got here so fast. "I don't know," I say, "but he has to know someone important."

We are all still standing in the hallway when the door opens and out walks David and Miguel. "See you in court, Officers," David says. Miguel is smiling, walking behind him.

"This is bullshit. How can he just walk out of here with murder charges over him? Can't we keep him in jail until the bail hearing?"

"No," says Conrad. "We can't prove that he killed Rosa, only for the attack on Shalimar."

"What about Rachael? That son of a bitch tried to kill her. Doesn't that matter?"

"Rachael is in no condition to verify Miguel as her attacker. We all know he did it, but until she is well enough to tell us it was him, there isn't much we can do about it."

"Attacking Shalimar should be enough to hold this son of a bitch."

"Obvious not if your lawyer is David Levin." I am so angry I just want to hit something or somebody, and that somebody is David Levin. How the hell is this possible?

I go home, shower, sleep for about an hour, and then get dressed for court. When I get there, Conrad, Rosie, the chief of police, along with a room full of cops and agents, wait while the DA and David argue for and against bail for this scumbag. Funny what can unite people who don't always see eye to eye. Here we all are standing together, seeking the same thing: justice for Rosa, Rachael, and me.

The judge is Walter Brown, who is listening to both sides of the argument. He seems to be paying close attention, and we are hoping that he will keep Miguel in jail. He asks the DA about bail; the DA recommends that he be remanded into custody. "Your Honor, look at the facts. His criminal background, his being here illegally, and with his obvious connections, he is a serious flight risk. He is also a suspect in the murder of Rosa Castillo and the attempted murder of Rachael

Mendoza. And on top of all of that, Your Honor, he attacked Special Agent Shalimar Blacque. There is no way he should be let loose. I am recommending that he be held without bail."

David stands up and gives some bullshit runaround about there being no evidence of murder or attempted murder. Rosa Castillo was his boss and also his girlfriend's mother, they had a great relationship. He has no reason to kill her. He had a wonderful working relationship with Mrs. Mendoza, again no reason to harm her. He was very upset when he was informed of what happened to both of them. As far as Special Agent Blacque is concerned, his client thought he was being attacked and was simply defending himself. He was scared and was doing what anyone else would have done in his shoes. How was he to know what motive Agent Blacque had in mind? "Coming from Mexico, where police are not always trustworthy, no wonder, Your Honor, he was scared. Also, Your Honor, my client has never been formally charged with any crimes back in Mexico. These are only allegations. I would also like to clear up the illegal matter. Miguel is here legally, but due to immigration's carelessness, an error was made in identifying him as he entered the country. He should not be held responsible for a mistake the government made." Under the circumstances, he would personally guarantee his client will appear in court and was ready to post whatever bail the judge saw fit. "Judge Brown, I would not be willing to stake my reputation if I did not believe that what happened between my client and Agent Blacque was a horrible mistake."

I tune out of the proceedings because I am steaming. Mad at all the bullshit that is coming out of David's mouth. All of a sudden all I hear is the judge saying that Miguel will be released on two million dollars bail. He will surrender his passport, and is advised not to leave New York. The court erupts as the judge is pounding his gavel for his court to be quiet. He goes into this long speech about how he is following the law, and he knows sometimes the decision doesn't seem fair, but he has no choice but to follow the rules of the law.

David has guaranteed that Miguel would show up for trial, and with that, they leave the court with a trail of reporters falling over each other for a comment. I can't move. What the hell just happened? Have you ever been so mad you want to cry? That is how I am feeling right now. I tell Rosie I don't care if it is the morning, I need a drink and now. Steaming is coming out of my ears, and all I want right now is a drink in my hand.

Leaving, we see Victor and Brad. "Join us for a drink?" We go to the local watering hole around the corner from the court.

CHAPTER 14

"We heard what happened," Victor says. "You must be upset."

"Damn right I am. Murder and attempted murder, along with assault on a federal agent, and he gets to walk out of jail. In what civilized society does that make sense? And how did David Levin get to be his lawyer?" We all know David is a mob lawyer, which means that this has something to do with the syndicate.

Brad is quiet for a while, then says, "I'm starting to believe you guys are right that what happened in Baltimore and the killings in Brooklyn are connected. There is no way that the gang in Baltimore could amass that much drugs and money without some help. We kept saying someone bigger is involved. I think the mob or the Mexican drug cartels are in bed together, or they are pitting one another against each other. That is the only thing that makes sense. Especially since David Levin is now involved."

The more we talk about this possibility, the more it starts to make sense. If both the mob and/or the cartel are involved, there is no telling how many people are on their payroll. This would also explain the large amounts of money and drugs and guns.

This shit is blowing up minute by minute. We go back to the office, and there is large envelope on my desk. There is no return information, just my name. I ask, "Did anyone see who put this on my desk?" Nobody pays much attention. I open it and on a piece of paper in cutout letters it reads: *JUDGE WALTER BROWN IS ON THE TAKE*. I nearly fall on the floor. "Rosie, come here, look."

He reads the message. "I knew it," he says. "That's why he let that shitbag off so easy." We stand there looking at each other.

"Rosie, everything just jumped off less than two hours ago. How did this get here so fast? And who sent it?"

"I don't know," Rosie says. "Maybe we have a guardian angel."

I get on the phone and call Victor, telling him what I have. He tells me he is not surprised. "There has always been the rumor that the judge was for sale to the highest bidder. He has a way of covering his ass. There was never any way to prove it. He has been under investigation before, so he knows how to play the game, and he has friends in very high places. Somehow or other the investigations always get dropped. Being that well-connected works for the scumbag."

We can't even go to the DA. They have tried and failed before to nail his sorry ass. Unless the evidence is so overwhelming that it can't be ignored, that is not an option, at least for right now. Going after the judge is a career-ender. We have no idea who he is in bed with. The DA is not stupid; he would never go into court charging a sitting judge with corruption without reliable witnesses and evidence. "I think it's time we get that evidence," I say. "This son of a bitch is as rotten as they come. He let Miguel walk after assaulting a federal agent. I don't give a damn what David Levin said in court, we all know he killed Rosa. We need to find His Honor's weaknesses so that we can hit him where it will do the most damage."

"His influence and reputation?"

"I was thinking more about money. That bastard is selling his seat on the bench. Everyone knows he has expensive taste. I can't believe he is risking all that he worked so hard for just for his influence."

We agree to meet after we talk to Conrad. Rosie and I go into Conrad's office and show him the note. I tell them about my conversation with Victor. Conrad smiles and says, "I think it's time we turn up the heat. Judge Brown was under investigation before. He's no dummy, so we have to do better than before. Let's see what his files show. I want to know how far the past investigations went. I want to know everything about that bastard we can get our hands on. I want this case to be priority number one."

We do a conference call with Brad and tell him what we had decided. "No problem," Brad says. "I will make sure that you have all the files we have on the judge. I would also suggest that we talk to the FBI. I am sure that they have more files to look at. The Justice Department at one time had their own investigation looking into the judge."

Conrad says, "I think it's also a good idea to put someone on the judge just so we can chart his every move."

"Good idea," Brad says.

"I will make sure that we put someone on Miguel as well. I want to know his every move, even when he takes a leak. Is it asking too much if we could catch them all together? The judge, Miguel, and that bastard David."

"Not in my book," Brad answers.

"I am not going to stop until we nail this son of a bitch," I say.

Brad laughs. "I love your passion, and I do believe he is going down this time."

"Damn, Skippy," I say. "It's personal. Attacking Rachael and then me, killing Rosa—I'm on a mission. I want his ass on a stick. He is being paid to throw cases, and God knows what else. I think he is our link to whoever the higher-ups are. Being a judge, I would think he has the most to lose. I say let's go after him." Brad says we will talk later.

"Shale, come with me," Rosie says. "One of my CI's has some information."

We drive to Brooklyn to an area that used to be surrounded by abandoned buildings and old brownstones that had seen better days. This area used to be a picture postcard for urban decay. But now developers have come in and made this area almost unrecognizable. Talk about a 360-degree turnaround. Brownstones are in various stages of being renovated. Some have been converted into condos and townhouses while keeping many as single-family homes. Commercial businesses will be opening soon, as well as several restaurants. There is now a small park that was once an open lot with only garbage and trash in it. They have even planted a small community vegetable garden for the residents. I cannot believe the transformation. It is absolutely beautiful now. Rosie says he is thinking about buying in the neighborhood.

As we wait in the car, a woman is walking toward us. She is tall and very beautiful. I smile to myself; of course she is beautiful. This is Rosie, after all. The closer she gets to the car, I start to see that this is no ordinary woman. She is wearing the shortest dress, and baby, it is hugging every curve on her body. She has on the baddest pair of Christian Louboutin pumps that I have never seen before. Her long black weave has hues of honey-blond streaks and curls that go on forever. "Hey, baby," she says to Rosie. He says hello, then introduces us.

"Cleo, this is my partner, Shalimar." We both say hello. So this is Cleo. Whenever Rosie speaks of her, it is only in terms of her being a reliable source. He never said anything about her looks or the fact that she is a special kind of woman. Not that it matters. It's just that he tells everything else.

Now I am secure in my own truth, so I have no problem saying that another woman is beautiful. Even in this case. Skin as smooth and radiant as butter, coffee-colored latte. Large doe eyes with thick eyelashes that go on for miles. When she smiles, two dimples magically appear out of nowhere. She has that kind of look that would make a man walk into a wall. Unless you are right up on her, you honestly could not tell. You still had to look real hard.

"I have heard a great deal about you, Shale," she says.

"All good, I hope."

"Nothing but the best. You are right, Rosie; she is beautiful."

"Rosie, you think I'm beautiful?"

"Of course," he says. "I only associate with beautiful women."

"You are so full of shit."

Smiling, Cleo says, "I tell him that all the time. Most men want me for my body; Rosie only wants me for information. Like the Yellow Pages or 411."

"That's not true," he says.

"No? What else would you want Cleo for then?"

He is giving me the 'shut the fuck up' look. And I am giving him my 'I don't give a damn' look because right now, seeing him squirm in his seat is heaven. Rosie hands her some money.

"I hear you are looking for Miguel Hernandez?"

"Yeah, we're looking for a Miguel Hernandez. Why?"

"Because I know where he is."

"How do you know that it is our Miguel?"

She smiles. "Honey, I know everything there is to know about these streets. Trust me, he's the one you are looking for."

"We know where he is, we have a tail on him," I say.

She smiles again. "How much you want to bet that he has lost your tail? Anyway," she says as she is looking at me, "a friend of mine tells me that Shalimar is cool peoples as long as she can stay away from your drink of choice."

We all start laughing. "Muffin," we all say at the same time.

"He was so upset about Miguel attacking you and wants me to do him a favor. I owe him one, so here I am." She hands the money back to Rosie. "This one is on me." She gives us an address and turns to leave, but before she does, she looks back in the car. "Please be careful. Miguel hangs around some pretty awful people. I mean real crazies. Rosie, I would hate to have anything happen to you before I get my hands on you." She blows him a kiss and walks away from us.

"Damn, she is beautiful," I say out loud.

"Yeah," Rosie says softly. "Too bad we have the same equipment."

I call out to her, "Cleo, I love those shoes."

"Thanks, love. Brand new designer. Just hit the U.S. market, but very big in Europe."

"Oh my God, please don't tell me Giovanni Lombardi."

She turns to face me. "I take it you like shoes."

Rosie is shaking his head. "Please don't get her started on shoes."

"Girl, I don't just *like* shoes, the word is LOVE."

"Me too. I have a friend in the shoe business; I'll hook you up. Rosie knows how to contact me."

Rosie is looking at me. "What is it about women and shoes?"

"Don't bother," I say. "You will never understand."

As Cleo crosses the street, a car stops. She goes over to the window. After a few minutes, she gets in the car.

On the way to the address she gave us, I check and sure enough, the agents lost Miguel. The house is about ten blocks from where the killings took place in Brooklyn. I tell the office to have a car to meet us at the address. "We are only doing surveillance, so send only one car."

Rosie and I have plenty of time to discuss what we are going to do once we get there. Traffic is a nightmare. A truck loses its cargo; construction has some of the streets blocked off, and a woman goes into labor. Son of a bitch. Wonderful New York traffic.

CHAPTER 15

By the time we arrive, the agents are already there. We get into the car they are sitting in. We tell them what we found out, and they tell us that Miguel is in the house. Just as they are pulling up, he gets out of a car with a young lady, and they both are carrying bags of groceries and beer. It looks like they are about to have a party.

The location of the house is in a grimy section of Brooklyn, and we are starting to attract attention. This car has 'police' written all over it. We need a better cover. We decide to leave and come back with one of our decoy vans, which will come with all the equipment we will need for surveillance.

Later that night we have the entire three blocks covered with federal agents and NYPD cops. After about two hours of not a lot going on, I am starting to get antsy. Light rain starts coming down, and I am wishing I was anywhere but here not being alone. Loud music begins to play from inside the house. Guess the party has started. No one else comes and goes from the house. Must be a private party for only the people inside the house. I wonder what they are celebrating and how many people are in there.

Another half hour goes by when suddenly there is a loud crackle that sounds like gunfire. We are out of the van in seconds, guns drawn, when we realize the sound we heard is thunder. The rain is coming down harder now, and the thunder is growing louder. Lightning is literally lighting up the night.

All of a sudden there is a very loud boom. For a moment we think it is thunder until we see flames shooting from the direction of the house. We come running from all directions. The house is totally engulfed in flames. There is no way that anyone could have survived that blast. A call had already been placed, so it is not very long before the fire department arrives on the scene. The rain has let up, but the fire continues to burn.

It takes a couple of hours before the fire is totally out. The fire marshal and his crew start going through the remains of the house. They find six bodies in the rubble, three in the front of the house, two in a top floor bedroom, and one in the hallway leading to the front door, trying to get out of the house, no doubt.

Two bombs had been planted, one at the front of the house, the other at the back. Whoever did this wanted to make sure no one escaped. There is nothing left to the house or the bodies.

We ask the medical examiner to put a rush on ID-ing the bodies. We can't imagine anyone escaping that blast, so is Miguel Hernandez one of the bodies? We play out this scene again in the middle of news reporters, police, and agents. We catch up Conrad about the details and what went on that night.

We are walking toward the van when one of the reporters runs over to me and asks how come every time there is a horrific crime scene, I am always there? I turn and smile and say, "Lucky, I guess. Now make sure you get my good side."

She turns to Rosie and asks, "Did anyone ever tell you that you could be a model?"

Getting into the car, he says, "I am one."

I'm so tired, and I don't feel like going home, so I bunk at the office. We have rooms with cots in them so we can sleep here if we have to, two for the women and four for the men. I fall asleep as soon as my head hits the pillow, but it is not a sound sleep. I see images of all the people who have died in the last few months. They are chasing me, and I am running, but it doesn't seem like I'm moving at all. They are about to grab me, but I take off running toward nothingness. I am frantically trying to find a place to hide, but there is no place for me to escape as the dead get closer and closer.

The whole damn Wolf family is the closest to me. Blood is coming from their eye sockets as they are gaining on me. Thomas is cussing that they will enjoy, as a family, killing me slowly. He wants to show his sons how it's done. Marsha has the look of a rabid dog, growling that she wants the first stab at me. Maurice is beside her with hands shaped like guns, pointed at my head. Bullets start shooting out of his fingers, hitting me all over my body. I run faster and faster but stand still in the same place.

I run around the corner, right into the arms of Left Eye and Miguel. Blood is still coming out of his missing eye, and the heel of my shoe is still hanging on for dear life. Miguel has the hands of Goliath, aiming straight at my neck. I run until I can't run anymore, screaming for help. No help ever arrives.

I wake up in a cold sweat. How long will these damn nightmares continue?

It takes a day for the results to come in. Miguel did die in the blast. The men and women who died in the fire were all Mexican nationals, and all had criminal records. They were all part of the Mexican cartel, involved in the drug trade. We are able to get all the information we need from the DEA because they had made a deal with one of the women to cooperate in exchange for a lesser sentence. The DEA is not sure if the killings were because she was made out as a snitch or because Miguel was now a liability. It really doesn't matter; they both are dead, and we still don't know everything.

I call to find out how Rachael is feeling and am happy to hear that she will be going home soon to recuperate with her family. Helen, one of the agents, goes to see her on behalf of the office with a beautiful bouquet of flowers and a nice-size donation along with a very big card signed by everyone in the office. She is very happy to hear that the man who killed her friend and tried to kill her is dead. She can't wait to get back to her normal life, and we can't wait for her to return. She is well loved around here. We consider her one of the family.

"Rosie, I've been thinking about Judge Brown. The man is not invincible. There has to be more in this for him besides money."

"Like what?"

"I don't know. Drugs, sex, high friends in all the wrong places. He is taking a lot of chances for someone in his position. He knows that he is under scrutiny, and yet he acts as if he doesn't care. Whoever he is in bed with has to be higher up the food chain for him to have his 'I don't give a fuck' attitude. There has to be a way to find out what his Achilles heel is."

We sit in silence for a moment, then it comes to us at the same time: CLEO. If she is that well-connected to the streets, she would be the one to ask about any dirt on our judge. "I'll call her, but you know something like this is gonna cost me."

"Oh, man up and take one for the team," I say, laughing.

The next day Cleo comes through. Rosie never did tell me what the price of this juicy information cost him, but I didn't care. Whatever the price, it was well worth it. We are sitting in Rosie's car with Cleo on the cell phone. Seems our respectable prudent judge is a big FREAK. He has a friend who owns a well-secluded, custom-built rustic mansion in the middle of 50 acres up in the Catskills. The house is not visible from the road and is surrounded by thick forest-like vegetation along with a very high-security fence. Supposedly the place is where the men can get away to fish, play golf, swim, and just relax without the old ball and chains. Every good wife knows that men need their space. A place where they can play poker, smoke cigars, tell dirty jokes. A real getaway from the stresses of working and living in the City. The best part is all this is less than four hours away.

But what the wives don't know is that they never fish or play poker, not the way they may think. What we are hearing makes this house a present-day Sodom & Gomorrah. Anything goes. If you want to do it or have it done to you, this is your kind of party. Drugs, underage prostitutes (male and female), swingers, whatever makes you happy. Some of the biggest names in the tri-state come to this house to be able to let their freak flags fly.

"Like who?" Rosie asks.

"You name them. Judges, politicians, police, lawyers, college professors. Look in the book of Who's Who and I can pick out names that would send shock waves throughout the country. Believe me, they come from all over the country, not just the northeast."

"To say I am speechless is an understatement. How could this be going on and this is the first we hear about this?"

"Sug, when you are dealing with this caliber of highfalutin people, they know what is needed for this kind of operation and where to go to get what they want. Money is no object. Besides, they are all in bed with each other, no chance of anyone spilling the beans."

Rosie makes a call to find out who owns that house and property. We want an answer pronto. I am fixated; I can't believe what I am hearing. "Cleo, you mentioned drugs. What kind and how much?"

"Please, girl, you name it, and it is all there for the taking. Start with A and stop at Z."

"How much?"

"As much as they want. There is never a chance that there would be no more drugs."

"Who brings the drugs?"

"Different people. It's never the same people at every party, at least the times I've been there. I can tell you they are not your everyday corner hood-rat dealers."

"How do you know?"

"Because hood rats are called hood rats for a reason. They stay in the hood. Their imagination could never imagine the kind of money I am talking about. Not all the money is illegal. You have all types: old money, new money, dirty money. Money attracts money. We are talking about titans of industry who have at their disposal all the money they will ever need. More money than most people will ever make in their lifetime. The cars, the yachts, the private jets, the mansions. Can you imagine having people at your beck and call? Every made-for-television movie pales in comparison. At some point hookers become call girls or escorts, unless slumming is your thing. Everything in this world has a price, and they can afford to pay it. Believe me, when they reach your price, you scream 'sold to the highest bidder.' I should know. A moment of silence, please."

Rosie asks Cleo if she knows who the drug dealers are. "I only know a few by name, but they are all Mexican."

Ding-dong—the light goes off. "Son of a bitch, we were right. It is not the mob, but the cartel."

Rosie is called back with the information on the house. The owners are listed as a corporation, MDC, Inc., but there is not much more than that. The agent says he will continue to dig for more information. "Thanks, Scott. Let me know as soon as you find out more."

"Have you ever heard of MDC before, Cleo?"

"No, it doesn't ring a bell."

"OK, Cleo, what about our favorite judge?"

"Your Judge Brown's personal favorite is role-playing and getting his ass beat. He likes to be dominated and kept in bondage. He has his own dominatrix who beats the hell out of him and makes him cry like a little baby. He is into all of it, the whips, chains, everything. The more pain that is inflicted on him, the better he likes it."

"No wonder every time I see him in court, he always has this expression like he is in pain. He never looks like he is sitting up straight. Welts will do that to you, I guess." We are also told that it doesn't matter to him if the dominatrix is male or female, as long as they are cracking that whip (fucking sicko).

"Listen, it's been fun, but I have to get ready for a hot date. Rosie baby, please don't be jealous. I would cancel this date in a heartbeat if you would only say the word."

"Have a nice time on your date."

"Chicken."

Oh my God, I swear I am hyperventilating right now. Rosie looks shell-shocked. I knew that bastard was dirty, but nothing I was imagining can match this reality. This is too good to be true. How to prove it is the question. "I need to get inside that house."

"Whoa," Rosie says. "What are you saying? Why does it have to be you?"

"This is too important to be left to an amateur."

"Look, Shale, you are not the only agent who will be working this case. Let someone else—"

"NO," I say. "This is personal, Rosie, and I want to be there when we bring those bastards down."

"You will be. But what I'm gonna need you to do right now is calm down. We are all taking this shit personally. Stop acting like you are Superwoman on a one-woman crusade. This is the big league with some very dangerous people who won't think twice about putting a bullet in the head of a cop. Especially a federal cop. It would give more bragging rights."

"But, Rosie—"

"No buts, Shale. I mean it. We are partners, but I still outrank you."

"What? Are you seriously pulling that outranking shit on me?"

"Hell yeah, and I will do it if it means keeping you out of harm's way."

"I have a daddy, you know, I don't need two."

"Well, stop acting like a little girl and start thinking like a trained agent. Besides, you really think I want to go against your father if I let something happen to his precious baby?"

I start smiling. "He would kick your ass all around New York."

"Damn, Skippy, he would." Laughing, he says, "Are you back?"

"Yes, I am."

"Now WE—notice I said WE—are going to be the ones to bring down Goliath. We just need proof. We need someone on the inside. Someone who is not recognizable to any of the players."

"You know that's me, Rosie."

"That is *not* you. Remember, the judge knows you. Besides, we don't know who all the players are yet. You could be in danger of someone else recognizing you."

"Damn, you're right. I hadn't even thought of someone else as a possibility." I'm so angry that I can't think straight. "Rosie, I need to be in the thick of things, but how? How can I get inside that house unnoticed?"

"Yeah, little old you will just walk up and ring the doorbell. Ding-dong, can I borrow a cup of sugar? No one would notice a six-foot Amazon."

"A good-looking Amazon, thank you very much. OK, wise guy, how do we get me inside?"

Rosie says, "It has not been decided that you are the one going in."

"Rosie, listen——"

"Shale, I am not going to argue with you anymore about this."

"No, Rosie, I was going to say I know the perfect person to get us in: *Cleo*. If it's that kind of party, she would fit right in. She wouldn't stand out as an outsider."

"I don't know," Rosie says. "This could turn dangerous, and she is too good of a contact for me to put her in that kind of danger. Besides, she has grown on me, but not in the way you think."

"Listen, I said WE would be there in case anything happened. I don't mean to send her in alone. Hell, I would go, but as you said before, that son of a bitch knows me. Talk to Cleo at least, see she if she would be willing to help us."

Rosie says, "I am hesitant about doing this, but I do agree that she is our best way in. I don't think she will do it, but I will call her."

"Don't ask her for her help over the phone. Take her out for a nice dinner."

"WHAT? And give her ideas? No, thanks."

"You just refuse to take one for the team. OK, what if I come with you?"

"You got yourself a deal."

He calls her and she agrees to meet us for dinner. "When?" she asks.

"Whenever it is most convenient for you," Rosie says.

"Let me check my calendar. How about tomorrow night?"

"You got yourself a date."

"Really, Rosie?"

"No, wait. I mean that we have something to talk to you about."

"WE?"

"Yeah, Shale will be joining us."

"Can't trust yourself alone with me, can you, Rosie?"

"No, that's not it at all. It's just that——"

Laughing, Cleo says, "Rosie, I have never known you to squirm and be at a loss for words ever."

Blushing, he says, "See you tomorrow night." He hangs up the phone, looking at me. "Don't you dare say a word."

"Who, me? I wouldn't think of it." LMAO—laughing my ass off.

We meet Cleo at our favorite restaurant. As we are being seated, people are staring at us. Who could blame them, two women over six feet and fabulous? I can only imagine what people are thinking, looking at the three of us. High-class working girls and who? You fill in the blanks.

We are seated, and we tell her to order whatever she wants, the agency is paying. "It must be one big fucking favor you want from me, Rosie. You never treated me like a queen before today. Why?"

We both are looking at him, me trying not to laugh. "I don't know," he says. "I'm sorry, I have no excuse."

Cleo looks at me, saying, "He is so full of shit, but damn, I can't help myself."

Before I know it, I am laughing out loud. This is the second time in two days that I have seen Rosie speechless and blushing, no less.

Cleo says, "I haven't eaten all day. It's not every day that a girl gets to eat on Uncle Sam. I am hungry," winking at Rosie. She starts with an appetizer, crab-stuffed mushrooms, then on to the entrée, Maine lobster, and for dessert a fancy exotic kiwi fruit tart. And of course, champagne to drink. She may be a beauty on the outside, but she can eat like every man I know.

As we eat, we tell her why we want to talk to her. "We need a way into that house without drawing too much attention. We want to bring these bastards down, and to do that, we need someone on the inside."

"Don't look at me," Cleo says. "This dinner ain't worth me dying. I love living too much. There are shoes yet to be worn. Do you know what would happen to me if I got caught? You would find my black ass floating in the East River, or not find my body at all."

FADE TO BLACQUE

"Cleo, all we want you to do is get me in. We would never ask you to risk your life doing anything other than that. We cannot afford to leave things to chance. We will only have one chance to do this right, and if it is done right, we will be able to get scum off the street."

Rosie says, "It makes me sick to my stomach to think about what goes on in that house, but to involve children in this sick fantasy, I want to castrate all these self-serving bastards."

"We need hard evidence to minimize the chance that they can walk due to shitty errors and obvious mistakes."

Rosie jumps in, "We also have to take into consideration that with the amount of money we are talking about, it's a good chance that someone could flee the country. From everything we know now, there are some people in high places who will have the resources to skirt justice. We will coordinate with local and other federal agencies to carry out this raid. We will play this close to the vest because we don't know everyone involved."

"It makes my blood boil to think about all they have been getting away with. No regard for anyone but themselves and their sick fantasies. Think about what you have been put through, Cleo, and ask yourself if you have a chance to right the wrong, would you? We will do whatever it takes to make sure you are not in harm's way. Once you get me in, your part is done. We know we are asking a lot of you, but knowing all of this now, we can't just sit back and let it continue. If I could get in without you, I would, but in this case, you have the right credentials. I don't know who all the players are and who else could identify me besides the judge."

Rosie looks Cleo in her eyes and tells her, "This is deeper than the freak show at this house. Judge Brown is in bed with the drug cartels and is using the bench to rule in their favor. They need to be stopped and now." Rosie adds, "I know this is a lot to ask you on such short notice. Please do not feel obligated to do this. If you say no, trust and believe, we will understand. You do not need to give us an answer tonight, and if the answer is no, we will think of something else."

She never says a word the whole time we are talking; we don't know if that is good or bad. I am trying to read her face, but all I see is this terrified blank look. Finally she says, "I always wanted to be a police-woman. This will be better because I would be a special agent. Do I get to handle a gun?"

"No," we both say at the same time.

She starts telling us about the first time she was at the house, and what happened while she was there. We listen as she goes into graphic detail about everything that went on, as well as the things she did while she was there. She goes quiet for a while; she has the look of someone who just told the biggest secret she had.

Rosie wants to know where they get the party people from. They can't just run ads in *The New York Times*—or can they? Cleo says a lot of the prostitutes are ones who appeared in their courtrooms. Pimps, those sorry sons of bitches, if they know they can make a shitload of money from one party, they would pimp out their own mothers. There are a lot of freaks out there who don't care. If you have what they need and want to turn on, they show up.

"Believe me, they have their own underground procurers who buy and sell anything or anyone. They have their own brokers who make a living in trafficking runaways who have no family ties."

"How old?"

"Young," is all she would say. "A lot of those old farts are pedophiles who will pay whatever the cost to satisfy their sick needs."

We sit in silence for a minute, trying to digest what we are hearing. She continues, saying how these old bastards love the prostitutes from the streets or, as they call them, street hoes. It makes them feel more superior. Most of the men would never acknowledge these women in public, but here they are the preferred choice of sickos. "As I said before, anything goes."

Rosie and I cannot finish our food. We both are sick to our stomachs. Cleo, on the other hand, eats everything on her plate. She looks at us and says, "Honey, when you have been to hell, nothing bothers you enough not to eat. Now, what's next?"

Rosie says, "What's next is now that we have you on board, we will need to talk to our bosses to facilitate all the planning that needs to be done. Coordinating all the different agencies and people is going to take some time. Conrad is going to have a baby when he finds out that we are using Cleo to help us. He hates using civilians in this way, but this is the best shot for us to close down these parties for good."

"I don't think he will mind when he finds out what is going on," I say. "Cleo, what's next for you is to find out when the next party is and how I can get in."

She smiles and says, "I think I know a way that you can be there, and no one would know it's you. I have an idea, but I won't say anything until I make some phone calls."

"Work your magic, girl," I say.

"Let me make a call." She excuses herself so that she can talk in private.

"Rosie, how much do you know about Cleo? Did you know that this is the world she inhabited?"

"She is only an informant," he says. "I know only what I need to know, nothing else. She comes through with the information that I need, and I pay her for it. We both get what is needed from each other."

She comes back to the table, smiling. "OK, it's all set."

As she sits down, we both say at the same time, "Who are you?"

She laughs. "I am a woman with many secrets. A lot of secrets. I know people who know people, and the next party is scheduled for next month."

Taking a sip from my glass, I ask, "You were able to do that with just one phone call?"

"No, it was already in the works. I just made a suggestion."

"Which was?"

"This next party should be a masquerade party."

"That is a brilliant idea," I say.

"Of course it is. This way I can get you in without anyone being the wiser."

"You are too much. Do you think it will work? The idea, I mean, do you think they will buy it?"

With a slight smile, she says, "Trust me, darling, it is time to start looking for a costume."

I am truly amazed. This woman has more connections than the President of the United States. I don't believe I know anyone more resourceful than Cleo. "Can I ask you a personal question?"

"Ask away," she says.

"How do you know the judge?"

"I was in front of him for prostituting, and he liked what he saw. He was waiting for me in his car after court and told me that if I didn't do what he wanted, he would make sure that I was someone's bitch in prison. He would personally make sure that it would be a maximum men prison. The thought of being locked up freaked me out. I cannot do prison. I would rather die. So I started sucking his dick and anything else he wanted. I know who I am and what I am, but the only time I feel dirty is when I'm with him and his cronies. I hate his soul, but what choice did I have dealing with a powerful man who could ruin my life at a whim?

"I don't know how, but he always knew where I was. I got picked up again and was in his court for the second time. This time he told me about the parties and how he had friends who would love to party with me. Again it was not a request; I had no choice. I am not ashamed of the things I do that I have control over, but when you are forced against your will, it belittles you and takes away what little self-esteem and dignity you may have. The one saving grace is that I get to beat the shit out of his nasty black ass. And I do mean beat. No more," she says quietly. "I feel sorry that this son of a bitch is getting away with this blackmail and using his authority to satisfy his nasty urges. Let's get this bastard." We all drink to that.

Cleo says, "I will call you in a week."

CHAPTER 16

he next day we fill Conrad in on our dinner with Cleo and everything she told us. We also tell him of the plans for the masquerade party, which is scheduled for next month. "Next month? Shit, that doesn't give us much time to get all of the clearance we would need for an operation of this scope."

"I know, Conrad, but the party was already a go," Rosie says. "Cleo just made the masquerade suggestion so we can get Shale into the party. We need someone on the inside. This operation is going to blow up in the faces of a lot of top officials and heavy hitters. We don't want these sons of bitches to walk on technicalities."

As we predicted, Conrad isn't happy about using Cleo this way, but concludes that this is the best avenue to pursue. "I will need to get clearance from DC," so he calls Buzz.

The three of us are on a conference call going over everything that Cleo told us. Every word coming out of Buzz's mouth is a curse word. "Here we go again. People who are supposed to uphold the law are the biggest criminals. Using the law for their own selfish gain makes me sick to my stomach. I can't understand any of this shit. Rotten bastards. I want to line them all up and blow their fuckin heads off. Rosie, you know this person. Do you believe her...him...hell, what do you—"

"You call her Cleo, Buzz. Her name is Cleo. And if you say anything stupid, I will kick your ass myself," I say. "She is willing to put her life on the line to help us, so cut the shit."

Rosie jumps in. "Yes, I believe her."

"This shit is beyond our agency; I will need to go to the top on this one. I will put in a call to the DOJ. We will need to get major clearance for something of this magnitude. It's going to take working across agency lines to bring down corruption at this level. I'll be in touch." Cussing, he hangs up the phone.

"Fuck," is all Conrad is saying. "Do you realize how much work this is going to take? My recommendation would be to use only senior agents after we vet their asses. We need to keep a tight grip on this investigation. No leaks will be tolerated. NONE. We also have to coordinate with the local city and state police."

One of the first decisions made is that it would be better if we did not meet in any law enforcement buildings. We still don't know who is involved; prying eyes don't need to know what we are up to. We start meeting at an office up in Riverdale that belongs to the brother-in-law of Victor.

We are working around the clock. I tell Jonathan what is going on, and for once he does not complain. He is as sick as the rest of us about what is going on. All he says is, "Make them pay." I make a promise we will.

We don't have a problem choosing agents for this task force. Only the best of the best are asked. Everyone is on board when they hear what is going on in that house. Buzz gets the OK from the DOJ after Cleo does a closed-door testimony held in Washington. We make sure that only the chosen few know what is going on.

A core team is put together from agents across agency lines. We meet every night to strategically plan our course of action. All our focus and energy is to ensure that our ultimate goal is reached: to nail the bastards. My heart is racing at the thought that the judge is going to pay for his crimes. I am going to make sure of it.

Cleo calls me a week later and wants me to meet her at this store in the Village that specializes in fetishism and dominatrix supplies. I have walked by this place a number of times and never paid it any attention until today. I guess I never needed to. When I walk in, Cleo is talking to a salesperson. I can't tell if it is a man or a woman but again, stunning. She comes over with a hug when she sees me. God, she is beautiful.

She gives me a tour of the store and tells me what to look for. I don't shock easily, but some of the things I see make me blush. Cleo acts like she is a personal stylist shopping for a famous client with money to spare. I must say she does have great taste, like someone we all know and love. Leather and feathers everywhere. Every time I try on something and look in the mirror, all I see is skintight leather with my ass hanging out. I start laughing. Who wears this shit?

As we continue to try on things, Cleo gives me the 411 on what to expect at this party. She tells me what to say, what not to say. Staring is not accepted; you have to blend in, like this is normal behavior for you. "Also, Shale, I know this will be hard for you, but don't be surprised if you are touched, pinched, groped, or worse. You are fair game for these animals. Your sole purpose is to let them do whatever they want, and you are expected to enjoy it. You are encouraged to do as many drugs as you want; it helps to take away inhibitions you may have."

"Cleo, the first time someone tries to touch me, I will blow his fucking head off. Both of them, if you know what I mean, and I think you do."

Laughing, she says, "Trust me, I believe you."

We look at whips and chains in all shapes and sizes. I am given a lesson on how to handle the equipment. I take a whip in my hand and crack that thing against a dummy that is in the corner. Damn, that felt good. What a great way to get your frustrations out. Cleo tells me the harder it is, the better the men enjoy it. I wonder if Jonathan would…(never mind).

After trying on about eight outfits, Cleo shouts, "This is the one." It is a skintight leather outfit in this amazing red color with a black design going down the back. I think I will keep this and try it out on Jonathan later. Because I can't just walk into this party, Cleo says we should also look for a mask. After all, it is a masquerade party. I try on about seven masks, and the one we decide on is the lioness. (I am a Leo, after all.)

We go for some drinks after leaving the shop. We make small talk at first, like two old girlfriends catching up. She asks me if I have a man in my life. I tell her about Jonathan. She asks me if I am in love with him. "I've dated some real jerks in the past, and I was tired of the bullshit. I swore off men for a while and decided to concentrate on my career. I have the greatest example of what real love is, and that is my parents. I decided that I was not going to settle just to say I have a man in my life. Growing up, I saw too much of that. Jonathan is the first man that I felt could measure up to my father. I guess that was a long way around to say YES, I am in love. We have our bumps in the road, like everyone else. He hates my job big time, and I don't like it when he is away for long periods of time. I just pray every night that our love can get us through. I swear the thought of starting over with dating again is not very appealing. What about you?" I ask.

"Well, I don't know about the kind of love you are talking about. I've been in deep LIKE before." We both smile. "Relationships—real relationships—are hard for me because a man looks at me and all he can see is the physical. That can get me any man I want. It's when they get to know the real me; that's when the trouble starts. A lot of men think of me as a fantasy. That way nothing can be wrong with them. They can have their cake and eat it too. But when it comes to something much deeper, it's 'see you later, it's been real.' There have been some exceptions, but those are few and far between."

She wants to know if Rosie has anybody in his life. "Yes, many. You know that nothing will ever happen between you and Rosie, right?"

She smiles and says, "I know, but a girl can dream." I am looking at her face and even with the beauty of it, I see sorrow in her eyes. I ask her about her life. How did she become Cleo? "You play the hand you are dealt," she says. I can tell she doesn't want to talk about it, and I don't push, but she does say growing up in her household was a living hell. Her father was not happy about his son who wanted to be a woman, so she was kicked out at a very young age. Her mother was a bit more understanding, but she could not go against her husband. She was as afraid of him as all the kids. She survived the best way she knew how living on the streets. End of story. I ask no more questions. One small tear rolls down her face, and the only thing I can do is to give her a big hug. I can see the pain on her face.

She changes the subject and tells me everything is arranged for the party. She goes into detail about what will happen after we arrive. I won't be able to go in with her because I wouldn't be able to have my face covered. No one can enter the house with their face covered. They don't want a reason to be concerned. Also they will have to go through security before they can enter. There is a side door next to the butler's pantry that she will leave open. Once I enter, I will need to have my face covered.

"How will you be able to get me in?"

"Leave that to me." Smiling, she asks, "Are you claustrophobic?" She tells me she will be going up the night before. "Please don't ask why." I don't.

I tell her about the work the task force has been doing and what we hope to accomplish. One of the things we would like for her to do before she heads up to the house is to meet with some of our tech agents. She will be taught how to operate and plant the small cameras we want her to place throughout the house. The cameras are so small, she shouldn't have a problem. They also come equipped with microphones as well. We want to see and hear everything.

I'm not happy about having her do this part alone, but she says she can handle it. "Have a little faith, hon. I got this."

"Are you nervous?"

"Yes. Every time I think about what is going to go down, I get this queasy feeling in the pit of my stomach, like I want to throw up. Then I think of all the hurt and misery they have inflicted on not just me, but everyone else who doesn't have a choice, and I feel brave. I just wish it hadn't taken me this long to get some courage. I should have confided in Rosie long before this, but fear had the best of me."

"Hon," I said, "you didn't have me. Trust and believe I will make it my business to see that you don't get hurt. I want you front and center when the shit breaks, and I hope one of the first persons that animal sees is you."

She gives me a big old bear hug. "I believe you."

"I think we should have another drink."

"You don't have to twist my arm," Cleo says. "We need to have something to drink to."

"SHOES," we both say at the same time. Laughing, I say, "Girl, we have more in common than I would have imagined. Let's see what else."

"Rosie."

"Lord, yes. New York City, definitely."

"Paris."

"Yes, I love Paris, especially when I'm with Jonathan."

"I wish I had a Jonathan," Cleo says softly. She takes a drink, then smiles and says, "And a Rosie, and a William and a Brian."

We start laughing uncontrollably. "Another drink?"

"Why not."

We tell the bartender to keep them coming. "Are you celebrating something special?" he asks.

We look at each other and say, "SHOES."

People are looking at us like, 'They are having too much fun for just the two of them.' A couple of men try to crash our party, but I say, "No men allowed."

Let me describe what happens next. As I am coming back to my seat after visiting the ladies room, I see this man walking toward Cleo, pointing his finger like a gun and winking his eye. Remember that old guy who was a player back in the day and is still hanging on for dear life, keeping hope alive that the hands of the clock will turn back? Well, he is still alive and walking toward us right now. His shirt is open down to the point where his stomach is sticking out like he is seven months pregnant. He has a thick gold chain that is lying against his sparsely haired chest. The big gap in his teeth is surrounded by three gold-plated caps. He is wearing a ring on every other finger, and his hair is slicked back with so much greasy hair product, you could fry enough chicken for the state of New Jersey. He pulls up a chair, uninvited, and starts telling us how beautiful we both look. Smiling that 'I hope my dentures don't fall out' smile, he proceeds to say how he sure would love to party with us fine young things. The smell of cigarettes is radiating from his skin like he took a bath in them. He pulls out a wad of money, saying to the bartender that the drinks are on him.

I am looking at this fool and am about to say the seventies are long gone, when Cleo leans over and, in this voice from *The Exorcist*, says, "Sure, baby. Are you a bottom or a top?"

He runs out of that bar like the Klan is after him. As he runs, his wad falls on the floor. He has a twenty on top and ten ones under that. I almost fall off the barstool from laughing so hard. "The old me is still in there somewhere," Cleo says. "I guess he didn't want to party with us fine young things."

We laugh the entire night. We don't leave the bar until it closes. We have a great time. It is nice to just decompress, knowing what we will be facing in a few weeks.

"Are you still on board?"

Walking to a waiting car, she says, "Absolutely." Smiling, I walk to my waiting car.

The weeks leading up to the raid are a blur. Things are moving so fast. We have been going over everything again and again. I see the plan in my sleep. Rosie has been working closely with the local authorities, working on the layout of the property, making sure that there are not multiple getaway exits, and calculating routes into and around the property.

CHAPTER 17

Cleo and I are in touch. She is keeping me up on the preparations for the party. So far everything is still on track. She lets me know that she is leaving for London but would be back days before the party; not to worry, she is ready to go. "I didn't think it would be a problem with me leaving since I know what I have to do. Talk to you in a few days," she says.

The closer we get to the date, the more anxious I am. I need to release some of this nervous energy, so I am working out with Hanshi Yamamoto two to three times a week.

We are pretty confident that the plans we have will assure us of success in getting vermin off the streets. We now have amassed a small army of federal, state, and local law enforcement. Everyone knows how important it is to continue to keep all plans confidential. After getting to know them as I have, I know in the end we will get not only the judge, but the high-level drug dealers of the cartel. I love it when we can get more than we bargained for, like two-for-the-price-of-one on shoes.

Cleo calls to tell me she is back in the city. She had already told me she would be going up the night before. I ask her if she is sure she doesn't want me to go up with her.

"You can't," she says. "I won't be driving myself, someone will be driving me. If you were with me without advance notice, it would be suspect. I will be OK. I have prayed over my decision, and I know this is the right thing to do. I met with your tech agents, and they showed me exactly what to do. Girl, let me tell you something I am learning: when you can smell freedom in the air, nothing can stop you. I am tired of what I have been put through. I want my life back, living on my own terms. I am so ready, Shale."

"Baby girl, I believe you."

"Because I am not driving up myself, I will need to use one of the cars at the house to meet you," Cleo says.

"OK, we will meet at the location that we mapped out. Do you remember where it is?"

"Yes, I remember."

"Cleo, please be careful. You will be on your own until the party. I don't want you taking any chances. Let us handle everything."

"Don't worry. I told you before, I love living too much to try and be YOU."

I laugh. "I know that's right. There can only be one Shalimar."

Before we hang up, Cleo says, "Shale, thanks for caring."

"What are friends for?" I say.

It is two days before the party. Jonathan and I are in bed, talking about what is about to go down. "I know, baby, that you are worried about me, but believe me, I will be surrounded by the best. This task force is on a mission, and from everything we have heard, I don't think we will have that much trouble. The only real danger will be if the drug cartel is there, and there is no guarantee that they will be there. Cleo said they are not at every party."

"I know all of this, but babe, that doesn't mean I won't worry about you."

"Jonathan, I know that, and I love you for your concern. I know how hard this is for you, and I promise that I will be extra careful. I have no plans on leaving you anytime soon."

He looks me in my eyes and says, "I love you, and I want you to know when all this hell is over, I am taking you to Paris and—"

That is all he has time to say. I start kissing him before he is able to finish what he was saying. Right now he is all I want to think about.

I go to see my parents, assuring them that I am going to be alright. My mother starts crying and my dad is pacing the floor. My father looks at me and says, "Please come home."

"I will, I promise, and I will see you tomorrow, Mother."

She looks at me. "Shale, before you go, I want to pray with you."

We hold hands as my mother begins to pray, lifting up God's grace and mercy for a successful end to our mission and my safe return. By the time she is finished, we are all crying. I leave, knowing that I have the greatest protection known to man.

On the drive up, we are in constant communication. Everyone on the task force is in their place. Conrad and Buzz are already at our command center. Rosie and I are quiet for a long time in the car. There is no music coming from the radio, no weather reports or local news broadcast. Just silence. "What's going on in that brain of yours?" Rosie asks.

"I don't know. I guess I am thinking about my family, Jonathan." I look at Rosie. "Mostly I am thinking about my Uncle Maurice. He would be all over this."

"He would be. He was one amazing man and one hell of a cop. He would be so proud of you."

"I hope so," I say.

We arrive at the command center, which is about two miles away from the entrance to the property line. We are using a house that is used as a vacation rental, owned by the chief of police of Greene County, which is where the house is located. Everyone is in position. We are just waiting for Cleo to contact us. Everyone is on edge because this raid has to produce results. Too much is at stake. If this fails, careers could be ruined, especially mine and Rosie's. We are the ones who pushed for this operation and put Cleo in harm's way. Our asses would be up a creek without a paddle. I won't let myself think about what this could do to Rosie. His reputation is stellar, not a blemish on his record. *STOP, Shale. This will work. I have faith that it will.* Time is passing slowly, it seems, but when I look at my watch, it is already 11 p.m.

Buzz comes over. "What time is Cleo supposed to call?"

"She didn't say exactly, just when it was safe for her to do so."

He looks at me. "Shale, you do know we are putting a lot of trust in the hands of a—"

"Don't you dare say what I think you were about to say, Buzz. I believe her."

"You mean *him*, don't you?"

"I wouldn't give a fuck if it is a Martian with four heads and nine dicks. We are going to nail this son of a bitch, and SHE is going to be the one who makes it all possible. Stop being a dickhead for once."

At that exact moment, Rosie's phone rings. "Cleo, I can barely hear you. What is going on? We are waiting for what? OK, I'll put her on. She said she was trying to call you, but your phone is not on."

"What? Yes, it is. Wait; let me check. Here, Rosie, see what the hell is wrong with this stupid thing. Cleo, yeah, sorry. What? OK, I'll be waiting. She is on her way."

"Shale, you have no signal."

"Son of a bitch."

Conrad notifies everyone that Cleo is on her way. Time for things to start moving.

She arrives in a beautiful BMW. "Sorry it's so late, but I didn't want to call you until the party was underway, and that doesn't happen until late."

"Yeah, we know. Our agents have been documenting the cars they see pulling up to the gate."

Cleo is wearing this itsy-bitsy French maid costume. Every man there is looking shell-shocked. Her body is banging. Notice I said 'her' because no man has a body like this.

Buzz leans over to Rosie. "Are you sure that is not a woman?"

"I am not so sure, looking at her now. I mean hell no, that is not a woman, not a real one, anyway."

I throw some shade at Rosie, who turns away. Looking at Cleo, I ask if she is OK. "Shaking a little, but I'm ready. Now you have to get ready. Why haven't you put on your costume?"

"I didn't want to sit around waiting for you with this bunch of morons."

"I can't be gone but for so long. Someone may start looking for me. Hurry."

"OK, it won't take me long to change." Looking at this bunch of knuckleheads, I can only imagine the response I will get when they see me in my almost-nothing-there costume.

I come out of the house in this skintight cat suit to whistles and cat-calls. "See, this is why I wanted to wait for your call."

"I see you in a brand new light, partner," Rosie says.

Conrad says, "Damn." Buzz has the biggest smile on his face.

"Pigs, all of you are pigs. When this is over, believe me, I am going to report all of you for sexual harassment. Come on, Cleo, let's go. Oh, wait." I reach into the inside of my right boot, just checking for my little friend. I want to make sure it is within reach. My gun is tucked in tight. "I'm ready."

"I want you two to be careful, especially you, Shale. Don't go acting like you are Wonder Woman. You have a team behind you. Remember that," Rosie says.

"I am so sick of you telling me that. What the hell do you think I am going to do?"

"We don't have time right now for me to tell you all the crazy shit you could get into. Just go. Buzz, get on the phone. Heads up, people. Shale and Cleo are on the move."

As we get closer to the house, Cleo pulls over. "Remember when I asked you if you were claustrophobic?"

"Yes."

"Well, the only way I can you through the gates is you have to get into the trunk. I told the guards that I had to run out for supplies, which I have in there now, so I will take them out and you will have to get in. It's the only way. Shale, I am so sorry it has to be this way."

"Girl, please, I'm ready, let's do this."

We take out the bags Cleo has in the trunk. "I picked this car because of the size. The trunk is supposed to be roomy. I hope you will be alright in there. You are not a short lady, you know."

"Yeah, so I've been told." Before I get in, I turn on the wire that I am wearing. "Rosie, can you hear me?"

"Loud and clear."

"I have to get in the trunk, so I don't think you will hear much."

"That's OK. The thought of you in that small space with that outfit on is enough to keep us amused for a while."

"Pigs. Right, Cleo. I'm ready."

I get in the trunk, and it's not as bad as I thought it would be. Cleo drives about a mile when I hear her punching in some number. "Who is it?"

"It's me, Cleo." The gates opening sounds like freight cars. Damn, these are some big-ass gates. She drives about another mile.

"About time your ass came back."

"I told you I had to get some supplies. Now help me with these bags."

"Keep talking shit and I will show you what will happen to you and that short-ass piece of cloth." Cleo doesn't say anything as the back doors of the car open. "Damn, how much shit did you buy?"

"I wanted to make sure that we didn't run out." As she starts walking to the door, I hear this smack and someone says to her, "When we get these things back in the house, I want you to do what you do best."

I am freaking out in this damn trunk. All I want to do is shoot this bastard, whoever he may be. My heart bleeds for her, because however bad I thought it is for her, it could never match her reality. It makes me sick.

About five minutes later, the car is moving, but it's not Cleo driving. My heart is pounding. Then I hear her voice saying, "He wants the car parked by the kitchen. He wants to take some things back to the city in the morning."

"OK, whatever he wants."

I can hear the sounds of music and voices. It sounds like a lot of voices. There is also laughter and what sounds like singing. I can't tell if it is music from some recording or it's live.

"Rosie, just checking if you can hear me."

"I can hear you, but there is a lot of background noise too."

About ten minutes pass, and I am starting to go crazy in the small and dark space. I hear someone coming to the car. I don't know if it's

Cleo or not, but I pull out my small revolver and take aim. I hear a knock. "It's me, Cleo. I will open the trunk, then run back inside. The side door to the butler's pantry will be unlocked. You will need to move fast. The car is not parked in any direct light, especially from the kitchen, so you should be OK."

I wait for about a minute, then slowly lift up the truck. I am out of the car and into the pantry's door so fast, Houdini could have taken lessons.

Once inside the pantry, I find the mask, and just as I am putting it on, Cleo walks through the door. We give each other a hug. "Rosie, I'm in."

"OK, listen, the both of you, be careful."

Cleo smiles. "Rosie, you do care."

Cleo starts giving me the lay of the land. I can smell food coming from the kitchen. "Damn, whatever they are cooking in there smells good, and I forgot to eat something."

"Stop talking about food and get to work," I hear Conrad saying. I stick my tongue out at him.

Cleo tells me that they use the same people for everything—cooking, bar people, clean-up, etc.—and pay them extremely well to keep their mouths shut. Most of the people are of the criminal persuasion anyway

She starts telling me who is here and what is going on already in some of the rooms. I want to know if the judge is here. "I checked, and he got here right after I left to get you."

"Hear that, boys? The devil is in the building." I ask Cleo what's next.

"Once your mask is on, you will follow me as we move throughout the house. We will start at the front of the house, where we will pass one of the bar areas that will have drinks on trays ready for us to pick up. Then it's just walking around, making sure that no one has an empty glass. Are you ready, Shale?"

"Hell yeah, let's go."

As we are about to leave the pantry, she looks at me. "Damn, girl, you look amazing. You look like you belong here."

"Cleo, that is not a compliment."

CHAPTER 18

This place is huge. The kitchen alone is bigger than most apartments in Manhattan. Cleo hands me a tray with drinks on it so that we can mingle with the crowd. Entering into this massive living room that could at one time have been a ballroom, I am struck by the sheer size.

All around the room are floor-to-ceiling windows that usually would light up the room with natural light just pouring in. Now the windows are covered with velvet drapes that look like they weigh a ton. Four large chandeliers with crystals dangle from the ceiling, which is painted in an art deco style. Stucco-color walls with very expensive paintings surround the room. Not much in the way of furniture. Cleo said the pieces that are usually there are taken out for the parties; too expensive for people to have sex on them. They have been replaced with cheap sofas and sectionals. In two of the corners are swings built for two.

This crowd is already in the party mood as the music is pumping. Drinks are flowing, along with anything else you could want. People in varies stages of undress are dancing or stumbling to the music, take your pick. They all look like they are in a trance of some kind.

People are huddled in groups; some are sitting and talking. Others are engaging in sex acts while still others are looking at the various monitors showing porn videos. People of every hue and color, all mingling together. Well, I'll be damned. This is one place where all people, regardless of their color persuasion, can stink like everyone else.

Some have on masks. Others had them on at one time, but due to their current activities, the masks have fallen off. Most of the women look like cheap hookers, and the men look rich and old. As we pass through the crowd, the drinks disappear, so we have to go back to the bar for refills.

All along the way, I see these guerilla-looking types walking around, doing nothing in particular. They are the only ones with no costumes at all, and it looks like they all have some type of modern-day walkie-talkies. Walking back to the bar, we see an old, fat-ass, wrinkled grand-papa type getting a blow job from a young girl who looks all of fifteen. Makes me sick to my stomach. I want to reach inside my boot and blow his fucking head off. But I am afraid I would hit the baby, so I am sure you know which head I was talking about.

I hear Conrad saying, "Shale, I swear if you kill somebody before the raid, you will be responsible for the cleanup. I know it stinks but stay the course."

Men are kissing men; women are kissing women. Threesomes and foursomes are in the corners doing each other. Women are naked, dancing on top of tables, and there are two women dancing on top of a very large piano with no clothes on and smeared with some kind of green cream. There are flashing lights like back in the Studio 54 days. As I walk around I hear foreign accents from every part of the world. From Europe to Africa, everyone is welcome. This fucking freak show is open to all perverts. The music is almost deafening. There are couples making out on this incredible sofa. One of the swings in the corner of the room is occupied with a naked man and woman not swinging. There is a lot of Sodom and Gomorrah going on in this place.

We pass another bar, where I pick up another tray filled with drinks. As I turn around, this old-ass man dressed in a clown costume, with his cock out, is trying to mount me from behind, his wrinkled dick trying to stay afloat. "I always liked tall kitty cats," he says. "I'm a climber," almost foaming at the mouth. Pointing to his dick, he asks, "Do you know what this is?"

"No," I say. "I know what it used to be, or I think I do. It's hard to tell [no pun intended], it's so small," and I walk away.

Cleo is laughing so hard she almost loses her tray of drinks. "Girl, I am so glad you are here." As we are walking away, I turn and see him downing a couple of the little blue pills, dancing all by himself. Damn— old, wrinkled, and no rhythm; sad, really sad.

I have never been pinched and touched so much in my life. All it is going to take is one more poke, just one. Now I know what bread in a store feels like. I am not happy, but I am here to do a job, so smile even if I feel like killing everyone in this fucking house. (I'm talking perverts only.)

The smell of marijuana is filling the air, and as I walk by this women dressed as a hooker scarecrow (don't ask), I hear her asking for the medicine cabinet. Making sure my tray is filled, I follow her into this very large room that resembles a library you would see in an old British mystery. There are floor-to-ceiling bookcases stacked with books going the whole width of the room. The room is filled with people enjoying their drug of choice. There is so much coke, you could have skied out of there. Heroin, crystal meth, Ecstasy, mushrooms, oxycodone— the list goes on. The DEA is going to love us. "Rosie, I hope you guys are getting this. We hit the mother lode."

With my last drink gone, I turn to leave, and I see more of the guerilla types standing by the entrance to the library. This time I see one of them has a gun tucked in his pants. As I am walking out the door, monkey boy grabs my ass. "I always did have a thing for pussy."

"Be careful. Pussy has claws and likes to scratch."

Laughing, he says, "I will see later how sharp those claws are."

"You can bet on it. Meow."

I wanted to drop the tray and do a leg kick to his Adam's apple, but I hear Rosie saying, "You can kill him later. Focus."

Walking away, I say softly, "I could have killed him too. Fucking idiot."

There is an orgy going on in one of the bedrooms on the ground floor. I have never seen anything like this in my life. I go to the bathroom and report back the things that I am seeing. The tech agents report that they are receiving great video despite the smoke, but the music is blocking out a lot of voices. Rosie wants to bust in now, but I tell him not yet. I need to find the judge. "Wait. Now is not the time."

I find Cleo and ask her about the judge. "He would be in the dungeon."

"Where is that?"

"Downstairs. Fill your tray and follow me."

After we refill our trays with drinks, we make our way downstairs. People are hanging out on the staircase, and we have to walk over bodies to make it to the basement. As we get to the bottom, one of the bodies grabs me from behind, pushing his nasty ass up on me. Cleo has to stop me from kicking him in his balls. He has an ape mask on, reeking of a nasty mixture of liquor, marijuana, and sex. He also smells like his body has not touched water in days. I manage to push him off of me without breaking his face, and we move on toward the back of the basement. He is lucky that I have more pressing issues, because I was ready to kick his ass.

This is no ordinary basement; this place is fabulous. There is a huge TV room along with a wine cellar that would make most wine sommeliers green with envy. A champion pool table is in the middle of the room, which is next to a home gym with more equipment than a lot of gyms I know. Around a little passageway is an Olympic-size swimming pool. Next to the pool is a sauna that could fit at least twelve people. Both are filled with people doing nasty things to each other. Everywhere you look, you see more depraved acts. The smell of marijuana is especially strong down here. I hope I don't get a contact just walking through the haze.

As we continue, we pass six bedrooms that are filled with people in them. What is amazing is that each one of the doors is named for a country: Japan, Sweden, Germany, Russia, etc. I ask Cleo why, and she says that whatever your type is will be in that particular bedroom. I just can't believe this operation. Who thought of this shit and how long has this been going on? This was thought up by a mastermind. If only they would use their brains for good. No ordinary street criminal could come up with this shit. No way. This is too elaborate for the everyday person.

There is this loud bell sound that comes and goes. "What the hell is that?"

"The doorbell," Cleo says.

I can't tell how many people are in this house, but there are a lot and they keep coming. We reach the last door, and through the noise of the people and the music, I hear the faint sound of a whip. I look at Cleo and she lets me know this is the room I am looking for. Before I enter, she tells me what to say to the person who is there so they will leave and let me continue. "Thank you, baby doll, for everything you did tonight. I don't know how we ever will be able to thank you."

"Just do your job, Shale, and don't let these sons of bitches walk."

"I promise. But now it is time for us to do what we do best, and time for you to leave. You know where to go to meet Rosie?"

"I remember." We give each other a big hug.

"Shale, please be careful."

"Now go and don't look back."

I open the door to a room set up as a dungeon. There are chains that are bolted to the wall. There is a table with holes at the top and bottom. The windows have been covered, so it is dark in the room. There are two chairs in the corner, and one of those contraptions that was used in the olden days for publicly flogging people. There in the middle of this contraption is Judge Brown, naked as the day he was born. He is blindfolded and is crying like a baby. The person with the whip is a very tall woman who looks like all she does all day is lift weights. She comes down so hard on the judge with the whip that the judge's body moves like it was being electrocuted. He moans like the pain is unbearable and at the same time is screaming how much he loves it.

I walk over to the dominatrix and say to her, "It's your turn, Romeo is waiting for you."

She smiles, hands me the whip, and leaves the room. I am looking at the judge with total disbelief. I am in total shock. I can't move. I'm standing there with a whip in my hand and one of the most respected judges in the country begging me to not stop, so I hit him, but gently. He yells, "Harder," so I hit him using more force this time. He is yelling, "Yes, more, please." With every slash of the whip, he seems to reach another orgasm. He is ejaculating semen like a running faucet.

The sounds that are coming from his mouth are like nothing I have ever heard. I hit him again and again. I almost get caught up in the moment when I remember why I am there. I take off my mask, drop the whip, and take my camera, which is the size of a dollar, from the inside of my brassiere and start taking pictures.

As I am clicking away, I am talking to the outside, letting them know what I am seeing. Rosie says to make sure to take off the blindfold so I can get pictures of the judge's face. He is still moaning as I go over and take it off. This fool has the biggest smile on his face, eyes closed. He looks like he is in heaven, except I am sure God wants no part of this freak. I say, "Keep smiling, Judge Brown, for the camera." He still has his eyes closed, but he is grinning as if he is reliving that last blow with the whip.

After I feel like I have enough pictures, I tell them to move in. "Rosie, please tell everyone to be careful. One of the goons has a gun, and if he has one, you can bet they are all packing."

Suddenly all I hear is the sound of Buzz yelling through a bullhorn that the entire property is surrounded. The bright lights from the helicopters are illuminating the house as if the place was sitting in the sun. People are screaming as they are running over each other to escape. Agents are moving in all directions as naked and half-clothed people are trying to find the nearest exit. Pandemonium has taken over the noise of music and sex. It feels like a panic when a bomb goes off in a crowded space. I hear a mixture of screaming coming from the people inside the house and the police and agents outside catching people trying to flee. Talk about a three-ring circus. It's a mess.

CHAPTER 19

As people are being rounded up, Conrad and Rosie come looking for me. The look on their faces is priceless as they walk into the room. There we are, the three of us surrounding a respected jurist who is butt naked, whip marks all over his body, sitting in a contraption from the dark ages, with the look of a man who just had the best orgasms in his life. He is so out of it that he still does not recognize that we are in the room.

Rosie looks like he has been hit by a locomotive. Conrad hasn't moved since he entered the room. Jesus, what a bloody nightmare. Conrad calls Buzz and tells him to bring the paramedics down to the basement; the judge will need medical care. Everyone who enters the room is speechless. You don't see this every day; all you can do is look.

Buzz comes in and has that same look on his face, a look of shock and horror. He pulls himself together and tells us we hit the jackpot. "Why?" I ask.

"Because in the crowd are some very bad people we have been looking for, for a long time now. We are going to be able to close the books on a couple of outstanding open cases because of this bust. I saw some familiar faces in that crowd. This is also going to make the FBI very happy. There are a couple of guys who are on their list. One of the guys working in the kitchen has been on the run for 13 years. Son of a bitch is wanted for a double homicide."

"Gives a new meaning to killer food," Rosie says.

"I spoke to the DEA supervisor, and he had the biggest smile on his face when he went into that library and saw the windfall in there. He told me to say thanks for the invite. We should do this again. Can you believe that in one raid we picked up members of the Mexican cartel, the Russian mob, and members of the Dirty Rice gang bangers? All this and not one shot fired. This is better than a trifecta at Aqueduct. This is one glorious night. You should all be proud. You got a lot of garbage off the streets tonight. I am so proud of you, Shale. You did real good, kiddo."

"Thanks, Buzz."

The paramedics come in with a stretcher and start to laugh at the sight. "Watch your step. With this mixture of semen, blood, and sweat, if you're not careful, you could drop His Honor on his naked ass." They untie the judge and take him to a private hospital that we had made an arrangement with, just in case.

"I don't know how long we will be able to keep this quiet."

Conrad says, "We won't. Just got word that the news crews are already here."

Rosie looks at me in my getup and starts to whistle. "Drop it," I say. "Remember, I know the real you."

Everyone starts laughing. "Yeah," he says, "you do know the real me." Looking around the room, he smiles and says, "This place is giving me ideas."

"Jackass. Please tell me you remembered to bring my clothes, and point me to the nearest shower."

"Stop the presses. World News Now. We interrupt your local broadcast for this special report…" Of course the press has a field day over this story. This is the biggest story on all the network and cable news outlets. Twenty-four hours a day you can see the faces of the people who were involved with this raid. Hookers telling their tales of woe, how they were forced with the threat of prison if they didn't cooperate, or worse. Businessmen in various stages of undress, trying hard to hide their faces as they are being led away in handcuffs. Police are having a hard time trying to wrangle people who are flying high on every drug known to man.

The house sits so far back on the property that we don't have to worry about people other than law enforcement interfering. The police did have their hands full trying to stop all the reporters who are trying to get on the grounds near the house. There is a circus gathering outside the gate as more and more reporters and neighbors arrive to try and get a closer look. Total shock is repeated over and over. Not in this respectable neighborhood. The faces are all showing disgust; only the most upstanding citizens live here. The couple next door says they can't understand how something like this could escape them. They were under the illusion that some famous doctor or lawyer used this place only for vacations. Some respectable doctor or lawyer. There goes that word again: respectable. What could be wrong? Well, right now I have a very respectable pain in my ass.

The only people who are not trying to hide their faces are the hookers, who seem to enjoy all the attention. Stoned out of their minds, they are blowing kisses and singing as they are led away. The hooker who was dressed as a scarecrow is handcuffed with two other hookers being led to a police wagon when a reporter who had managed to get close to the girls asks if she had anything to say. She says, "Yes, I do. Tell that fat bitch who lives next door: I hope you like kissing your husband, because every time you did, you tasted me. The big freak. Did you know he loves soul food? Tell him to call me; he has my number." They are laughing so hard they have trouble getting into the wagon. Brings a smile to my face.

The underage prostitutes are taken into CPS custody, along with the SVU police department. The parade of characters goes on and on and on. The judge will be kept in the hospital for a few days, but his respectable wife is filing for divorce and is bent on taking him for everything he has. She is surrounded by the media in New York City, crying about the shame she feels and how all this information coming out about her husband has her in shock, trying to make herself cry fake tears. Make way for another horrible liar. She almost has a smirk on her face. Crying all the way to the bank.

There are 183 other "respectable" gentlemen sharing a jail cell. We have a couple of married senators; judges, state and federal. A few police officers as well as a couple of police captains. We have a couple of senior partners in a top New York law firm. Don't you just love highfalutin people when they get their comeuppance? People who walk around with their noses up in the air like their shit don't stink. Where I grew up, we have a saying: When the shit hits the fan, don't be wearing white. (What the color has to do with it, I don't know, but I'm going with it.) Well, let me tell you, there is a lot of shit up in here.

There are also a few lesser public officials, such as schoolteachers and college professors. One very well-known Hollywood director married to a young actress (and I use that term loosely) who was caught with a man I take it is not his wife. Oh, the assorted nuts we found when we dug deep. And would you believe David Levin, attorney at law, caught with a 15 year old male prostitute? I make sure that as he is led away in handcuffs, I am one of the first people he sees. "Hey, David, how's that reputation you care so much about going these days?" I have the biggest smile on my face.

The grand jury indicts all on multiple counts ranging from child sexual abuse to drug trafficking, witness tampering, blackmail, malfeasance in office, obstruction of justice, compounding a felony and conspiracy. This is one of the biggest stories to hit not just New York State but the country in a long time. International news outlets are also running away with this fiasco.

As we are rejoicing over this victory in the name of justice, elsewhere the mood is more somber. Not everyone is as happy as we are.

• • •

The four men in a small room in back of a rundown building are sitting around a table with a small TV, watching as the report of the raid is playing nonstop. "Son of a bitch, can you believe that bastard got himself arrested? All that kinky shit was bound to catch up with him. Now what are we going to do? We have a shipment that can't be delivered without our usual protection, all because of this shithead."

A cell phone rings and the voice on the other end of the phone is cursing obscenities in Spanish. "We heard the news all the way down here in Mexico. What the hell is going on? I can't believe that bastard Brown got his ass arrested. None of you are worth shit. I can't count on any of you assholes to do anything right."

"Listen, boss," one of the men is trying to say, "not only that, but our drugs were confiscated, along with Hector and Manny."

"Shut the fuck up. I did not plan on coming to New York so soon; now I'll have to rearrange my plans. I'm on my way."

• • •

It is going to take forever to handle all of the paperwork associated with this case, but we manage to get a good head start because of the time we took to make sure to plan ahead. All of our preplanning worked perfectly. Conrad tells us to take a few days off. We both deserve it, he says. So we do. I can't remember the last time I was in my apartment; it's a wonder that my cats remember who I am. Gary and Rob took such good care of them in my absence.

I sleep almost a whole day, get up, do some cleaning around the house, and return phone calls. Later I go to my parents' and have lunch, catching them up on the case. My dad tells me I look good in front of the camera; maybe I should have been an actress. That's my daddy.

I call Cleo and invite her to dinner. "What about tonight?"

"Tonight it is," she says.

Looking at her now, you can see the stress has gone completely from her face. She really is beautiful. "I don't know how to repay you for all you did for us," I tell her.

She smiles. "I'm just glad that the judge and his cronies will get their due. They hurt a lot of people and made me feel like shit. He took away any degree of self-respect that I might have had. Thank you for wanting to know the truth," she says. "You are a woman of your word, and I will never forget that." We sit around drinking wine for a couple of hours, talking about the case and what more she will need to do as far as the district attorney is concerned. "I spoke with him and for now they don't need anything more. The closer it gets to the trial, his office will be in contact."

"What's next?" I ask.

"I am going on vacation with someone very special."

"Do you know where?"

"Europe is all I know." We both smile: Paris. "It better be part of wherever he wants to take me, girl. You know how much I love Paris. How much we BOTH love Paris." Her cell phone rings. She goes over to the window. "My date is here, I must be off. But before I leave, I have something for you."

"Cleo, you don't need to give me anything, I should be giving *you* something."

"You have, Shale. You gave me back my dignity." She walks to the car and returns with this beautiful bag with words written in Italian all over it.

"Oh my God, please tell me this is not what I think it is."

"I don't know, you will need to open the box."

As I lift off the box top, I start screaming, "Shut the fuck up." Inside is a pair of Giovanni Lombardi shoes. He is the IT boy in shoe design. "His shoes have only been in the U.S. for about six months. How the hell did you—"

"I told you before that I know people who know people. I made a phone call. I wanted you to have the shoes before I left on vacation."

The shoes are bright red with a three-inch heel that is phat. The design is to die for. No one else will be walking around town in these bad-ass shoes. Nobody. "Cleo, I don't know what to say."

"You don't have to. The look on your face says it all."

We hug as she leaves. "I will call you when I get back, and I hope we can be real friends."

"I know we will," I say. I go over to the window and watch as she gets into the back of this very long limousine. "Go head, girl," I say, smiling.

Jonathan comes by later, and I model for him the outfit I had on during the raid. It doesn't stay on for long. There is nothing in the world like making love with a man you are in love with while wearing a brand new pair of Giovanni Lombardi stilettos. We don't bring up anything about me leaving my job, which makes this time more precious. I hope he is learning to trust me and know that I am good at this job and how much I love it.

He tells me he will be leaving in a couple of days for a jazz festival in Ireland, and I should come with him. I would love nothing better, but I can't leave now in the middle of the biggest case of my career. I make a promise that as soon as this madness is over, I will go with him wherever he wants to go, "and you can take that to the bank."

Back at work, Rosie and I both look refreshed after being off. After the raid is when the real work begins, so it's not as if we can completely relax. We've got a lot of work ahead of us. All of the top brass is assembled to discuss how to handle this mess. The press is relentless, and when they smell blood, they will do whatever it takes to be the first at anything related to the case. It seems nothing else is going on in New York, and with all the news cable channels, it's all news all the time. I can't remember the last time this many big fish were fried at one time. I guess I can't blame the press in this case.

High-priced lawyers are bidding for the chance to get involved in this case with all the money that is at stake. Nothing but the best for the dogs at the top, but what about the little fishes? I don't see the same attention given to them. Manny and Hector are sitting in jail because they were denied bail—flight risk and their connection to the Mexican cartel. Rosie and I decide to go and speak to our little fishes at Rikers.

We decide it is best to talk to them separately, Manny first. He is waiting for us in the interviewing room. He has an angry look on his face that does not change the entire time we are there. He is not talkative, but we keep up with the questions. "Why were you at the house? How do you know Judge Brown? Who brought the drugs into the house?" This goes on for over an hour. The only thing he says is, "I want a lawyer."

Next we try Hector, with the same results: nothing but "I want a lawyer."

As we are leaving the room, Rosie turns and says, "With all the charges you are facing, you will never see the outside again. How old are you, thirty? That's a long time to spend in the joint before you die, because you will never make parole. Maybe you won't make thirty-one. Whoever your bosses are, you can bet they are going to want to tie up loose ends. Are you a loose end, Hector? If I were you, I would start talking; maybe the DA will cut you a deal. Think hard about that."

If we were not there, I do believe he would start crying.

CHAPTER 20

Two days later Hector has a meeting with a lawyer. "About time someone showed up," he says. "Get me the hell out of this shithole now." The lawyer looks like one of those high-priced 5th Avenue types. Again, what is a high-priced lawyer doing here for this scumbag? The cartel obviously pays well. How much do you want to bet he is not a public defender? What fool would take that bet?

He tells Hector that things are being worked on, but with a couple of their judges out of circulation, they have to do things legally, and that will take time. "If you hadn't let your sick urges get the best of you, we wouldn't be here. You and that stupid Judge Brown. That son of a bitch was living the life."

"Fuck the judge. You are here to talk about me." Hector is furious. "If I am not out of here soon, I will start talking."

The lawyer looks at him and says, "That is not a good idea. Better to keep your mouth shut and let us handle things."

Hector jumps up as if he is going to hit the lawyer. "Get me out or I will make trouble for everybody, and you know I can. Guard, I'm ready." Hector storms out of the room.

The lawyer is on the phone as he sits in his car. "I think we need to cut our losses now. He will not cooperate."

The voice on the other end of the call says, "I will take care of our little problem."

The next morning, while they are in the shower, both Hector and Manny are stabbed to death. A fellow inmate, a lifer, is charged with the murders. I hang up the phone after hearing the news. Looking at Rosie, I say, "I guess they both were loose ends."

With the deaths of Hector and Manny, Judge Brown is freaking out. He knows that he either will die in prison or be killed as well. He is what is considered a big loose end. If he gets jail, he knows he will be in there the rest of his life. With all the shit he has done, he will need to be in solitary confinement; there is no way he can be in the general population. I guess they will have to build a prison for one. Life as he knew it was over. His lovely gold-digging wife will get everything, his career is in the toilet, and he will never know the sweet sound of a whip again. He is a disgrace to all who know him. At his age he knows that he will die in prison.

I get a call from his lawyer. "The judge wants to see you."

"When?"

"In about an hour."

"OK, tell him we will be there."

"Judge Brown says he only wants to meet with you."

"The judge is in no position to make demands on anything. We will be there when we get there."

Rosie and I meet the judge in a special room within the prison. He looks like he has aged 50 years since the last we saw of him. For one thing, he has clothes on. I should have said this before, but he is not a bad-looking man and had a great body for someone in his sixties, if you overlook the welts on his body. He has beautiful cocoa-brown skin and little gray streaks throughout his hair that, in a matter of days, had turned completely white. Not a bad-looking man at all. Of course right now he just looks sad and pathetic. I wonder how he explained things to his wife; she had to have some idea. She had to know but didn't care as long as the money was coming in. She is seventeen years his junior. I guess it doesn't matter now. Looking at him now through the window of the door, he looks like death.

As we walk into the room, Rosie asks, "Where is your lawyer? You shouldn't be talking to us without him."

"I don't need a lawyer for what I am about to say. He argued against me talking to you alone, but I insisted."

"What do you want?" I ask.

"I know my life is over; I have nothing left to lose. I want to make a deal."

"Sorry, Judge, we don't work for the DA's office. You need to talk to them."

Rosie says, looking at me, "Maybe if you can tell us something worthwhile, we can speak to them for you. No promises," he says. "Also, I want to tape the conversation. Do you understand that?" He nods his head yes.

The judge starts to cry, and for a split second I almost feel sorry for him, but it doesn't last long. "Come on, Judge, we have things to do. What do you want?"

He takes a deep breath. "What do you want to know?"

"Everything," I say. "Start at the beginning."

He says he was approached by someone who knew his dirty little secret and threatened to expose him if he didn't start working with his boss to fix cases that came before him. "At first I said no, but when I was told how much money I would be paid, I changed my mind. I've always had expensive taste, and I knew the perks would be the icing on the cake. Most of the cases were drug-related, then murder, prostitution, you name it. As long as the money flowed, I was happy."

"How much money and for how long?" Rosie asks.

"Over twelve million in the last four years."

We are all quiet for a minute. "What a son of a bitch you are," I say. "I hope your ass rots in jail, and you live a long time."

"What else?" Rosie asks. "How long have these parties been going on?"

"Too long to remember," he says, almost smiling.

"I take it back," I say. "I wish we had the death penalty. Jail is too good for you." All I can think of are those underage prostitutes with those old-ass men. It makes me sick.

"We know you don't own the house. It belongs to a dummy corporation, we know that much. Who is MDC?"

"I don't know."

"You are a bald-faced liar." I am screaming. "You got us up here to bullshit us. I knew it, Rosie. Let's go."

"Wait," Judge Brown says. "I am telling you the truth. I don't know anything about MDC, but I do know who the real owner of the house is."

"Well, who is it? Don't keep us waiting."

"He is a very powerful man. He is very smart and very ruthless. He knows people who will take care of any problem that may come up. He is well connected, and I don't just mean in business. He also has family connections." Looking up at us, he said, "Chief Assistant DA Taylor Perez."

Time just stops at that moment. The silence is so deafening you can hear our hearts beating. I have to take a seat. "Taylor Perez, Judge? Are you serious?"

"Yes, I'm serious. He is the one who first approached me. I don't know how he found out about my addiction, but he knew everything. He said he knew people who could give me everything my heart desired, and he was right. The money, the women, and the trips anywhere in the world we wanted to go. He owns houses all over the world. His offshore bank accounts each have millions in them, and I lost count of how many of those he has. It wasn't until about a year in that I found out he has a very strong connection to the cartel."

Our mouths drop. Rosie says, "We want everything now."

Once he starts talking, he can't stop. In-between bouts of crying, he tells of the corruption within the police department, city and state government, and federal as well. "Can you give us names?"

"Yes, but not now. I need some kind of leverage."

"You sorry son of a bitch. You will need to take that up with the DA."

By the time he is finished, I am numb. Rosie and I are looking at each other with confusion and disbelief. We knew this was big, but this surpasses anything we could imagine. "He is power-hungry and greedy. He has had the taste of power for some time now. He will not want to give it all up so easily."

"It's not up to him," I say.

Rosie asks, "Besides owning the horror house, what other part does he play? Is he only a part of the freak show or is he more involved?"

"He is a very big part of all of this. The money he makes on the parties alone is more than the two of you and half of the NYPD makes in a year. He is a freak too; he just does his shit behind closed doors. I have never seen him participate in any of the activities, but I have seen him observing some of the action that was in play."

Looking at this sad excuse of a man, I ask, "Why? Why throw away your career, your reputation? You were sitting pretty. You were writing your own ticket. The prestige, influence, stellar reputation. Not only that, but the historical achievements you made as a black man in the justice system here in New York. There are not a lot of judges in your rank who look like you. I don't understand how you could just throw it all away."

He is quiet for a minute, then says, "I'm weak. The money was just too good to say no to. The lifestyle was something that I wanted. As you now know, I have certain needs that had to be met. Who wouldn't go for it if it meant having all your needs fulfilled?"

"Someone with morals and a sense of truth," Rosie says. "Ask yourself now: was it worth it? Losing everything you worked hard for? In the end, was it worth it?"

"Before hell exploded, yeah, it was worth it," he says.

What can you say to that? Nothing. "Was there anything else?"

"No," says the judge.

"Are you sure?"

He looks up with tears in his eyes. "Why would I lie now?"

Rosie stops the recorder and we leave. "What the hell have we stepped into, Rosie?"

"I don't know, but I do know that we have to be very careful who we tell this one to."

"Do you believe that the judge was telling us the truth?"

"Why would he lie now? His ass is going to jail for life."

"I know, but Taylor Perez? That is mind-boggling. I need a drink."

CHAPTER 21

On the way to the bar, we stop by the office. We want to look up as much information on Taylor as we can find. We put together a file that we want to go through outside of the office.

As we are leaving, Conrad stops us. "Where the hell are you two going?"

"Off to meet a CI."

"Yeah, right," he huffs as he goes into his office.

As we sit and go over the files we brought with us, we are trying to paint a picture of Mr. Perez. Taylor Perez is tall, dark, and fine. He is the product of a black mother and Latino father. He was a rising star in the DA's office at a young age. He is a New York City boy born and bred. He grew up in the Brownsville section of Brooklyn, the oldest of five children. Because of his surroundings, his mother pushed education as a way to get out of Brownsville, and he excelled. Scholarships to John Jay College and Columbia Law School. He graduated with honors from both, got a job right out of college within the DA's office, and never looked back. He rose very quickly and made a name for himself as someone who not only respected the law but loved the law. Everything by the book. Justice will prevail.

He was the poster child for not letting where you grew up dictate where you could go if you only applied yourself. Both Latinos and African Americans were equally proud of all he accomplished and of the way he was giving back to his community. He did a lot working with inner city kids, trying to keep them on the straight and narrow, arranging to have other people of color go into schools and after-school programs to let the kids see that anything is possible. No matter what your race is or where you come from, you can achieve anything you set your mind to.

At 48 he has everything a person would want who is considered successful. He was never married, but he has dated some of the most beautiful women in the world: models, actresses, you name it. He has very grand taste in women and everything else. He works hard and plays harder. His track record at work is exceptional. There is not a hint of scandal anywhere near this man. His pristine record is intact. What would make men like the judge and Taylor give up everything they worked for to become monsters?

"Rosie, it doesn't make sense. They both had everything most people can only imagine. They had everything."

Rosie, shaking his head, says, "They wanted more. Greed knows no boundaries. Look at all those Wall Street types. Look at what some of them gave up, all for this god known as money. I've been at this game a long time, and nothing surprises me anymore when it comes to what people will do for the almighty dollar. We need to proceed very carefully. If he has managed to keep out of the limelight this long, he has to know even more powerful people who are enjoying their lifestyles and will stop at nothing to protect it. We start with him."

I call Cleo and leave a message. I want to know what she can tell us about Taylor. Rosie calls in some favors to help us paint a better picture of Perez, but for now we will need to keep it between the two of us. Rosie and I will work on our own, so we decide to meet at my apartment.

A week later I call Muffin. He has been lying low due to fear, but I know what to say to him to do me a favor, like, "Jail will make a woman out of you." I ask him to talk to his lowlife friends and get me whatever he can on Taylor; I want all the dirt he can find. "I need to hear from you as soon as you hear something. I mean it, Muffin. Don't make me come and look for your raggedy ass."

Later Cleo calls. "Sorry, girlfriend, I was out of the country or I would have called you back before now."

"No problem. I was going to ask how you are, but it sounds like you are doing OK."

"I am wonderful. I have my life back, thanks to you and Rosie. How is he?"

"Hold on, I will put you on speaker. You can ask him yourself."

"How are you, sweetheart?"

"I am great," he says. "I hear you have been out of the country."

"Yeah, I was in Jamaica, then off to London."

"It must be nice not working a nine-to-five."

"It has its advantages," she laughs. "OK, Taylor Perez. What do you want to know?"

"All the dirt."

She says, "I always knew he was dirty, but to tell you the truth, I don't know a lot. He keeps his dirt covered very well. He dated this model that I knew just as an acquaintance for about a year. She told me that after a year, she still felt like she didn't know him at all. She couldn't put her finger on it, but there was always this distance between them, and when she would ask him, he told her it was all in her head. She did say he has a temper, but it was never aimed at her. He is extremely careful about his business and personal life."

"Cleo, did you know he owned the hell house?"

"NO. WHAT, are you kidding me? I would never believe that he was involved. I never saw him there. I don't know of any connection between him and that house except he was friends with that bastard judge. I was told to mind my own business, and that is exactly what I did. I only found out through you guys that the house is owned by some corporation. I remember you said MDC. Up until then I never heard anything about MDC. I can't believe it, Taylor Perez. Not Mr. Perfect. How will you get anybody in New York City to believe the worst of this man who champions doing the right thing, whatever it takes? He is fine as hell, though."

"Yeah," I said, "and underneath all that fineness is the devil. Cleo, we need to find out as much as we can about every aspect of his life."

"Shale, honestly, I have only heard whispers about him, but I will see what I can find out."

"Thanks, babe. Welcome back to the Apple."

"I will call you soon."

"Dinner?"

"Absolutely. Rosie, was this only a business call?"

"Yes, it was. I did miss you, I have to admit."

"Thanks for that, love, but you are too late. I think I found my Jonathan."

"You go, girl," I say.

"Cleo, wait, before you go, are you still in contact with that model you were talking about?"

"No, poor thing."

"Why, what happened to her?"

"She died about seven months ago from a drug overdose; they said it was a suicide."

"Do you know why she wanted to kill herself?"

"No, but if I had to guess, I would say it was over Taylor. She really wanted him to marry her, and I think she was pressuring him to do so. When that didn't work, she ended it."

"I know you didn't know her well, but did you get the impression that she was using?"

"Not the few times we were together, and I never got the impression that she was depressed either. She was living life. Her career was taking off, and she was in love with Taylor. But who really knows what someone is going through in their private time? She was a very sweet girl. Her name was Nina Reed, and I liked her. We'll talk soon, gotta run."

After Cleo had hung up, Rosie says, "My ass is twitching. In my experience, to pressure someone you have to have something to pressure them with. I wonder what Nina had on Taylor that she thought was enough to get him to marry her."

"I don't know, but I say we find out. The more I find out about this bastard, the more I hate his guts. I would love nothing more than to blow his brains out in Jesus's name."

Jonathan and I are watching television when a commercial comes on about a charity function DA Taylor Perez is having in memory of his mother. She died from a brain aneurysm, so this issue is near and dear to his heart. The affair will be held at the newest hotel in New York, the Grand Hotel. There will be celebrity guests, fine wine, and food prepared by a surprise celebrity chef. This will be the premier black-tie event in New York this season.

There are pictures of Taylor with survivors of brain aneurysms smiling and talking about how thankful they are to be alive, but that more research still needs to be done to prevent more people from going through the pain they went through. The association is very lucky to have a friend like Taylor Perez who can help get the word out and help raise money for further research. I put my finger in my mouth like I was trying to throw up. "What an asshole."

Jonathan chuckles. "Tell me how you really feel."

"My blood is boiling. He has the whole world fooled. New York City's very own Prince Charming. Not me; I see his true colors, and if it's the last thing I do, I am going to bring his ass down."

"You don't have to convince me, baby. I believe you." Jonathan has a look like he wants to say something.

"What is it, love?"

"Shale, I didn't want to tell you, knowing how you feel about our wonderful Assistant DA, but I am playing at the event."

"WHAT? When were you going to tell me?"

"Babe, I didn't know how. Look at you now, ready to jump through the television and strangle his ass. I agreed long before all this shit about him surfaced. It's too late to back out now; it's a done deal."

I don't say anything for a while. My mind is going a mile a minute. I turn to Jonathan. "I want to come. Is it too late to get me a ticket? Can you arrange for the love of your life to be your date? Pretty please? I promise I will be on my best behavior."

"I don't know, Shale. I would hate for you to embarrass me."

"Jon, I would never think of doing anything like that."

"Shale, I know you. The first time he says something you don't like, all hell will break loose."

"I double-pinky-swear I will be a perfect lady for a night on the town with the man I love. Besides, when was the last time we played dress-up? Please with sugar on top?"

"Shale..." I start kissing and rubbing him. "I can't say no to you, can I?"

"No, sir, you can't." Lights out. "By the way, can you get two tickets for Rosie?"

This event is the only thing people are talking about. Rosie agrees that this is a great way to get close to the bastard. I call Cleo and ask if she will go shopping with me to pick out an outfit to wear. "Absolutely," she says. "We will make a day of it. I know of some small designer boutiques hidden in the cut. You won't look like anyone else at this fake function. I know the designers; you have the kind of body they like to dress."

"I'm ready. See you tomorrow."

We meet for breakfast early and start the search for the perfect gown and shoes. We are all over the city, looking mostly in the smaller stores, trying on gowns in every color. Some I like, some I don't. Stopping for a long lunch, we have a ball. We are two women out for a day of shopping.

Our last stop is this very small fashion boutique with no curb appeal at all, but once we enter, it is like stepping into a very famous designer showroom. The first thing I notice is the beautiful colors, bright hues of red, blue, orange, black, pink. There is a small section for the metallics—the silvers, the grays—dresses that light up the store with shine from sequins and sparkle. Cleo greets the designer and introduces us. He and Cleo go way back. Listening to them talk, they are New York. That Cleo. What is there about New York that she doesn't know? He takes my measurements and the hunt is on.

I have on gown number five and am walking back to the dressing room when I see it. There in the corner of the metallics is my dress. It is a skintight silver number with the back cut low and no straps. I try on the dress, and baby, let me tell you, they had to pour me in this dress. "This is the one, Cleo. I know it."

"Jonathan's eyes are going to pop out of their sockets when he sees you in this dress," Cleo says.

"I believe you are right."

We walk out of there with my dress and three pairs of the most beautiful shoes ever made. "This was a great day," Cleo agrees.

I ask Cleo if she is going to the event and she says no. "I might know some of his friends, and I don't want to go down that road ever again. I have my own special night planned. Besides, my BFF will be there in person to give me all the dirt."

"Absolutely I will."

Rosie can pick and choose who he will bring, and I applaud his choice for this event. Rita Standing is one of the best pediatric surgeons in New York. She not only is beautiful but one of the coolest people around. Of all the chickenheads I have met—and there have been many—Rita is the exception. She is truly a woman of substance and the one I hope will be the lion tamer. He needs someone on his intellectual level and not just big breasts and a big ass. Rita is beautiful, well-read, has a great sense of humor, and a body to die for. I know she is good for Rosie. He may not admit it, but he knows it's true. He's running scared, but I say a prayer every night that he will face the truth before he loses her.

Finally it's the night of the party, and Mommy is looking good. Not a hair out of place and a gown that is fitting like a second skin. "Damn, baby," is all Jonathan can say. "That dress is..."

I give him a kiss. Nothing else needs to be said. "Watch out, Professor. You are looking like a black Adonis yourself. I have always said you look good in a tux."

"I ain't gonna lie, baby; we look fabulous," he says.

We meet Rosie and Rita at the hotel. We go in the side entrance because of all the press and paparazzi in front. We don't want to draw too much attention to ourselves. It could bite us in the ass down the road.

"Damn, partner, you clean up real good. And I thought you looked good in that catsuit."

"Why, thank you, kind sir. May I say you look very handsome? Rita, I love that dress. That color blue looks good on you. You are looking beautiful, as always."

"Thanks, Shale. Long time no see."

"Whose fault is that?"

Rosie clears his throat. "Shall we go in?"

The party is in full swing. All the beautiful people of New York are out in droves. Jonathan excuses himself so he can check on his band.

Rosie pulls me aside. "Listen, Shale, I don't want any shit from you tonight. All we are here to do is scope out Taylor. That is it."

"What the hell is wrong with you and Jonathan? You act like I am going to pull out my gun and shoot the bastard."

"You brought your gun?"

"Of course I did. See, it fits nicely in this small purse."

"Oh my God, Shale, why the hell did you bring your gun?"

"Rosie, a woman is always prepared. Now Rita and I need a drink. How about you?"

We head for the bar. Rosie is holding his head. "Drinking and a gun. This can't be good."

The champagne is flowing. Jonathan's band starts the music off right. You name them, they are here. Hollywood is well represented, as is Broadway. New York politicians as well as bimbo models who are running over people to get to the bathroom to throw up what they just ate. They do serve a purpose in that I don't stick out so much in the height department. There are actually women in the room a little taller than I. Everybody who is here, is here to celebrate the golden boy of New York. The celebrity chef is doing the damn thing. I never heard of him, but the food is delicious.

We're about an hour in. Walking around the room trying to get a feel for the place, I ask Rosie if there is any sign of our illustrious host. "Not yet. The trumpets haven't been blown and the red carpet hasn't been rolled out yet."

Rosie and Rita are on the dance floor, looking like the perfect couple. I wish he would take another chance on love again. He is older and
Rita is not that witch woman he was married to before. But according
to him, that will never happen again.

Jonathan's group takes a break so I can have him to myself for a short
while. We tear the dance floor up. Surprisingly, I am having a great time.
Great company, good food, and even greater champagne. This is what
I call a party. I even get Rosie on the dance floor. "Come on, Grandpa,
show me what kind of dances they were doing in the fifties."

"This grandpa still got it." Boy, does he ever.

CHAPTER 22

Sudden the music changes and in walks the man of the hour, strutting like he is King Tut arriving so his subjects can adore him. All eyes are on him and his date as he enters, shaking hands as he makes his way to the center of the floor. He takes his date in his arms, and they slowly start to dance as people are clearing a path like Moses did when he parted the Red Sea. 'Amazing' is the only word I have for the charisma this man has. All the women are wishing that he was dancing with them, and all the men want to *be* him.

His date is this bleached-blonde WASP type who comes from money. Her father is a bigwig in state government. There are whispers that Taylor is thinking about running for mayor.

Trash is trash; I don't care how you wrap it up and put a pretty bow on it. Rosie disappears for a moment. When he comes back, he whispers that he saw a friend of his who worked in the DA's office and wanted to say hello. "I wanted to ask about some of the men who are around Taylor; they don't look like they work in the DA's office." They don't, his friend said; he had no idea who they were.

"They look more like bodyguards to me."

"My thinking too," he says.

The dance ends and people start clapping like he just successfully negotiated a hostage release.

"What is it about this man that has these people so hypnotized?"

"Rita said it's the power. They smell it on him. He can do no wrong as far as they are concerned. It's like a drug. I see it sometimes with doctors and their patients. They feed off each other. The more success they get, the more they start to believe what everyone says about them."

Taylor is going around the room, laughing and shaking hands with the very rich of New York. Rosie pulls me over. "I think some of these bodyguards are cops. I recognize a few of these faces. If they are, then they are packing."

"See, Rosie? Aren't you glad I brought my gun?"

"No, it scares the hell out of me."

We see Taylor leaving the hall, so Rosie decides to follow him. As soon as Rosie leaves, three goonies run after him. Rita looks at me. "Is this one of your undercover operations?"

"Well, yes and no."

Shaking her head, she says, "I don't want to know anything more. I might regret it later."

Rosie comes back. "He went to the bathroom, but then he went into this room next door. I don't know what's in there, but it looks guarded." I start to move in that direction. "Oh no, you don't."

"I was just going to see if I could—"

"I know what you were going to do, but now is not the time."

"Rosie, I was—"

"Shale, do you want me to get Jonathan?"

"NO. God, we know he's dirty."

"Let's prove it the right way. We can't get too close. We don't want him to see us, not just yet."

We spend the rest of the evening watching every move he makes, taking mental notes on faces and every time he leaves the room. I go back and forth to the ladies room, trying to see what is happening outside the ballroom, but from this angle, I can't see much. Every time a loony goon whispers something in his ear, he disappears. We need to get into that room somehow. I don't see that happening tonight; there is a man posted in front of the door.

He finally takes the mike and says he wants to thank everyone who made tonight such a success. The money raised will go a long way in helping people who have had an aneurysm and hopefully can prevent more people from having one. He is grateful that they had come a long way in diagnosing and treating this condition. He just wished that his mother and father were here today to see the progress that has been made since they passed away. By the time he is finished, there isn't a dry eye in the place. I am looking at him, with this smirk on his face like he just pulled the biggest con job in the history of the U.S., and he did. Makes me hate him even more.

All in all, we have a wonderful night. I wish I could have gotten into that room, but as Rosie said, we will get him, and when we do, it will be even sweeter.

Note to self: Check out those loony goons to see if they are cops. I manage to take some pictures with Jonathan's cell phone. I had to leave mine at home; no room with my gun in my bag.

A few days later Rosie and I are sitting around the living room, going through the reports and files we brought from the office. "Shale, we were lucky the night of the party."

"How so?"

"All those city bigwigs. Thank God the chief of police wasn't there, because he would have surely seen us."

"I know. I was wondering why he wasn't there, or the commissioner."

"I don't care why. The fact that they were not there works for us."

My cell phone rings. "Hey, beautiful, it's me, Muffin. I am outside your apartment with my friend Stack."

I go to let them in, but I stop them before they enter. "Let me tell you two Negros something. If I find anything missing, I will come after you and shoot you between your eyes. Do you understand?"

"Oh, come on, Shale, you know us better that."

"Yeah, I do. That's why I said what I did."

They come in and sit near Rosie. "Can I get you something to drink? I have wine, sangria, beer, water." They both say wine (big surprise). I bring them wine in plastic cups, and after they take a sip, the look on their faces makes me laugh.

"Boy, that is nasty," Muffin says. "Thank God we brought our own, thank you very much." He takes out a bottle of that ghetto blaster that his mother pulled out of her pocketbook at the hospital. "This shit could start a train engine. The kind of crap that will leave burn marks down your throat." He takes a gulp out of the bottle before handing it to Stack, who does the same. "Boy, that is good," Muffin says. They both look like they just opened a thousand-dollar bottle of champagne.

"Sorry-ass Negros." I pour out my wine and pour the wine they bought. "Here, use a cup and act like your mothers taught you some manners."

Stack says, louder than he realized, "Upper, ain't she."

"What did you say, Stack?"

"Nothing, Shale, nothing."

Rosie just laughs.

So help me God, how do I describe Stack? He looks like a taller JJ Evans from *Good Times*. He is six feet six inches and weighs all of 150 pounds soaking wet. He is called Stack because he reminds you of a chimney stack. He and Muffin have been friends from childhood; they are the ghetto's Abbott and Costello, only skinnier.

We settle down to business. Rosie and I go over what we know about Taylor's background. "Now you fill in the rest."

The picture that we are getting is one of a man who is driven, who likes the finer things in life, and who has come a long way from the Brownsville projects. Taylor's mother died from a brain aneurysm when he was ten years old. His father seemed to be lost after that, so the kids were raised by their grandparents. His mother's death was a blow to Taylor because he loved her so much; his relationship with his father is hard to read.

We start talking about his parents and his mother's passing and how it tore the family apart when Muffin says, "The family was torn apart way before that. Taylor's father used to beat the shit out of his mother. He had a very violent temper, and it didn't take much to set him off."

I go through the paperwork, looking to see if there are any reports of domestic violence. There is nothing noted. Muffin says, "She never reported it, but it was well known in the neighborhood."

Stack says his mother told him that the beatings were the cause of her aneurysm. There is a love/hate relationship between Taylor and his father. It could be because after his mother had passed away, his father was not around as much. Stack says, "I heard Taylor blamed him for his mother's death, and he was the reason the family was split up, and the kids had to go live with their grandparents. His brother and sisters didn't have much to do with the father after that. Can we get something to eat? My stomach is talking to me," Stack belts out suddenly.

"Yeah, that is a good idea," Muffin chimes in. "Gotta feed the liquor."

Walking into the kitchen, all I can say under my breath is, "Sorry-ass Negroes."

We stop long enough to eat something. Knowing my guests as I do, I figure fried chicken and potato salad would suit them just fine. They eat that chicken like it is about to take flight. Rosie and I sit amazed at how fast that food disappears. The way they attack that food, I am surprised at how skinny they both are. I guess the liquor burns up what food they do eat. Can I tell you how these Negros had the nerve to ask me for some of my nasty wine after they polish off their bottle? Muffin says the wine tastes better after they eat.

Stack wants to know if I will be serving dessert. "Hell no, there will be no dessert." Rosie is on the phone while I go back to reading. We are trying to sort out what we've been told so far.

I ask Rosie if he has any information on the father now. "Looks like he drank himself to death about four years ago. Maybe he felt guilty about the abuse, or the fact he didn't stay with his children after his wife died."

Muffin and Stack look at each other with a look of bewilderment. "Rosie, what are you talking about? His father is not dead," Stack says.

"What?"

"No, he is not dead."

Jumping in, I say, "Yes, he is dead. He died four years ago."

"No, he didn't," Stack says adamantly.

Rosie and I look like we were slapped with a subpoena. "How do you know he is not dead?" Rosie asks. "All of our information says he left New York after his wife died. He didn't want the responsibility of the kids. That's why they were raised by the grandparents."

I look through the papers to find a death certificate, and there is one, with a date four years earlier. Muffin says with a smile, "This is why you need us to set you cops straight."

"I don't believe you, but let's hear the rest. What else do you know?" Rosie asks. "Is he still in the state? The country? If he left New York, where did he go? I see that he was from Mexico. Did he go back there?"

"Where the hell do you guys get your information?" Muffin asks. "Listen, Shale baby, you need to call me more often. Let a brother help a sister out, because it looks to me like you guys need all the help you can get. He is not from Mexico; he is from Colombia."

I almost drop my drink. "WHAT? Muffin, are you sure?"

"Stack, is I sure?"

"You are solid sure, my brother."

"Can you repeat what you just said?"

"I said that Taylor's father is Colombian."

Rosie says, "There is none of this in the file."

Looking dazed and confused, I am wondering how could we get it so wrong.

Rosie gets on the phone and starts dialing. "I love you two idiots right now," I say. Stack and Muffin came through big time, and I will need to treat them both better as soon as we can verify this new information. I tell them to keep us updated on anything they hear. "But don't be stupid. Call my cell phone night or day."

They leave my apartment with money in their pockets and smiles on their faces. Rosie and I are dumbfounded. "Colombia. He is from Colombia." My mind starts clicking. "Why did we think he had died? Why are the records so screwed up with some many errors?"

Rosie says, "What I want to know is how is it possible for someone to be such a high-profile individual and we not know his real story?"

Later that night I can't sleep. My mind is going a thousand miles a minute. The last six months are running into each other. I hear my uncle saying, *Trust your common sense, baby. Slow your mind and put things in perspective. In time the whole picture will be made clear.* Tossing and turning all night, trying not to think. Nothing is working. Can't shut off the noises in my brain. I end up looking at my cats sleeping like they don't have a care in the world. I watch the sun come up, drinking a cup of coffee, TV on but not watching when breaking news interrupts the regular programing. "We have reports coming in that Judge Walter Brown committed suicide early this morning. He hung himself by tearing up his bed sheet and tying it to the bars in his cell." Damn, what a way to start the day.

I get to the office early and the suicide is all anyone is talking about. Son of a bitch couldn't face a lifetime of jail time, so he ended it all. Rosie and I click coffee cups together. "Bastard bites the dust. Hell is getting crowed," I say out loud. Time to concentrate on Taylor.

"We still don't have anything concrete to go to Conrad with yet," Rosie says. "I think we need to pay a visit to the medical examiner who signed the death certificate. What is his name?"

Looking through the files, I find the name Doctor Hue. I call the ME office and make an appointment to meet with the doc. "Better come now, I will be leaving early today." We are on our way.

Twenty minutes later we are walking into his office. "Thank you for seeing us on such short notice, Dr. Hue, but this is very important."

"No problem," he says. "You caught me at a good time. I am leaving on vacation this afternoon."

CHAPTER 23

"I pulled the report you asked for. How can I help you?"

"We need to know how this man died."

"He was shot seven times. The first bullet killed him instantly, it went straight through his heart. There really was no need for the other six shots if killing him was the only motive. The bullets really did a number on his face. Not much left to work with for identification purposes." He shows us autopsy photos and explains exactly what was done to him.

"Wow, whoever did this wanted to make sure he was dead. Or to send a signal," Rosie says.

Looking at the pictures, I ask, "Doc, who ID the victim? Like you said, not much to go on."

He goes through the report. "He was identified by his son Taylor."

"He could tell this man was his father looking like that?"

"I was suspicious that he was able to ID him, but the victim had a snake tattoo that he could identify. He also had a copy of his dental records with him."

"Just like that, he came to ID the victim with the victim's dental records? Didn't you find that strange, Dr. Hue?"

"Not really. When my office called him, we told him to bring whatever ID he had because we were going to need help."

Looking at Rosie, I ask Doctor Hue if he can check another death for us. "The name is Nina Reed. She was twenty-six or twenty-seven, died about a year ago."

He goes to the computer. "Here we go. Nina Reed died from an overdose of heroin that was almost one hundred percent pure."

"Can you tell if she was using long?"

"No, she most definitely was not a user. This was probably her first time. But with the heroin almost pure and her being a novice, she didn't stand a chance."

Rosie and I look at each other, smiling. "Thank you, Dr. Hue. You have been more help than you know. Enjoy your vacation."

"This was no fucking suicide. He either killed her himself or he had one of his goons do it. This is what she found out, his cartel connection. Rosie, I think it's time we pay Mr. Perez a visit."

We call to make an appointment to see Taylor for that afternoon, but are advised by his secretary that he is too busy to see us today. Rosie tells her, "This is very important. We need to speak to him about Judge Walter Brown and the raid that took place at the house he owns."

"What raid are you talking about?"

"Just tell your boss what I said."

She says, "Hang on." Where the hell has she been? What raid, she asks? A few minutes later she says, "He believes he can spare an hour."

"Funny how he was able to clear some time for us."

"Yeah, really funny."

When we arrive, his secretary informs us that he is on a very important call and we should wait. I whisper to Rosie, "I wonder who he is talking to."

Half an hour later we are escorted in to his majesty. He is sitting behind one of the biggest desks I have ever seen. Must be compensating for some shortcoming, if you know what I mean, and I think you do. Mr. Perez is more handsome in person than any picture I have seen of him. He even looks better than he did at the fundraiser.

He comes from behind the desk and says, "Hello, pleased to meet you." Handshakes all around. "Please be seated. How can I help you?"

Before we can say anything, he says, "Your reputation precedes you both. What a pleasure to finally meet you in person. I know the people of New York are sleeping better, knowing we have you to protect us, fighting crime, making our streets safe." I give him my 'you are a shit-hole' smile. "My secretary said you wanted to talk to me about Judge Brown. Isn't it a tragedy what happened to the judge? I called his wife, Diane, to offer my condolences. I still can't believe he killed himself. What a terrible loss all the way around, especially to the legal system. He was a pioneer in legal matters and a personal friend. He will be greatly missed." The entire time he is talking, I think to myself he would have made a great actor. What a bullshitter.

He continues, "What a mess Judge Brown created for himself and for me. If I had known what he was using my house for, I would have never allowed him to use it."

"Oh, you didn't know about his freak show?"

"No," he says. "I was told he used it for poker parties with his friends."

"Well, in a way——"

I shoot Rosie a look. *Be quiet.*

"Speaking of the house, when we looked into the ownership, we found that the owner is listed as MDC. Can you tell us why the house is not listed under your name?"

"Yes, the house was purchased as a corporate retreat. The only time we use it is for business. I do rent it out from time to time to help pay for the upkeep. As you saw for yourself, it is quite large. It takes a lot of money to maintain a property of that size. That is why it is not listed under my name."

"What does MDC stand for?"

"It stands for Money Distribution Corporation."

"Which does what?"

"Financial. We help in the building and rebuilding of the Americas. We help throughout South America, Mexico."

"Doing what, may I ask?"

"Infrastructure. Providing the basic needs of the people. I am very excited about the project we are currently working on—water production and filtration. Did you know that a lot of diseases are caused by not having clean water to drink? I am very passionate about this project. We just started but I know it will help a lot of people, especially the elderly and young children, who are at a greater risk of getting sick or dying. We are also building new schools and affordable housing. Putting in roads where there were none. I feel very blessed by what I have been able to achieve, and I want to share it with not only people outside of the United States, but also right here in New York. 'Brooklyn do or die' is still my motto." He returns to his seat like he just won Popeship. I hate him so much. He makes my skin crawl.

Rosie says, "I applaud you for the work you do. Getting back to the judge. What I can't figure out is how he got away with so much shit and was never caught. I just can't believe that he carried out all this mess alone. There is no way he was able to do all he did and nobody knew. I mean, the man had been under investigation more than once. I can't remember, was your office ever involved in any investigations on the judge?"

"Not this particular office, and never under my watch," he says.

"Well, the authorities are still processing the house, but we are here due to the volume of drugs that was found there. If they have not already, I'm sure the DEA will be paying you a visit. We just don't believe that the judge acted alone. Do you have any ideas?"

He is giving me this look like, 'Bitch, get the hell out of my office.' Clearing his throat, he says, "I had nothing to do with the judge except that I let him use the house when he asked."

"That's it for a close and personal friend?"

"I never said he was a close friend, more a business associate. If I were a betting man, I would say that you don't know everything about your partner. Am I right, Agent Jenkins?"

"No, you would lose that bet. I know everything about Shalimar. Right, partner?"

"Right, Agent Jenkins."

"I can tell you the few times I was at the house, there was never any sign of drug use or drug paraphernalia to be found. There was never anything out of order."

Rosie smiles and says, "You never saw the dungeon that he used as his whipping room?"

"No. Like I said before, if he had all that shit there, then he hired the best damn cleaners in the world. If I had known of all the shit that the house was being used for, I would have called the police myself."

"Even on a personal friend?" I ask.

"I would also like to add that I never had any complaints from any of my other guests that rented the house."

"That's because they were all there at the same time," I say under my breath.

"I don't have anything else to tell you that I have not told the police. Now if you don't mind, I really am very busy." As we get up to leave, he turns his chair around so that his back is facing us.

"Bastard," I whisper.

Rosie and I are smiling after leaving his office. He is dirty and we both know it. "Rosie, I thought you were going to bring up his father or Nina?"

"After looking at his smug face, I didn't have to."

I am flying. Things are starting to make sense. Thank you, Uncle.

I call Brad. "I know you guys are busy, but we need to meet at our office. We are on our way there now."

● ● ●

As soon as we leave, Taylor is on the phone. "I just had two federal agents in my office asking a lot of questions. No, I played dumb as usual, but we have to move fast. I could tell that bitch didn't believe me. I don't care how you do it, but keep my name out of this shit. I have the most to lose and I don't plan on losing."

The man on the other end of the phone hangs up and says to the other men in the room, "We have to move fast. The feds are sniffing around a little too close."

One of the other men says, "We can't do anything until the boss gets here on Friday."

"You're right. I better call him now and update him on the situation."

• • •

Rosie and I get back to the office. Brad and Victor are waiting for us in Conrad's office. We break down everything we have learned and the things we suspect. "Damn, that son of a bitch. He has been the poster child for justice, and the whole time he is laughing behind our backs."

Brad and Victor have been working almost around the clock to identify dirty cops. "Almost every piece of paper in the files is fake. I doubt if anything is real except Taylor's name and his mother dying."

Conrad says the key to this whole thing is to find out the truth about Taylor's father. "We need to know if in fact he is alive and what his real name is. I will get some agents on this right now."

Rosie says, "Conrad, we now know that not all crooked cops work for NYPD. We have some rats in our closet too. You need to be careful who is assigned to this case."

With a look of sadness, he says, "I know. Victor and Brad are still working on who falsified the records. They will let us know as soon as they know something."

Sitting at my desk, I keep looking for something that we missed. Anything. Rosie comes back with lunch, but I don't feel much like eating.

CHAPTER 24

It's only Wednesday, and I wish it was the weekend. I need the rest; my brain hurts from too much thinking. Things are coming together. It's the little pieces of the puzzle that I can't place. I say a silent prayer: *Uncle Maurice, where are you?*

• • •

In an abandoned warehouse in Brooklyn, three men are sitting in a windowless room. "Good to see you, boss. Glad you made it in before Friday. We really need to step up our operation. Did you have any problems getting back in the country?"

"I never have a problem. That is why I come and go when I please. It's all in who you pay. Greed is the son of a bitch that works well for us. Now get me up-to-date."

They tell him of the phone call from Taylor, the investigation into the judge. "What an asshole. I'm glad he killed himself, saves me the trouble of blowing his black ass up."

"We have to move quietly, boss. The authorities are all over the place."

"What about our people that we pay for?" he asks.

"So far so good, but a couple of them are getting scared. What should we do?"

"Pay them more money. We still need them. After that, kill them."

• • •

Thursday Brad calls. They found two of the dirty cops who work in records, and they have them under surveillance. They back into the dates and times. Brad says they are pretty sure it's them. "Officer James Mason and Officer Sean O'Malley. We are monitoring everything they do, will keep you posted."

I love it. Things are in motion. It makes me sick to the stomach that cops turn their backs on what is right for money. The only thing worse than a dirty cop is two.

• • •

There is a lot of activity near the abandoned warehouse. A couple of big trucks have been coming and going. Watching from a distance, taking pictures, trying not to get caught, our neighborhood heroes are taking matters in their own hands. "Man, hand me the bottle," Muffin says to Stack. "Shale will be surprised when we go to her with this evidence."

"Yeah, but evidence of what?" Stack asks. "We don't know what the hell is going on."

"It doesn't matter, man," Muffin says. "It's late at night and that warehouse is abandoned. What's with the trucks? We're gonna find out. Now shut up."

From the warehouse, one man says, "Look, someone is getting out of the car. He must be the boss. See how the guy is holding the door for him? Take another picture." There is a flash of light.

"Look, I told you someone was out there. I know what I saw. Maybe the cops?"

The boss says, "Go look, and if someone is out there, bring them back."

Two of the men get in the car and drive around to the other side of the building. Muffin and Stack are so busy drinking, they don't realize that the men are standing behind them. "Is anybody there for us to take another picture?" Muffin asks Stack.

"No, I don't see anybody. Pass the bottle."

By the time they realize that the men are behind them, it is too late. "Look what we have here." Stack drops the bottle of wine as they both try to run. The men pick them up like they are picking up garbage. They both struggle to break free, but the hold the guys have on them makes that impossible. Muffin is hit so hard that a tooth flies out of his mouth. Stack is hit with such force that he throws up on the man who hit him, which makes the beating just that much more severe. After beating the shit out of them, they placed them in the trunk of the car and drive back to the warehouse. They don't notice that the cell phone had dropped in the grass.

By the time they are taken into the warehouse, Muffin and Stack had been beaten to a pulp. They bring them in front to the boss. "Who are you?" he asks. "What brings you out this late at night?" He nods his head, and they both are hit again. Muffin is crying like a baby. Stack is totally out of it. "Hit them again," the boss says. Blood is flying into the air like dust particles in the abandoned building.

• • •

I fall asleep on the sofa with the two cats, TV blaring in the background.

My cell phone going off wakes me up. I answer, not quite awake yet. "He's not back yet," the voice is yelling in the phone.

"Who is this?"

"Pookie. Muffin is not back yet. I know something is wrong. He wouldn't stay out this late. Shale, help him, please. Something is wrong, I tell you."

I try to calm her down, but she is not listening. She is freaking out on the phone. "Pookie," I yell, "shut the fuck up. I can't understand what you are saying." I hang up the phone.

She calls right back. "OK," she says. "I'm sorry." Then she starts crying. "Something is wrong. I think my Muffin is in trouble."

"Why do you feel this way?" I ask.

"He was supposed to be home by eleven. It's three-thirty a.m., and he is not home yet."

"Pookie, you know Muffin. He's probably with Stack and the boys, drinking somewhere. Wait, where are you and why are you calling me?"

"I am back in New York. Muffin said it was OK to come back. Please, Shale, help him."

"Listen, Pookie, I can't help you. Muffin is a grown man. I still don't know why you are calling me."

She raises her voice. "Because **he is working for you, that's why**."

"What the hell are you talking about, working for me?"

"He told me that he was helping you with a case."

"He told you what?"

"Yeah, he said that you needed his help. What the hell have you gotten my man into? Why the hell don't you do the job that you are paid to do? Now go get my man, bitch."

"Call me a bitch again and I will kick your ass all the way back to Mississippi, Pookie. I am trying to understand what the hell you are talking about. I never asked Muffin to help me with shit."

"Then why did he tell me he was working for you? Oh, damn that son of a bitch. If he's fooling around on me again, I will kill him. I ain't going through this shit no more, me with seven babies. I will take his sorry ass to court. And do you know how much money I can get with seven children? Shit, I won't even need to be on welfare with all that money I would be getting."

"Pookie, shut the fuck up and start talking sense. What exactly did he tell you?"

"He told me that he heard something about a big shipment of drugs coming into New York, and he knew where the location would be. You told him to stake out the place and take pictures for you."

"I never told that fool anything like that. Oh my God, Pookie, I gotta go. Wait, did he tell where this location is?"

"Somewhere over where those four men were killed."

I hang up the phone and call Rosie. "What the hell is going on? Why the urgency?"

"Muffin and Stack are going to get killed if we don't move and fast." I fill him in on the phone call from Pookie.

Before I run out the door, I put on a pair of my specially made boots. Something tells me I will need them tonight. Oh my God, I hope those fools are still alive. What the hell possessed them to go out on their own?

We sound the alarm and wake everybody up. Conrad puts the whole agency on high alert. I call Victor and tell him what is going on; he will contact Brad. All local and state authorities are activated. The DEA and the ATF agents are moving their people to try and find this location. Brad issues warrants for the two cops in records. We try to time everything so that no one is tipped off to what is going down.

The building where the killings took place is torn down, but that whole area is nothing but old warehouses and abandoned buildings. They could be anywhere. We split up in groups, each searching a particular area. We are working fast; we need to find them before the sun comes up. One of the agents reports that he sees a light in the farthest warehouse. We converge on the sides of the warehouse but all is quiet.

Rosie and I are with Victor as we move closer. I am saying a quiet prayer that Muffin and Stack are still alive when I trip over something on the ground. There is so much debris around here, God only knows what it could be. Rosie gives me his hand to help me up, and when I look down, I see that it is a cell phone in the middle of all the debris. I pick it up and the phone comes on. I search the phone and discover that the phone belongs to Muffin.

My heart is racing like it is about to jump out of my chest. This is the place. The call goes out, alerting everyone that we found the building. We have this entire warehouse surrounded, plotting our next move.

We see this Town Car pull up. The building door opens to let the car in, and Conrad says he can see that the man who opened the door has a rifle in his hand. The man steps out of the warehouse, surveying the land before he goes back in and closes the door.

"They have to have Muffin and Stack in there; we need to move and fast."

"Yeah, but we can't just go in with guns blazing. If they are still alive, they would surely kill them."

"I can't stand this waiting, I need to do something."

Tony, one of our team members, reports that he sees an opening at the back of the building but it is not very big; looks like the size of a manhole. "It's not on the ground level, but there are piles of concrete blocks and enough discarded building materials to lift someone up to the opening. A small man or woman maybe can get through it."

I take off running. "Wait," Rosie says as he tries to catch me.

I make my way to the back where the opening is. "Look," I say to Rosie, "I can get through there."

"No, it's too dangerous for you to go by yourself."

"You can't stop me," I say. "Now are you going to help me or will I have to do it myself, DAD?"

"Alright, I will, on one condition: you get in and report what you see without trying to take on everybody in there. You have no idea how many men are in there and what weapons they have. I mean it, Shale."

"I promise." Turning to face him, I say, "Rosie, remember our signal. No matter what you hear, wait for my signal."

"Yeah, I remember. I don't like it, but I remember."

"Good. Now help me get to that opening."

I manage to squeeze through the opening, which leads to a small bathroom. The smell almost makes me throw up. From where the opening is to the floor is not a bad drop for someone six feet tall. I wait a bit before I jump to the floor, trying not to make too much noise. I hit the floor. Oh God, I hope no one heard me. I wait behind the door, making sure I don't hear anyone moving in my direction.

Nothing; I don't think they heard me. I hear loud laughter coming from inside. I have my gun in my hand as I slowly leave the bathroom. The place is dark except for a group of small lamps scattered throughout the room. From where I am crouching, I can see most of the room. It looks like there are several big barrels in the center of the room, along with a small van. I see two big round tables with a couple of the lamps on each side, along with four money-counting machines.

Two of the men are pulling money from bags and running it through the machines. One of the men is taking bundles from one of the barrels and placing them into the van. Another is weighing and pouring what looks like cocaine into small plastic bags on a smaller table next to the big round table. Movement is with clockwork precision as they continue the process of moving drugs and counting money.

I am trying to move so I can see the other side of the room where laughter is coming from. My heart is beating so hard, I'm afraid someone may hear. I am trying to make out how many voices I hear to count the men in the room, but there is Spanish in the mix, so I can't be sure exactly how many are here. I can see the Town Car parked with the trunk open. I stay in my position for a minute before I try to move. I move very slowly because I can't see what is in front of me. I feel around me as I slowly move toward the sound of the voices.

Just as I turn to move to my left, I hear someone coming in my direction. "Yeah, I'm coming. I have to take a leak." He walks past me and enters the bathroom without closing the door. I look back and I can see his backside standing in front of the toilet. I have a decision to make. Do I let him leave or do I stop him in the bathroom?

I decide to stop him. I sneak back to the bathroom and before he can turn around, I grab him by his neck and twist. I am taller than he is so I am able to catch him before he hits the ground. Swift and silent. I drag him to the side and go back to where I was before.

I move farther to the left as I hear, "What the hell are you doing in there, shitting up the place? C'mon, man, we are ready to go." Moments later I see someone running to the bathroom. "Jesus, what's wrong with you, man? Coke, what happened? Are you OK?" He goes over to the man lying on the floor. "Hey, man, what the fuck." Reaching down to shake him, he realizes that he is dead. Running out of the bathroom, he shouts, "Somebody's in here! Coke is dead."

I hear the sound of feet running all around me. There is a space in between some boxes, so I move as fast as I can. I hear someone cursing in Spanish. Then I hear, **"FIND THE BASTARDS. TEAR THIS PLACE APART. IF YOU CAN'T FIND THEM, I WILL KILL YOU."** Then I hear, **"PUT THE BARRELS BACK ON THE VAN NOW."**

CHAPTER 25

see two men run past me with guns in their hands. I am glad now that there is no more light in the room; it's my perfect cover. Moving in my direction is this tank of a man pushing things out of the way. Every time he moves something, I move. I try to get in the position where I can kick him in the face with my boot. I can almost feel his breath when he pushes back the last box in front of me. I take my right foot and hit him dead in the face with my heel. He yells as he falls back. Blood is rushing from his nose.

By then my cover is blown, so I come out shooting. I shoot the closest man to me, then shoot the man I kicked in the face as he is trying to get up. I get the guy who came from the bathroom right in his kneecap. He goes down screaming. I see two men jump in each of the two trucks heading straight to the door. One of the men is running to get into the Town Car as he is shooting at me. I manage to hit him in the back of his leg. He falls into the car as it is about to drive away.

That's when I see Taylor and a man holding Muffin and Stack with a gun to their heads. They are alive but not by much. "Drop the gun or we will blow their heads off." I am praying that Rosie and Conrad will wait before they bust in, even hearing the gunshots. Rosie will know what to do. I look at the man standing next to Taylor and immediately know he is his father. "Walk toward us slowly or they die," Taylor shouts.

As I get closer, he recognizes me. "I knew your black ass was trouble when you came into my office asking all kinds of questions. Where is your sidekick? You never go anywhere without him."

"I'm alone," I say.

"Bullshit," he says. "Pops, meet Federal Agent Shalimar Blacque. She is the one I told you about."

"Damn, you are fine. Too bad we had to meet under these circumstances, this being your last day on earth."

"For a dead guy you look pretty good yourself," I say.

He smiles. "You are my kind of woman. Fucking you would make my day. I like my women tall, black, and with plenty of attitude. You remind me of my late wife. You and I could have a whole lot of fun."

I smile. "Funny, that's not what I heard. Didn't you use her head as a punching bag?"

Taylor is in the background yelling, "Stop talking about my mother, bitch, or I will kill you myself."

"Like you did Nina?"

"Shut the fuck up. If she had minded her own damn business and wasn't snooping, she would never have found out about me. Can you imagine, she was trying to blackmail me into marrying her? Blackmail me, the little cunt. We made sure to send her out in a cloud of white snow."

Taylor's father comes over and looks me in the face. "I don't believe we have been properly introduced. My name is Aguilar Perez, and I will be the one to kill you." Looking directly into my face, he smiles. "If I had met you before now, who knows, you could have been one of my women."

I roll my eyes. "I seriously doubt it."

"You'd be surprised. Power is a powerful aphrodisiac, so don't look at me like it would have been impossible. Look at my son. All he has to do is look at a woman, and the panties come off. Like father, like son."

"Sorry, but you don't do it for me. I like my men taller and not so greasy."

The smile disappears as he walks over to me and slaps me hard in the face. A tear rolls down my cheek. He puts his gun to my head. "You have no idea who you are talking to. I am the head of one of the biggest drug cartels in Colombia. I can have any of my men kill you, but I will leave that for myself to do. They can't have all the fun." He slaps me again, but this time he spits in my face.

I have no choice but to stand there, being outnumbered by both manpower and gun power. I close my eyes, saying over and over in my head, *I am going to kill both of you slowly.*

As I open my eyes, I look at Muffin and Stack and my heart bleeds. They look like they were in a plane crash. Muffin is trying to look at me, but his eyes are so swollen, it's a wonder if he can see at all.

"We need to move fast," Taylor says. "I don't believe for a minute this skank is here by herself. Kill her now, Dad, so we can get the hell out of here," Taylor is screaming.

"No, we need her if you are right and she has friends outside. These two will not be missed if we kill them now. We will need her for leverage. Tie her up now; we will deal with her later."

One of the guys comes over and jerks my hands behind my back. Once he is sure my hands are tied, he comes in front of me and hits me hard with his fist. I fall back and hit the ground. I can see Muffin crying. I am in pain but too mad to cry. "Never let them see you cry" is playing over and over in my head.

"Are you sure she isn't alone? Why would they leave her here to die after hearing gunshots ringing out?" Taylor's father says.

"I know she is not alone," Taylor says. "These two are tied together at the hip."

As I lie there, I am praying that Rosie sticks to our code. He knows what to do.

● ● ●

Meanwhile, on the outside, Conrad is ready to send in the Marines, but Rosie says no. "How do you know she isn't lying in there dead? We need to help her."

"Listen, I know my partner. We have made plans for situations like this. Please believe me. Now is not the time, or she will die."

Conrad is not convinced but says, "We will wait one more hour, that's it."

Rosie turns and whispers, "Shale, I pray I am right."

• • •

They have me tied to a chair with my hands tied behind my back. Aguilar comes over and rips my blouse open. "I need to see if you are wired. This will be a pleasure." My bra opens in the front, so he starts unhooking my bra from the bottom, all the while rubbing my breast. The only thing I am thinking about is killing his greasy ass.

Muffin starts crying and shaking uncontrollably, making moaning sounds like a wounded elephant. If you didn't know better, you would think he was having a seizure. Everyone is looking at him. "What the fuck is wrong with that skinny son of a bitch? Shoot him," Taylor is screaming. I know that Muffin is doing this to stop Aguilar, and my heart melts.

While all eyes are on Muffin, I am able to slide my right foot back to where my hands are tied. There is a tab on the top part of my boot that I am trying to reach. The idiot who tied my hands didn't do a very good job, so I am able to wiggle the tie enough to loosen it. Muffin is close to death, so with everything I have in me, I am able to pull out the tab on my boot. The end of the tab is a very sharp knife, not very big, but very long and sharp. The knife slices the tie, but I keep my hands behind me as if I am still tied.

"Kill him," Taylor is screaming again. One of the men standing the closest to Muffin points his gun.

I scream, "NOOOO." This makes everyone turn toward me. "Don't kill him," I say.

Aguilar looks at me. "OK, we'll start with you first. I was hoping to fuck you before I killed you, but since you want to be the hero..." He comes over and leans in my face like he is about to spit again, but before he has a chance, I jerk my hand from my back and jab the knife in his throat. I push that knife like I was pushing out a baby. I push the knife in and down; he falls back, yelling in pain. Blood is running like a river out of his throat.

The move takes everyone off guard. I jump up and kick the gun out of the hand of the man standing closest to me. I catch the gun before it hits the floor. I fire off two shots, killing the man next to me and the one in front.

Taylor runs over to his father, crying as Aguilar is twisting in pain. He cradles his father, trying to decide if he should remove the knife. One of the guys jumps into the Town Car, trying to get away, but I turn the gun on the car, shooting out the front tires. He jumps out of the car, running in my direction with a shotgun in his hand, cussing me and getting off one shot before I hit him in his face.

I run and pick up the shotgun, shooting the hell out of one of the lamps till it catches fire. Rosie can see that a fire has started. "NOW, MOVE NOW."

Things are moving so fast it feels like slow motion. Confusion runs rampant. Men are running in all directions trying to escape out of the building while police are running into it. Gunshots ring out as bullets fly, looking for someone to hit. A bullet hits one of the lamps nearest the round table, and in a second a fire starts, spreading to the table with the money and cocaine on it. Someone is trying to escape in the van but is stopped by a police car coming through the door.

I see that the fire is spreading fast. I hear someone say, "Get the cars and the van out of here before the fire can reach them." Somewhere in this nightmare, I hear the sirens of the fire department. A blanket of smoke is starting to engulf the building. I hear Rosie calling out my name. "Over here," I say. "I am looking for Muffin and Stack. There is no way they would be able to make it out on their own."

I hear the moaning of someone in pain, so I move in that direction. I see Stack not moving, lying on his back. Rosie calls out loud, "We need paramedics over here, we got two people down."

I run over to Muffin, who is barely breathing and looks like he is dead. "Muffin," I cry as I pick up his head. "Can you hear me?" He is not moving, but I can feel a faint heartbeat. The paramedics arrive with two stretchers. "Get them out of here now." We all need to leave as the smoke and the fire are spreading. The fire department has started spraying water on the fire, but this thing is moving fast.

As we turn to leave, I see in the corner of my eye Taylor still cradling his father. He has a gun in his hand and will not let the paramedics touch him. He is surrounded by Conrad and the other officers at a distance but is not moving. We can't tell if Aguilar is alive or not since Taylor won't let anyone near him, but the smoke is getting thicker. We may have no choice but to take them by force. One of the paramedics is talking to Taylor, who seems to be in a trance. Finally we have no choice; the cops are able to make him drop the gun as Taylor is pried from his father by a couple of police officers as the paramedics take out his father. The firemen are yelling for everyone to get out of the building before the roof collapses on top of us.

The police are leading Taylor out of the building when he suddenly turns and runs back in the building, grabbing me as he goes in. Rosie tried to hold onto me, but Taylor has a better grip on my arm.

We are back in the building as fire is dancing all around us. I hear Conrad and Rosie screaming my name as he pushes me deeper into the building. We end up in a small area at the back of the building. I can barely see due to the smoke and fire, but I can see that Taylor has a gun in his hand. Where he got it from, I don't know.

"You black bitch." He is seething. "You ruin everything. You killed my father and destroyed my life. Now I'm going to take yours. We both will die in this hellhole. It's poetic justice, don't you agree?" I am looking in his eyes, and all I see is pure hatred.

Because we both are breathing in smoke, things are starting to get hazy. I feel like I can't breathe much longer, so I say a prayer and lunge at him with everything I have. We hit the ground just as the roof caves in on top of us. All I remember is the sound of the world ending.

EPILOGUE

My head feels like a ten-ton truck hit me at frightening speed. I try to move, but the pain is excruciating. The light in the room makes opening my eyes next to impossible. I hear voices in the background, but I can't make out what they are saying.

After a few minutes, my blurred vision begins to focus, and the first person I can see is my father. My mother is beside him, along with Jonathan. "Welcome back, baby girl," my father says.

My throat is on fire as I try to speak. "How long have I been here?"

"A week," says my mother, "but you have only been awake since yesterday afternoon."

"May I have some water?"

Jonathan walks over the table next to the bed, pours some water in a cup, and puts the straw in my mouth. The feel of the cool liquid hurts at first, but the more I sip, the better it feels. "Do you remember what happened?" he asks me.

It takes me a minute to try and remember. I'm confused, so I'm not sure in what order I remember things. My mind takes me back to a fire. There is a man with a gun, smoke all around us, and the roof caves in. I think I hear someone calling my name, but the noise is so loud I can't be sure. "What happened to the man with the gun?"

"He died," my father says.

"Thank God that son of a bitch died, because if I got my hands on his sorry ass, I would have killed him myself. Who was the man?"

"Taylor Perez."

Hearing that name brings it all back to me. The warehouse, the drugs, the money, the fire—it's all coming back to me now. "What happened to his father? Wait, where are Muffin and Stack? Are they OK? Did they make it?" I try to sit up, but my body will not have it.

Jonathan lays me back down. "Stop," he says. "Muffin and Stack are here in the hospital. They took a really bad beating, and they had also suffered from smoke inhalation. The doctors said they will make it. Stack was the worse of the two. He has had two surgeries already. Muffin had broken bones, and he lost a couple of teeth. He was in surgery again last night, but he is in a room. Pookie is with him now. I went to see him this morning. He had a message for you. He told me to tell you he is not cut out to be a federal agent; he is leaving all this up to you."

I smile. "He protected me when Aguilar was going to..." I can't finish what I was about to say.

I am about to ask about Rosie when Conrad walks into my room with a big, beautiful bouquet of flowers. "Glad to see you awake. You had us scared for a minute."

"Glad to see you too. Thanks for the flowers, they are beautiful."

My mother takes the flowers. "I will see if I can find a vase big enough to fit them."

Conrad says, "The two of you will be the death of me yet."

"The two of us?"

"Yes, you and Rosie."

"Why? What happened to Rosie?"

"That nut went in after you and Taylor. The roof fell on him as well, but he was lucky. He wasn't as far in the building as the two of you. He only suffered a broken leg."

"Where is he now?" I ask.

"Home," says Conrad. "He has around-the-clock care." I try to laugh along with everyone else, but it hurts too much. We all know what type of care he is getting. "I'm not going to stay too long. I wanted to make sure you were awake. All I want you to do right now is get well." He turns to leave.

"Conrad, what happened to Aguilar and his crew?"

He looks me in my eyes and smiles. "He's in hell along with his son. We got them, Shalimar. We got them all."

A week later I am recuperating at home. I have around-the-clock care from my parents, and when they are not here, I have the Betty Crocker Patrol. I am sleeping and eating more now than I ever have in my life. My babies know that I am not well because they refuse to leave my side.

Rosie hops over to see me, along with his latest nurse. He is looking good and rested. His leg is healing nicely. He hates being on crutches, but it could have been so much worse. He tells me I look like I have gained weight. "How could I not with all this home cooking from my mother and Rob?" I tell him I remember most of what happened, but that some things are still fuzzy for me to remember. He fills me in on what happened.

He ran in after us but didn't get far before the roof came crashing down on us. Taylor was standing beneath one of the large beams that crushed him to death. I was lucky because the way the roof fell, it created a small barrier between the two of us, or I would have died with him. His father died on the way to the hospital. He probably would not have made it anyway, because the knife did some serious damage, but it was the smoke inhalation that killed him. "We rounded up all of Aguilar's men who were not killed. There is no telling how much cocaine and money went up in smoke. We didn't stop drugs from coming into the Northeast, but we put a damn big hole in it for now. Aguilar Perez was a big fish in the cartel who will never again hurt anyone."

I am lying in bed looking out of my window at the brightest moon I have ever seen. I am grateful to God that I am still here to see it. A lot has happened, and I have had plenty of time to think. I am well aware that I could have died, but I know that I am here for a purpose, and I want to do everything in my power to carry out that purpose.

Jonathan and I will need to work on our relationship if it is to survive. I know the love is there. Once I am well enough, I will meet him in Paris. Not for anything but to be with the man I love. We still don't know by whom and why I was involved in all this mess, but I guess I will have to wait and see what happens next.

As I drift off to sleep, I see my Uncle Maurice smiling and giving me the thumbs-up. "I am so damn proud of you," he says. "I love you."

I smile. "I love you too, Uncle Maurice."

Tomorrow is looking brighter. Thank you, God, for your armor of protection.

Just as sleep is surrounding me, the phone rings. "Hello…"

ACKNOWLEDGEMENTS

There are so many people I need to thank.

To my mother Louise I love you for your encouragement and love (I told you one day).

My sister Rita and niece Tarshanda (Smurf) thanks for believing. Hugs and kisses.

Thanks Bo for getting the ball rolling.

Thanks to:

Saudeia, Janice, Dalevonne, Nelly, and my crazy friend Janet.

Deangela Williams, you are a true friend indeed. Thank you so much for your friendship and advice. You have no idea.

Mary Beth Parker, you are an amazing friend who stepped in and offered to help without hesitation. Who knew all those years ago on a trip to the Bahamas, I would meet a crazy family who has become my family.

Gary who I have known for too many years to count, and Michael (stay crazy) I love you both.

Patty thank you for the great job you did of taking my word and turning them into a book.

Special Thank you to Denise Revell, God places people in your life for reasons not known at the time. Words cannot express how much you have changed my life. Saying thank you for your inspiration, prayers, and FBCG, just doesn't seem enough.

Introducing me to strong women of God has only helped me in my spiritual growth. You are known by the company you keep, I am Blessed. Thank you so much.

Lastly a big I love you to my four legged fur baby Ochie (he's in the book) who drives me crazy in the most cat like fashion, thirteen and still going strong.

God Bless you all for being in my life.

ABOUT THE AUTHOR

J. P. Dallas is a New Yorker, even if she did originate in New Jersey and now lives in Maryland with Ochie the cat (who crops up in *Fade to Blacque*).

A one-time biker chick with a deep love of God, animals, and world travel, Dallas began writing when she turned fifty-six. *Fade to Blacque* was inspired by her interest in forensics, British murder mysteries, and all aspects of law enforcement.

70629801R00134

Made in the USA
Columbia, SC
10 May 2017